LOVE IS THICKER THAN WATER

RAISE A GLASS, BOOK TEN

MARY E THOMPSON

Love Is Thicker Than Water

Raise A Glass, book ten

Copyright © 2019 Mary E Thompson

Cover Copyright © 2022 Mary E Thompson

Cover Photo (vineyard) from depositphotos, Copyright © AlexGukBO

Cover Photo (couple) from depositphotos, Copyright © gum92

Published by BluEyed Press, All Rights Reserved

Ebook ISBN: 978-1-944090-52-4

Print ISBN: 978-1-944090-53-1

❀ Created with Vellum

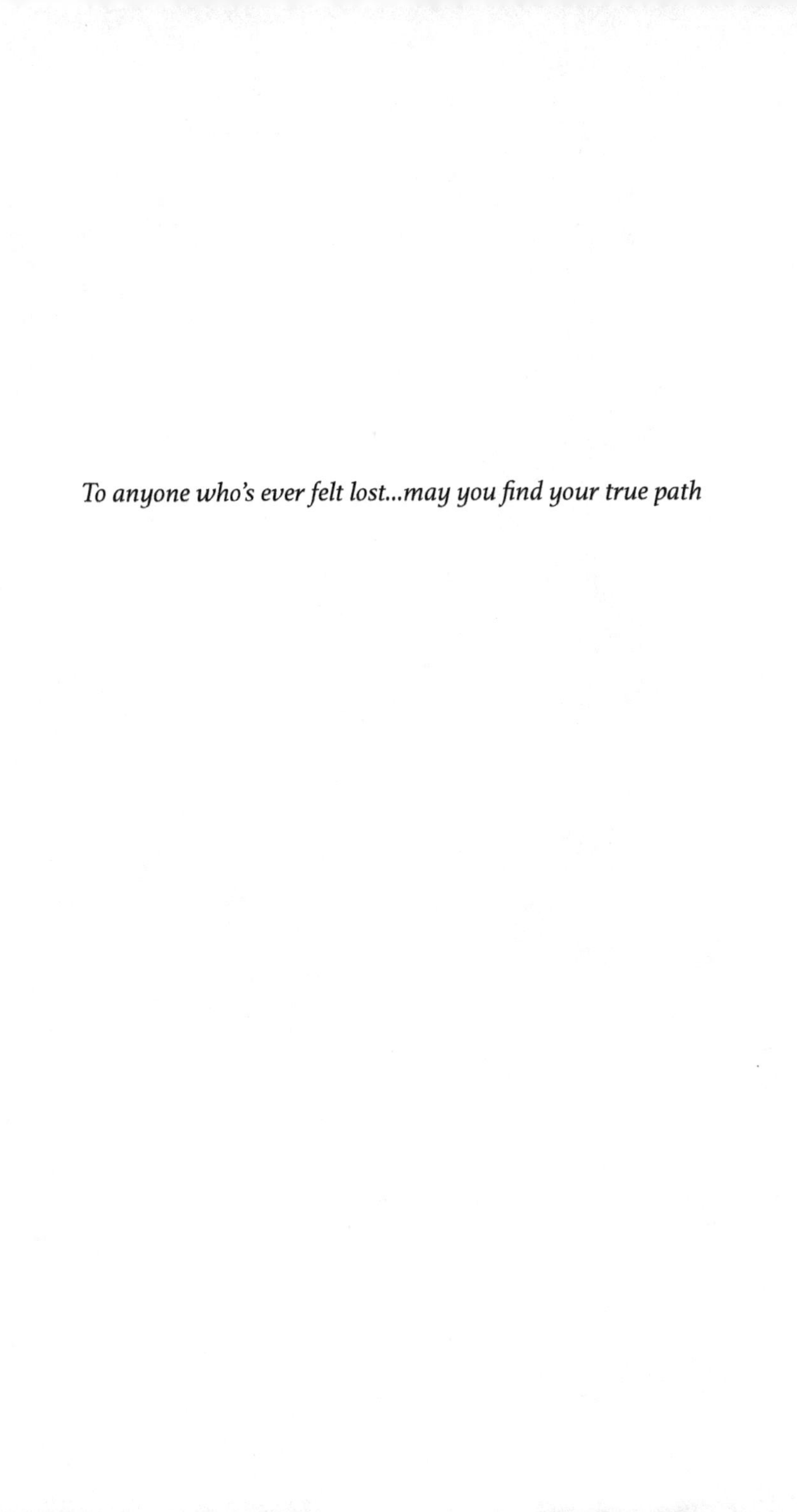

To anyone who's ever felt lost…may you find your true path

1
—————

RYAN WILSON SAT TO THE SIDE OF THE PARTY AND SIPPED HIS wine. He was the only one not enjoying himself, but how could he? The party was to celebrate the second anniversary of his father's death. As far as Ryan was concerned, there was no reason to celebrate.

The rest of his family disagreed with him, so he sat and watched them enjoy themselves.

He wondered what his father would think of the family if he were there. Two years didn't feel that long, but two years without the man who made him a man was an eternity. In two years, his brother found love, just like many of his cousins. Some of them had kids. The cousins had officially taken over the vineyard, and everything was different with them in charge. Different in a good way, but different.

Ryan hoped his father would be proud of him, but there were plenty of times he doubted it. He was twenty-eight and hadn't done much with his life. Yes, he loved his job, and he loved being with his family every day, but his dad always said his greatest achievements in life had nothing to do with work. He hoped Ryan would find love, but as the last of the nine cousins who was still single, he hadn't done what his father asked.

Wasn't the first time he let down the man he never wanted to disappoint. Probably wouldn't be the last.

"Why are you pouting in the corner?" Ryan's grandmother said. Tina, Nonna to the cousins, was as feisty as they come. At eighty-nine, soon to be ninety, Nonna was the matriarch of the family and lived up to the title. She was a ball-buster, but she loved all of them with her whole heart.

"I'm not pouting," Ryan argued, wrapping his arm around Nonna's shoulders. She was nearly a foot shorter than his five-eleven, but you'd never know it once Nonna opened her mouth and told you what to do.

"That look on your face says otherwise. Not enough women here for you?" she teased.

Ryan snorted. "Considering I'm related to all of them, definitely not."

Nonna chuckled. "Good answer. Want me to set you up? Maggie and Violet have some pretty granddaughters."

Ryan laughed and shook his head. His grandmother's cronies were wonderful ladies, but their granddaughters were too close. They were like extended family as far as Ryan was concerned, which made them all off limits.

"I can find my own dates, Nonna."

She shrugged. "Just trying to help. Your mother worries about you."

"You don't?"

She shook her head. "Nah. You can take care of yourself. None of you have ever had trouble finding someone to warm your beds."

"Nonna!"

She shrugged again. Her petite frame barely nudged his shoulder. Nonna, like the other women in his family, was small but not thin. Ryan grew up thinking that was how women were supposed to be. Small enough that he could wrap his arms around them and tuck their heads under his chin, but not so thin he felt like he'd break them with one touch. He'd slept with women of all shapes and sized, but the ones he considered hanging onto for longer than a few nights were always the curvy ones.

"Don't pretend you don't. I might not live with you, but I know how you operate. All of you were the same at one point in time."

Ryan shook his head. The last person he wanted to discuss sex with was his grandmother. His father sat him down when he was barely a teenager and had the talk with him, but his talk was more about how to treat a woman than it was how it all works. At the time, Ryan was too young to let his dad's words have much of an impact, but as he grew up, he knew every word was truth and lived by the same code. Women deserved respect, especially when they were willing to take their clothes off for you.

"I need a dance partner. Since the rest of your cousins are taken, how about you take me for a spin?" Nonna suggested.

Ryan wasn't in the mood to dance, but he couldn't deny his grandmother. He nodded and offered her his hand. Nonna took it and followed him to the cleared area they were using as a dance floor. An old slow song played through the speakers as Ryan slid his arm around his grandmother and smiled at her.

"Your grandfather loved this song," she said with a sad smile. "It was one of his favorites. Your father was a lot like him. They'd only met a couple times before Nonno died, but your father and he were so similar it was scary."

"I wish I'd met him."

Nonna nodded. "I wish all of you had. He would have loved this. The whole family together. It was what he always hoped would happen. He was the mushy one of the two of us."

Ryan laughed. "I can definitely see that."

Nonna rolled her eyes. "I care."

Ryan grinned. "I never said you didn't, but I can't imagine you getting emotional about a lot. You're a dirty old woman."

"Hey! Who are you calling old?"

Ryan laughed again. "You're only proving my point."

Nonna winked at him. "Yes, well, I got a smile out of you. That's all I was after."

Ryan grinned and nodded. She was right. He'd been feeling like shit as the date approached. If things were busy, it would have been better, but the vineyard was quiet in the winter months, and his second job as a volunteer firefighter was quiet, too. It was strange, and it sucked.

Leading up to the first Christmas without his dad, everyone was on edge. His mom cried most of the time, and the rest of the family felt the loss as acutely as they did, but this year was their second Thanksgiving, Christmas, and New Year's without his dad. Two wasn't as significant as one, so it passed for everyone else like it was nothing. Sure, his mom and brother felt it, but for them, it was a moment. For Ryan, it felt like someone opened him up and scooped out his heart and forgot to give him a new one.

"Are you sure you're okay?" Nonna asked, her brown eyes knitted with worry. Her hair had even more gray than the last time Ryan really looked at her.

Ryan nodded. "I'll be okay. Tonight is tough, but I'll be okay."

Nonna nodded, accepting Ryan's words without question. He'd become more than skilled at lying when people asked if he was okay. It wasn't a talent he set out to improve, but it was one he'd learned over the last two years. He couldn't fall apart when his mother was, or when his brother was, or when anyone else was, so he faked it and lied. If any of them knew how hard it was for him to be in that room, they'd sit him down and feed him because for Italians, food fixed everything. All Ryan really wanted was a little quiet.

Ryan finished his dance with Nonna, then went back to the corner to watch the family. He loved his family, but they were too much for him at times. The laughter and joy in the room was starting to get to him. He itched to get a call for a fire, but immediately felt guilty for hoping for a fire. He just wanted to get out.

His phone didn't ring, and his family didn't stop talking until late in the night. The ones with kids headed out early, but the others stayed and helped clean up, which meant Ryan was there long past dark. He did his part and helped out, and walked his mom, grandmother, and Aunt Marie to their apartment at the front of the inn the family ran on their vineyard, Amavita Estates.

"Thank you," Nonna said at the door. She kissed his cheek and took Aunt Marie's hand, walking inside.

"Thank you for this," Ryan's mother said. Jo had aged in the two years since her husband died. Ryan used to see his mother as young and vibrant and barely old enough to have retired. As the youngest of the four Richliano sisters, she could have worked another decade, but the kids were ready to take over. And she was ready to see the country. She and Victor were in New York City when an aneurysm killed him two years ago.

Ryan nodded. "Of course. It's always nice to celebrate Dad."

Jo smiled. "He was so proud of you and your brother. I know he would have loved to see the two of you today."

Ryan shrugged. "I'm not much different than I was two years ago."

Jo huffed a laugh. "We're all different. Maybe not as much as we'd like, but we're different."

"Are you okay, Mom?" Ryan asked.

She nodded and patted his cheek. "Yeah. Just missing your father. He was the love of my life, and knowing I might have a few decades without him is tough. I think it's finally sinking in these days."

Ryan sucked in a breath. He knew the feeling. Every day when he walked the vineyard, he looked for his father. Two years wasn't long enough to erase the man who made the place home for him. Victor taught Ryan everything he knew about running a vineyard. Sure, he went to college and got had a degree in viticulture, but he also learned a lot from his father. By the time he was in college, he knew half of what he learned because of the education his dad gave him. It was impossible not to see him everywhere.

"Anyway, I'll let you head to bed. You looked tired all night," Jo said. "I'll see you tomorrow, honey."

Ryan hugged her and kissed her cheek. "Good night, Mom."

"Night, honey. I love you."

"Love you, Mom."

Ryan waited until she was inside the apartment and the lock slid shut before he turned and walked through the inn. The dim lights illuminated the hallway, but the entire place was quiet. The guests they had upstairs were likely asleep, and with the rest of his cousins gone, the inn was quiet. Just like Ryan had been hoping for all night.

He didn't want to go home. He shared a house with his cousin, Leo, and Leo recently moved his girlfriend, Sara, in with them. Ryan liked Sara, but the idea of going back there right away was less than appealing.

He walked out of the inn, making sure the door was locked behind him, and drew in a breath of the frigid night air. January in the Finger Lakes was cold. Ice coated the vines, but snow was coming soon. They had a few inches of snow for Christmas, but it all melted shortly after. The green grass wouldn't last long. A winter wonderland was coming.

Ryan looked toward his house, in the distance, and shook his head. The walk would be good, but he needed more time than that. He turned toward the lake and decided to head that way. Getting in wouldn't be a good idea, but he always loved the old dock and the big tree near it. It was as good a place as any to sit and think and be alone for a little while.

Bella Chase sat on the edge of the dock and took a deep breath. The water helped clear her head. She longed to dive in and float around in the dark water, but she could see her breath, and even she wasn't crazy enough to think swimming in that weather was smart.

She pulled her jacket tighter around her and closed her eyes. It was peaceful there. Quiet. She felt like she could breathe for the first time in far too long. The pain in her chest eased as she sucked in one after another deep breath.

Going home was the right thing to do. Her father was

probably worried about her. She almost laughed out loud. Her father. She spent the first twenty-seven years of her life thinking he didn't exist, and after one conversation, she'd moved in with the man she never knew. Of course, she had nowhere else to go, but she didn't expect him to open his home to her, or to be so welcoming to her.

Bella laid back on the dock and promised herself she'd go in a minute. It was hard to walk away from the place, even though she knew she didn't belong.

"Are you okay?" a deep voice came through the quiet, foggy night.

Bella sat up, startled and curious. She was sure she was alone. She turned toward the voice and found a man not far from the end of the dock.

"Are you hurt? Did you fall in the water?"

Bella shook her head. "No, I'm fine."

"Good," he said. "Then mind telling me why you're trespassing?"

The harsh edge in his voice sent a shiver down her spine, the kind of shiver she hadn't felt in far too long. She liked men who took charge, mostly because then she didn't have to think. She spent her entire life letting everyone else take care of her, and old habits were hard to break.

"I was just enjoying the moonlight. I didn't realize it would be a problem," Bella lied. She knew it was a private vineyard, and even though it was open during the day for tastings and meals, she understood that being out there at night wasn't okay. Neither was wandering around a vineyard. At least, that's what her father told her.

"This is private property. Unless you're a guest of the inn, you shouldn't be down here. Even guests are asked not to wander the vineyard. The vines are delicate."

"You sound like you know a lot about it," Bella said,

turning on her flirtatious tone. She knew how to make men forget she wasn't supposed to be doing something. And even though she couldn't see the man in front of her, she could tell by his voice he was young, maybe close to her age.

"I do," he said gruffly, crossing his arms over his wide chest. He wore a dark coat and jeans with heavy boots. His hair was short and dark, and he was tall. She wished he'd take another step toward her so she could see his face.

Bella stood, surprised at how far the man towered over her. "I'm Bella. I'm new to town. Maybe you could tell me all about making wine?"

"We have tastings available during the day. Whoever is in the tasting room can answer your questions," he said. "I think it's time for you to go. How did you get here?"

Bella shrugged. "I walked."

"From town? It's a bit of a hike. Especially this late."

"Should I be worried? Is it safe?"

The guy nodded. "Yeah, Bereton is a safe town. You don't have to worry about that. The worst that would happen is getting chased by someone's dog or walking home with people after a night out. Do you want me to call you a ride? We don't have Uber around here, but there are locals who will pick you up if you need it."

Bella shook her head. For some reason, she didn't want him to know where she lived. "I'll be fine."

She walked off the dock and stopped when she was next to him. She looked up at him, and he finally met her gaze. His eyes were too dark to see what color they were, but she could finally make out the rest of his features. A straight, narrow nose, full lips, thick, dark hair, and stubbled jaw. He was gorgeous. And not just because she hadn't been able to bring herself to sleep with anyone since her mom died, but because he was honest-to-God hot.

"I'm sorry about the trespassing. It won't happen again."

The edge of his mouth curled up and he laughed. "I doubt that. You don't strike me as a rule follower."

She grinned back at him. "You never know. There's a first time for everything. Maybe I'll surprise you."

He nodded. "Maybe you will."

Bella started to walk away, then paused. "You never told me your name."

"Ryan," he said.

"It's nice to meet you, Ryan. I'm sure I'll be seeing you around."

He chuckled. "Hopefully not at midnight on my property again."

She grinned and waved, then walked up the path. She stopped at the side of the inn and looked back at the water, but the tree blocked the view of the dock. She wondered if Ryan was still there.

She shook her head. She wasn't there to meet a guy. She was there to get to know her father.

She took a breath and kept walking, up the driveway and across Highway 89 to her father's vineyard, Perry Mount Vineyards.

2

———————

BELLA WOKE UP MID-MORNING THE NEXT DAY. SHE STRETCHED then stilled, waiting to see if there was movement in the house.

It was odd to her that Albert welcomed her in as quickly as he did. She wasn't sure what she expected, but he never once questioned her story or its accuracy. All she had to say was she was his daughter, and that her mom was Melanie Chase, and he let her in. No questions asked.

Bella expected a fight. Hell, she went there looking for one. After her mother died, Bella felt lost. The car accident that claimed her life was sudden, and she didn't suffer, but Bella suffered enough for both of them. She ached for her mother. Right up until she discovered her mother lied to her. For her entire life.

Bella eased her way out of bed and looked around the room she was staying in. Albert said she could stay as long as she wanted, but Bella wasn't sure. Her home was two hours away, but it didn't feel like home after her mom died. The people she was close to were her mom's friends, and

Bella wondered if they were all laughing at her. Thinking she was foolish for believing the lies her mother told her.

Even if they weren't laughing, Bella couldn't face them. Not now. Not when they'd all try to talk her out of hating her mother.

Bella opened the door quietly and peeked out. Albert's house was small, but well-maintained. The room Bella was sleeping in was a guest room, but was clearly not used often. Boxes were stacked along the walls and the bed had piles of paperwork when she arrived. He insisted she could stay, but she still felt like she was putting him out.

Bella skipped across the hall to the bathroom. She flushed and washed her hands, rolling her eyes at herself in the mirror. She was hiding from the man she went there to meet. She needed to get over herself.

She opened the door and walked down the hall toward the living area of the house. A large, open kitchen dominated the space. He had a wall of wine that divided the kitchen from the dining room. A family room with a stiff couch and a recliner that Albert sat in at night completed the house. There was a fireplace and above it a TV, but neither were on as Bella walked into the room.

"You're awake," Albert said with a smile. He folded his newspaper and got up from his seat at the dining room table. "Can I make you breakfast?"

Bella shook her head. She wasn't a morning person, and breakfast never appealed to her. She couldn't figure out how she only ate two meals a day and still wore size sixteen jeans, but she supposed she had her mother to thank for that. Melanie had hips for days and passed them on to Bella the same way she passed on her chestnut hair and ice blue eyes. Her narrow nose, full lips, and heart-shaped face all came from her father she learned.

"I'm just going to get some coffee, if that's okay," Bella said.

"Of course! I was going to try to clean out some of the boxes in your room today so you have space for your things. If you don't mind me being in there. Most of the boxes I can just move to my room or the office. But I don't want to be in your way if you were going to be in there," Albert said.

He smiled and ran a hand through his thinning gray hair. The pictures Bella found of him and her mom when they were younger showed a man who looked the same, but almost thirty years younger. He was handsome in that nerdy way that Bella herself never really understood. He wore glasses now, mostly for reading it appeared, but he still had a nerdy look. Pressed pants instead of jeans. Button down shirts instead of something more casual. Like he was always trying to look ready to impress, but fell short in the style department.

"The boxes are fine. You don't have to worry about them."

"Oh," he said, his smile fading.

Bella sipped her coffee. She was already getting a headache. She didn't know him well enough to know what the single word meant, but he was clearly not happy with her answer. "If you really want to, it's fine. It's up to you."

Albert shrugged. "Well, if they're not in your way, that's okay."

Bella drew in a breath and forced a smile. She stayed on the other side of the kitchen from him, still not sure how she felt about the man her mother said never wanted her.

"Can I ask you a question?" Bella said after a minute.

Albert nodded. "Of course. Anything."

Bella set her coffee down on the counter and looked at him. She could definitely see the resemblance between them, but before meeting him, she never picked up on the ways she looked more like him than her mother, right down to the way the edge of his mouth twitched impatiently as she worked on how to ask the question.

"Why didn't you want to be in my life?"

Albert blanched. He pressed his lips together and stared at the table.

Immediately, Bella regretted asking the question. Tears burned her eyes as humiliation sank into her gut. She didn't really want to know the answer. Just that he seemed happy she was there. If he was happy she was there, why hadn't he ever made an effort to be a part of her life before?

"Never mind," Bella murmured. She grabbed her coffee and moved toward the hallway to escape him again. The time she'd been there was filled with enough awkward silences and uncomfortable questions, like what her name was, but she asked the hardest one so far.

Maybe it was time to move on. To accept that her father was being nice to her, but he really wasn't a replacement for her mother.

"I never knew about you," Albert said softly when Bella was almost to the hallway.

She froze, stunned in place. He was going to lie to her? Really?

She finally found the strength to turn and face him. "My mother said she told you. She told me you didn't want me."

He raised an eyebrow. "Was this before or after she told you I was dead?"

Dammit. He had a point. Bella didn't want to think about how many lies her mother told her. The biggest one of all was that her father was dead, but she only said that after Bella pestered her mom about meeting her dad one day. A father-daughter dance was coming up at school.

Bella thought maybe her father would be willing to go, even though she'd never met him. Her fragile ten year old heart thought if she was good enough, he'd be willing to give her a chance. She wasn't a baby anymore, and she could make her own lunches for school and studied hard and promised not to cry. She told her mom she wanted her to call him and invite him to the dance, but Melanie refused. When Bella pushed, Melanie shouted that her father was dead.

Bella never asked about him again.

"I'm sorry I wasn't there when you were growing up, Bella. I wish I could have been. I'd love to tell you I would have been a good father, but I don't know. I'm sure your mother had reasons for not wanting me to know about you, or you to know about me. I wish I knew what they were, but I am happy you're here now. That I have a chance to get to know you now."

Bella nodded. She pressed her lips together to keep the emotions inside. They threatened to spill from her eyes, so she nodded again, then turned and rushed down the hall to her room so she could be alone.

He didn't follow. She knew he wouldn't. It was how she wanted it. She was alone. And even though she had a dad for now, she knew it wouldn't last forever. At some point in time, she was going to have to figure out what the hell she was doing with her life.

One day.

~

RYAN SAT in the back of the rig as they wove their way through the streets of Bereton. He was hot and sweaty and dirty, but he felt good. Damn good. He smiled at Matt, another one of the volunteer firefighters he worked with, and the goofy ass look on his face.

"What's so funny?" Matt asked.

"You. What the hell's wrong with you?"

Matt flipped him off. "I've been up twenty-four hours. I'm fucking exhausted."

"New baby giving you hell?" Ryan asked.

Matt nodded. "Natalia is a saint, but this one is taking a toll on her. I think she might finally be done."

"She doesn't want to go for five?" Ryan asked.

Matt shook his head. "Fuck, I hope not. I can barely keep up with three. Now with four, we're going to be lucky if we survive. I don't know how I can keep doing it all."

Ryan's brows drew together. "Are you giving this up?"

Matt shrugged. "I don't want to, but money's always tight and I don't have time for a third job."

"But you love this," Ryan said, baffled at what his friend was saying. Matt was one of the first friends Ryan made when he decided to join the Bereton Volunteer Fire Company. Matt used to be a firefighter in New York City, but Natalia wanted to raise their family in a small town, so they sold everything they had and moved to Bereton. At the time, they were just talking about having kids, but four kids later, Ryan could understand the struggle.

"I do," Matt said. "I want to keep doing this, but we just have to see. You'll understand when you settle down. If you ever settle down."

Ryan rolled his eyes. It was a running joke between them that Matt was the old man and Ryan was the young stud who couldn't be saddled. Matt was younger than Ryan's older brother, Henry, but he and Natalia started having kids in their early twenties. By the time he was Ryan's age, Matt had two kids with a third on the way.

"I like things the way they are."

Matt grinned. "Yeah, yeah. Hey, how did everything go the other day? I haven't seen you since."

For a second, Ryan thought Matt was asking about the mysterious Bella. Then it clicked that he was talking about the party for his dad and the pain came back in a flash.

"Not easy. My family wants to celebrate, but I keep thinking he died without ever finding proof that Perry stole from our family. My dad swore it, but Perry insists he never did anything. I just wish I could bring him some peace."

"Something tells me he isn't the only one who needs that peace," Matt said. "What's to stop you from digging into it again?"

Ryan shrugged. "I don't even know where I'd look. If he has something, I wouldn't think it'd be out in the vineyard. He'd have it hidden. And I have no way of getting onto his property and searching. Not to mention it isn't legal."

Matt shook his head. "Don't get arrested. But what about going through your dad's stuff. Maybe you can find something there. Something he missed. You're a fresh set of eyes."

They paused their conversation as they helped unload the gear from the rig. Once everything was stored and cleaned and ready for the next emergency, Matt turned to Ryan again.

"You need this. And I think your family might, too. Perry did what he could to make your father look like he was crazy. He told anyone who would listen that your father was trying to set him up. I don't blame you for still being pissed and wanting justice. You should get it."

Ryan nodded. He knew Perry tried to ruin his dad, but Victor was well respected in the community. It didn't stop Perry from trying. Then the asshole had the nerve to show up at Victor's funeral. Henry almost didn't make it through his eulogy when he saw the man there, again, making himself look good in front of the community when Ryan's family had no choice but to stand by and let it happen.

"I need to talk to my brother and my mom. If I'm going to do anything, they need to know about it. I don't like people thinking my father was the one who lied all these years," Ryan said.

"If you need anything, let me know," Matt said.

Ryan chuckled. "When do you think you can help? You already said you don't sleep."

Matt nodded. "Yeah, well, I'd figure something out if you needed me."

Ryan grinned. "Thanks. For now, go home and get some sleep. Morning will come far too early."

Matt looked tired just thinking about the morning. He turned and headed out. Ryan checked in with their supervisor for the shift and confirmed he wasn't needed either, then headed up to the bunk room. If he got called in for a fire, or if he was on call, he usually spent the night at the station. Most of his fellow volunteers went home, but Ryan preferred the quiet of the fire station to the quiet of his home, especially when he wasn't sure his home would be all that quiet.

He settled onto one of the cots and turned onto his stomach. He closed his eyes and smiled to himself when darkness was all he saw. He was almost asleep when the alarm went off again.

It was going to be a long night.

RYAN WAS DRAGGING the next day when he forced himself out of bed for lunch. The best thing about working on his family's vineyard was the free food at his constant disposal. He knew how to cook, but he much preferred to let his cousin, Zach, do the cooking while Ryan enjoyed the fruits of Zach's labor.

He trudged to the inn and went through the front door. Andie, another cousin, was at the desk at the front, talking to guests who with suitcases next to them. She smiled at him and held up a finger, so he waited while she finished and opened the door for them to leave.

"Hey," Andie said happily. She looked almost as tired as Ryan felt.

"Hey. You okay?"

Andie nodded. "Mia is kicking my butt. She hasn't been sleeping well lately. I should have taken off a year like Cody wanted me to."

Ryan chuckled. "Alyssa tried to warn you."

Andie rolled her eyes. "One day I'll learn to listen. I stopped you because there's a woman here for lunch. She asked if you were around. I got the feeling she knows you, but I wasn't sure how well. I told her you weren't here when she got here and didn't offer anything else. She still went for lunch."

"What does she look like?" Ryan asked, wondering who would be there looking for him.

"She's pretty. Shoulder length hair, a really pretty chestnut color. Blue eyes so light they look like ice. She's about your age. I didn't ask her name. She looks familiar, but I can't figure out where I know her from."

Ryan shrugged. The description wasn't ringing a bell for him at all. "I'll let you know when I see her. I don't have any crazy ex's hanging around lately, so I don't know who this one is. If you hear me scream, call 9-1-1."

Andie chuckled and rolled her eyes. Ryan winked at her

and walked down the hall toward The Drunken Grape. Leo and Kristen were behind the counter in the tasting room and waved, but they were busy since it was a Saturday. Even in the winter, they got plenty of visitors on the weekends to make it worthwhile to have it staffed.

Ryan made his way into the dining room and looked around for the woman Andie mentioned. There was only one woman sitting by herself, but she had her back to Ryan. There was no guarantee she was the one looking for him, but it was possible.

He scanned the dining room once more and didn't see anyone flagging him down, so he headed toward the woman by herself. If she didn't look familiar, he would sit at the table just beyond her and she'd never know he was trying to figure out if they knew each other.

She looked up at him when he passed by. Those eyes. Damn. He would have remembered those eyes if he'd seen them before. Ice blue, just like Andie said. He scanned the rest of her face, trying to place her. She was familiar, but he couldn't put his finger on it. Where did he see her before?

"Ryan?" she asked, her plump lips turning up on the edges. "I almost didn't recognize you."

"Really?" he asked. "Well, thankfully you did."

She smiled. "Do you want to join me? You don't have to, but if you're not meeting anyone, you can. It's up to you."

Ryan nodded and took the seat across from her. She was beautiful. Her eyes lit up when he sat down, and her smile hit him in the chest like a laser. He wanted to reach across the table and take her hand just so he could touch her, but there was only one problem.

He still had no clue who she was.

3

BELLA FELT LIKE AN IDIOT SHOWING UP AT AMAVITA ESTATES again, but she needed a break from Albert. Since he didn't have a restaurant, yet he told her, she went in search of food. Instead of turning her car toward town, she drove across the street, remembering she saw a sign on her walk the other night that mentioned a restaurant.

Walking into the inn and asking the woman at the desk about Ryan was stupid, but obviously it was okay since Ryan was there, in the flesh, looking at her like she was better than any of the food on the menu. And it was a yummy looking menu.

"I haven't ordered yet. I've only been here a little while. I did get a glass of wine, though." Bella had a tendency to ramble when she was nervous, and looking into Ryan's brown eyes definitely made her nervous.

She couldn't see him clearly the other night on the dock, but she recognized his jaw when he walked by her. She purposely faced away from the entrance to avoid staring at every man who walked in, but when he walked by her, she knew it was him and blurted out his name before she could stop herself.

"I'm guessing everything is good here, right?" she asked.

He still looked dazed, like he had no idea what she was saying.

"Um, Ryan?"

He shook his head and nodded. "Yeah, everything's good. Sorry. I was up all night."

"Oh," Bella said, a little shocked. She really didn't want to hear about his sex life. She didn't even know his last name.

"Too many people fall asleep with their space heaters on, or with candles on, or trying cheap ways to heat their homes. It makes us crazy."

"Us?"

He nodded and took a sip of the water on the table. "Firefighters."

Bella felt silly for her thoughts and laughed. "That's why you were up all night?"

Ryan nodded. "Yeah. You didn't know?"

She shook her head. "No. Sorry." Bella wasn't sure how she would have known that, but she wasn't going to ask.

"Yeah, it's been a while. There are a lot of guys who are available during the summer, but since I'm basically out of work all winter, it fits my schedule."

"You're out of work?" Bella gasped. "Why? What happened?"

Ryan chuckled. "I work in the fields. The vines are dormant all winter, so my job is pretty quiet. I don't do a lot through the winter."

"So you fight fires instead?"

Ryan nodded. "Yep. It keeps me out of trouble."

Bella grinned.

"Oh, hey, Ryan," the waitress said, walking to their table. "I didn't realize you were joining her."

Bella wondered if there was a hint of jealousy or if she imagined it. She tried to tell herself it was all in her head, but the glare the waitress shot her said it wasn't.

"Yeah, I just got here. It worked out well to sit together."

"Oh, so you're not actually together?"

Ryan shook his head. "No, not now?"

Bella tilted her head in question. Was he asking her? She shook her head slowly.

"No. We're just friends now."

Bella pursed her lips to avoid laughing. He had no idea who she was. She smiled up at the waitress, who wasn't wearing a name tag, and said, "Ryan and I go way back. The stories I could tell you about him."

Ryan's smile faltered then pressed right back into place. "Yep, old friends. So, can we order?"

The waitress nodded and dug a pen out of her apron. "Absolutely. What can I get you, Ryan?"

"I'll start with a glass of Riesling, and I'd like the Caprese salad and the linguine and shrimp for lunch. Zach knows how I like it."

The waitress leaned forward and set her hand on his shoulder. "Don't worry, I'll make sure everything is exactly how you like it."

Ryan nodded, but Bella had to give him a little credit for not checking out the woman's boobs. She had to be a little younger than Bella, maybe just out of college, and clearly looking to land a man.

When she didn't turn to Bella after a long moment, Ryan shifted and nodded to her. "Um, can you take my friend's order, too?"

The waitress laughed like what he said was hilarious, then glared at Bella. "What do you want?"

"I'll start with a Caesar salad, and have the manicotti for lunch please, with an order of breadsticks, too," Bella said with a wide grin.

The waitress scribbled it all down then slid her gaze down Bella's body. She wanted to whither under the insulting look, but she refused to give in to bitchy bullies. Bella had accepted her body, and even though she didn't always love the way it looked or moved, she knew it was the only one she was going to get and worrying about other people's opinions of it wasn't worth it.

"That's all, Amy," Ryan said after a minute, handing her the menus.

Amy was all smiles for Ryan again, taking the menus and thanking him before she walked away. Bella wanted to roll her eyes, but she had no idea if Ryan liked women like that. If he did, she was going to write him off immediately.

"I'm sorry about Amy. She's not usually that bad."

Bella shrugged. "I'm the one invading your personal life here. Then again, since we're old friends, I shouldn't be surprised she's falling all over herself to get your attention."

Ryan leaned back in his chair. "Well, you would know I've never had too many problems finding a woman to spend my time with."

Bella nodded, playing along. "True. But what we had was short-lived. I forget how many other women you've spent time with."

Ryan nodded. His brows drew together. Bella almost laughed out loud. She grabbed her water to avoid blowing the whole thing. She wanted to make him squirm.

"It hasn't been that many," he defended himself.

Bella shrugged. "It's really none of my business. We were

only together one night. There was no commitment. I knew what was happening. I didn't expect more."

"So, why are you here? I mean, it's been a while, so why now?"

Bella shrugged and thanked God when Amy interrupted them with Ryan's wine. He thanked her, but she lingered, asking if he needed anything else before the salads were ready.

Ryan assured her they were fine and plastered on a smile, then sighed when she finally left. "Should I assume you're here for the same reason she's acting like that?"

Bella raised an eyebrow in question. Better he let him hang himself than admit to anything.

"You know everyone else is off the market. I'm the last of the cousins still single. So, you figure now's the time to reel me back in? Catch me before someone else does?"

"Everyone else?" Bella asked. She really needed to hear that story.

Ryan sighed and leaned back. "Yeah, well, Dillon, Zach, and Henry are married, and Sean and Leo probably will be soon. And just in case, Alyssa and Andie are married, and Kristen is living with her boyfriend. I'm the only one of the nine cousins who's single. But I'm not looking to change that. Not right now."

His dark gaze was firm and not friendly. Bella leaned back at the look, hurting for him that he felt he had to defend himself against women looking to take a piece of what was his.

She shook her head. "I'm not here for that. For you. Sorry to disappoint you, but I'd rather be with someone because *we* have a connection than because *he* has a connection."

Ryan held her gaze for a long moment then nodded. "Okay, so if that isn't it, why are you here?"

Bella shrugged. "I like talking to you, and I thought it might be a good distraction."

"From what?"

"Everything going on with me right now. My life's gotten a little...complicated, to say the least. And I just wanted to see a friendly face," Bella admitted. Ryan wasn't overly friendly when they met, but she had a feeling he would be someone she could relax with when she wasn't trespassing on his family's property.

And he was the only person she'd met since she came to Bereton besides her father, and he put everything happening at the front of her mind instead of the back.

"Did someone hurt you?" Ryan asked. His voice was low and deadly. Like he was going to rip the head off someone, even though he still didn't know who she actually was.

Bella was quick to shake her head. "No, it's nothing like that. It's not that big of a deal. I just wanted to talk to a friend. I can go, though..."

"No," Ryan said quickly, setting his hand on hers.

Was she the only one who felt that zip of electricity?

He pulled his hand away and sat back in his chair. Bella followed suit, putting distance between them.

"So, it's been a while. What have you been up to since we last saw each other?" Ryan said, sipping his wine.

Bella grinned. "Oh, wow. Since we last saw each other? Not much. Sleeping and eating mostly."

"Working?" Ryan asked.

Bella shook her head. "Not since I last saw you. No."

Ryan blanched. "Wow, um, good...good for you. Did you win the lottery or something?"

Bella grabbed her wine and shook her head. "Not in the last few days."

"But before that? When did you stop working?"

The question reminded Bella of her last day at work. She was pissed and ignored her mom's calls, sending her to voicemail. She wasn't ready to talk to her mom yet. Except the calls weren't coming from her mom. They were calls from the police, using Melanie's phone to try to reach Bella to let her know her mother was killed in a car accident.

"I'm sorry. I wasn't trying to be so nosy," Ryan said, his thick, dark brows pulling together again.

Bella smiled. "It's fine. You didn't know."

"Did, um, did you lose someone?"

She nodded, wondering how he knew. "My mom."

He sucked in a breath. "I'm sorry. I lost my dad, too. Two years ago. Earlier this week."

Bella thought back to the night she was there. She heard the party when she walked by the inn and assuming it was some kind of celebration, but now she wondered. "Tuesday?"

Ryan nodded. "Yeah. How did you remember? Most people have forgotten by now."

Bella looked up at him and forced a smile. "That was the night we met, Ryan. I'm Bella."

BEFORE RYAN COULD RESPOND, Amy was back with their lunches. She set their plates down and was all smiles for Ryan as she asked if he needed anything else, then ignored Bella and walked away. Ryan would have been pissed if he wasn't anxious for her to leave them alone again.

"Old friends? Only one night together? You haven't

worked since we last saw each other? Jesus, you had me going crazy trying to figure out how I forgot you. Those eyes. I knew I wouldn't forget your eyes," Ryan admitted.

Bella smiled and ducked her chin.

"You're something." He laughed and shook his head.

"I figured you deserved it."

"Oh, really? And why is that?"

Bella shrugged. "I'm sure you did something to deserve it at some point in time."

He shook his head again and pointed his fork at her. "Not to you."

"You threw me out."

"Well, you don't live here. And...I was having a rough night."

"I'm really sorry about your dad," Bella said. She offered him a sad smile. "I didn't know."

He nodded. "Thanks. It sucks, doesn't it? Losing a parent."

Bella nodded again, pushing her food around on her plate. Her pain was visible, but he understood not wanting to talk about it, especially with a stranger.

"So, you must be new around here. I would have remembered you," Ryan said, changing the subject.

Bella flashed him a grateful smile and nodded. "I am. I just got here a few days ago."

"Just got here? That sounds like you're visiting."

Bella shrugged. "I don't really know what I'm doing right now. Other than eating lunch."

Ryan laughed softly and nodded. "I like the sound of that."

"Sorry you had a long night," Bella said after a minute.

Ryan shrugged and met her gaze. "It's part of the job. Last night was really cold, so people did more dumb things.

They're trying to survive. This is a great area, but most of the people here are middle class. Every penny counts. If they can get away with a cheaper way to heat their homes in the winter, they're going to try."

"It's not cheaper when they burn the house down," Bella countered.

Ryan nodded and chuckled softly. "That's what I keep telling them. We had a fundraiser here over the summer to educate people about the dangers of space heaters and leaving them on unattended. We had a bunch of people turn them in for newer models that didn't get as hot, but a lot of people refused to hear the risks. I love what I do, but it's definitely frustrating to know these fires could be prevented."

Ryan was intrigued by the woman in front of him. There was obviously something bothering her, but he didn't know what it was. Hell, he didn't even know her last name. What he did know was that she was beautiful, and he wanted to erase the pain he saw in her eyes.

"What do you do, Bella?" Ryan asked.

She drew in a breath and sat back. She stalled by sipping her wine, then wiped her mouth on her napkin and met his eyes. "I'm kind of in between jobs right now. I have a degree in psych, but you can't do much unless you have a master's, which I don't have. I was working at an accounting firm for a while, but I left that job."

"So, what brought you to Bereton?"

"Is it shallow to say the wine?"

He barked a surprised laugh, and she smiled back at him. He shook his head and grinned. "No, it's not shallow. It's why most people come here. Although most people come in the summer when the weather is a lot more bearable."

Bella shrugged. "I grew up a couple hours from here, so I'm used to the weather. It doesn't faze me."

"Where are you from?" he asked, wondering if maybe they had crossed paths at some point.

"Outside Binghamton. A little east."

Ryan nodded, knowing it was highly unlikely they'd ever met. There was still something familiar about her, something more than meeting her a few nights earlier. "I've been through that area a few times, but never for long."

Bella grinned. "There's not much to stick around for."

Ryan chuckled again. "Is that why you're here? Didn't want to stick around there?"

Bella nodded. "That definitely had something to do with it."

The sadness was back in her eyes. Whatever was bothering her had to do with her home. He wondered how long ago her mom died, and if that was it, or if it was something else. For him, two years wasn't long enough to get over losing his dad. He didn't think a lifetime would be long enough, though. The pain might dull from time to time, but it never went away.

"Well, I'm happy you're here now," Ryan told her honestly.

"Me, too."

Amy returned with a pitcher of water and a big smile for Ryan. She asked how their food was and thanked him when he said it was wonderful, as if she had anything to do with it. Ryan was losing patience with her, and after she ignored Bella for the third time, he almost pulled her aside.

Bella put her hand on his, drawing his attention. She shook her head, and he felt his body calm almost instantly. Amy's gaze fell to their hands as Ryan turned his palm over and captured Bella's hand in his.

Amy walked away in a huff, but Ryan barely noticed. All he could see was Bella. She tried to pull her hand back, but Ryan was reluctant to let her go.

He finally gave in and released her hand. She smiled at him, a shy smile that went straight to his gut. What was it about her? He didn't know, and at that moment he didn't care. She made him feel better. She calmed him. It had been far too long since he knew someone who had that same effect on him.

Two years, to be exact. Two years since he could look at another person and feel better just knowing they were there. He never thought he'd feel it again, but he did. He didn't know what it meant, but he was going to figure it out.

4

———————

72 years ago

TINA VINCENZO BRUSHED HER LONG, BROWN HAIR BACK OVER her shoulder and smiled at herself in the mirror. It was going to be a good day. It was always a good day when it was her birthday, but she was eighteen, so she knew it was going to be a really good day.

She walked out of her bedroom in her new dress, the one she worked hard on over the last few weeks. She wasn't as good at sewing as her mother, but she was getting better. The hem of the dress was slightly crooked, but once she put it on it wasn't that noticeable. She was proud of it, and she felt pretty in the dress.

"Good morning, Mama," she said with a kiss on her mother's cheek. "Papa." She kissed him, too.

They both returned the greeting and sat her down. Her siblings weren't there, but she figured they were outside playing. She was sure she'd see them later.

"You are eighteen now," Tina's father, Peter, said. "You need to start making plans for the rest of your life."

Tina groaned. Her parents had been telling her that for months. Once she turned eighteen, they made it sound like her life was over. She liked the idea of finally being free, but it felt like she was walking into a prison instead.

It wasn't that she didn't want to get married someday, but someday was not today. She hadn't met anyone who made her feel the way her mother did about her father, and she wasn't interested in settling down with a boy she didn't at least like.

"Do I have to decide this today?" Tina asked her father.

He shook his head. "No, but you need to decide soon. I have friends who want you to marry their sons. Now that you are eighteen, they expect a decision."

"Well, you can tell them I've decided not to get married yet," Tina said.

Her father's dark eyes went darker. He'd never raised a hand to her, but the threat of it was always there. She knew better than to talk back to him.

"Tina," her mother hissed from behind her.

Tina immediately ducked her gaze. "Sorry, Papa."

He breathed deep, and she dared look at him again. The angry look was gone from his face, but he didn't look happy. He slid a look to her mother, one that said she was going to have to deal with Tina. She was used to it. Her father had his hands full with work and her brother, and her mother ended up being the one who talked Tina into doing whatever it was her father wanted.

"I need to go to work. Spaghetti for dinner tonight?"

Her mother nodded, accepting his request that wasn't really a request.

"I expect an answer when I get home tonight," he said to Tina.

She resisted the urge to tell him she already gave him an answer and simply nodded.

He walked through the house and out the front door. It closed behind him with a soft click, and Tina turned to her mother.

"Does he really expect me to marry someone? I just turned eighteen."

Her mother nodded. "And that means you're of a good age to have children. If you wait too many years, no man will want you."

"There's more to life than this, Mama. I want to see the world. To explore. To do more than just cook and clean and chase children."

Her mother threw the dishtowel on the counter and got in Tina's face. "You can stand there and judge me all you want, little girl, but there is nothing wrong with my life."

"Mama, I didn't—"

"No," Maribel Vincenzo said harshly. "You didn't. You didn't think, you didn't care, you didn't listen. You never do it, and that's why we're here. Because if you'd listened to me for the last year, you would have known this day was coming, and you would have made an attempt to get to know the men your father was interested in you meeting. He's worked hard for this family, and you have to do your part. These boys are all your age, Tina, and they want the same thing you do."

"To travel?" Tina asked excitedly.

Her mother shook her head. "To get married and have a family and live out their lives right here in our town."

Tina fought the urge to roll her eyes. She knew it would only get her a whack on the butt. "That's not what I want, Mama."

Maribel sighed, the sound full of all of the frustration

Tina had put her through over the last eighteen years. She was a disappointment. The oldest child and the most rebellious. Her brother and sisters always did as they were told, but Tina? Tina pushed and pushed and pushed until things blew up.

"Tina, it no longer matters what you want. You were given the chance to choose. You were told to meet these men and decide for yourself. You refused. So now, your father is going to decide. And I'm going to let him."

"What? No. You can't. He can't!"

Her mother turned her back on Tina and said, "He can, and he will."

Tina froze. Her mother had never dismissed her like that before. She always listened to her. But her one and only ally had turned against her.

Tina ran from the house, slamming her way outside. She didn't care where she was going as long as she was going away from her home. She wanted to run far away. To escape. She couldn't handle being there. Not when her life wasn't her own.

She knew how things worked. She was from a family who was comfortable. Her father worked hard in his bakery, but so did her mother. Her brother and sisters helped, and Tina herself kept up the appearance of a stable, comfortable family life. But she thought once she was eighteen, she would be able to go. To find her own path.

Instead, she was being told her path was predetermined by her father. That he had all the power, still, and she didn't get a say.

Tears stung her eyes, but she kept running. Past the dusty fields and through the small town she'd called home her entire life. Small buildings lined the main road, but Tina ran right past all of them. She needed to get away, and maybe if she ran far enough and fast enough, she would get away before her parents found her. She could escape. She could see the world. She could do the things she wanted to do.

Tears streamed down her cheeks, but she didn't care. No one stopped her. Eventually it would get back to her father where she'd gone, but he wouldn't be able to catch her if she got far enough. She just had to get far enough.

She ran blindly. She didn't care where she ended up, but she needed to go. She took a corner at a full sprint, then ran into a wall and bounced back and fell on her ass.

Rubbing her head, she looked up at the wall she knew wasn't supposed to be there. Not a wall. A man. A man she'd never seen before.

He was large with dark hair and the brightest blue eyes she'd ever seen. His olive skin glowed in the morning sunlight.

He reached for her, offering her his hand to help her stand. "Are you hurt? I didn't see you. Are you okay?" he asked in rapid succession.

His accent was slightly different from hers, but still Italian. Tina found herself unable to speak, which had the stranger's brows knitting together.

"Did you hit your head? Can you understand me?"

Tina shook her head to clear the fog.

"No? No to which question?"

She finally found her voice. "I didn't hit my head. I'm sorry. I was running, and I didn't...I wasn't paying attention to where I was going."

He offered her his hand again, and this time she took it. Sparks of lightning pulsed through Tina, and when she met the stranger's crystal blue eyes, she felt the power of it through every inch of her.

He pulled her to her feet in one swift movement as though she was one of the skinny girls in her class and not one of the chubby ones. Her mother was the best cook in town, and Tina's belly and rounded bottom were proof of it. She loved the way she looked, and if she were reading things right, so did the stranger whose eyes trailed down her womanly body.

"Thank you," Tina said. "I should be paying more attention."

He smiled. "It's hard to do when you're running through the streets like your bottom is on fire. Did someone hurt you? You've been crying."

Tina shook her head. "No, nothing like that."

"Then what has a beautiful woman crying like this?"

She smiled. "It's nothing. It'll be okay."

He raised his eyebrows and squeezed her hand, then released it. Tina couldn't explain the feeling she had when he stopped touching her, but it felt like a piece of her heart went missing. Like she wasn't whole without the stranger's touch.

"I hope it is because I don't like to see you cry."

"Do we know each other?" Tina asked.

He shook his head. "No. I definitely would have remembered a woman as beautiful as you."

Tina grinned. She'd kissed boys in her class, but none of them ever spoke to her the way this man was. There was an air of confidence around him that Tina had never known. He wasn't like the boys in school, the ones who were barely turning eighteen themselves. He had to be older. Wiser. Stronger. A man instead of a boy pretending he was a man.

"Do you live here?" Tina asked.

The man shook his head. "No. I live in Molveno. I'm here

for supplies. And apparently to save a beautiful woman from harming herself."

Tina smiled. Her cheeks heated with his compliment. "Thank you."

He grinned back and offered her his hand. "I'm Carmelo Richliano."

"Carmelo?" She rolled the name around on her tongue. She liked the way it felt. Like he was hers even though they'd only met moments ago. "I'm Tina Vincenzo. It's nice to meet you."

"The pleasure is all mine, Tina. And unfortunately, I need to run or I'll lose my position. Hopefully I'll run into you again sometime."

Tina nodded. "I definitely hope so, Carmelo."

He paused another moment before releasing her hand and continuing around the corner. She watched him until he disappeared from her view, then danced home on a cloud.

Carmelo Richliano was going to change her life. She just knew it.

Present Day

BELLA WANTED to believe it was the lake that drew her to the docks on Amavita Estates again, but it would have been a lie. She was hoping to see Ryan again.

After their lunch, she couldn't get him out of her mind. She barely knew him, but she felt a connection to him. Maybe it was the loss of their parents, or maybe it was the freedom that came with someone having no preconceived notions of who she was, but it was intoxicating being with him.

The moonlight guided Bella down the hill toward the water. She heard the gentle lapping of the water against the shore. She wondered if Ryan would appear again, but even if he didn't, she wanted to be there.

She was trying to get to know her father, but it wasn't easy building a relationship with a complete stranger. Especially when there were so many expectations. He wanted to know things Bella wasn't sure she was ready to talk about, like her mother, and Bella didn't really know what she wanted. Albert said she could ask him anything, but she didn't know what to ask. She just knew she wanted to meet him, and yell at him, but she never got the chance, and it left her feeling a little lost.

Her feet crunched along the frozen ground as she moved toward the water. It sounded loud to her ears, only to be drown out by the sound of her breathing.

The dock looked wet when Bella got closer. She wasn't sure if it was ice or just water, but she wasn't sure it was smart to test either one when there was an ice cold lake beneath the dock.

A small bench sat to the side of the dock. It was going to be cold through her jeans, but Bella wasn't ready to turn around and go back just yet. Something told her to stay there a little longer.

She lowered herself onto the bench and hissed when the icy wood seared her jeans and froze her ass. It didn't matter that she expected it, it was fucking cold.

Bella wiggled her butt to make sure she wasn't actually frozen to the bench then settled and blew on her hands. Her gloves were warm, but her fingers were always cold. Her heavy boots kept her toes from getting too cold, but she chose fashion over sense when she wore jeans only instead of long underwear beneath her clothes.

Too late now.

She sat there and listened as the water sloshed quietly along the shore. A part of her wished she'd arrived there in the summer and could swim at night instead of just staring at the water, but she planned to be long gone by the time the lake was warm enough to swim in.

Bella got lost in her thoughts, trying to decide where she was going to go once she left Bereton, and didn't hear the crunch of footsteps until they were almost to her.

She jumped and spun toward the newcomer, only to scare him and have him shout and take a quick step backward. He tripped over a root or slipped or something, and before she knew it, he was sprawled on the ground and groaning.

"Oh, my God. Are you okay?"

"Bella?" he croaked.

"Yeah. Sorry. I..."

"Was trespassing again?" Ryan said with a trace of humor in his voice.

"Well, yeah. And I was hoping to see you."

He pushed himself to a seated position. "You might get to see more than you bargained for. I think I ripped my damn pants."

A snort worked its way free from Bella's throat. She slapped her hand over her mouth, but it was too late.

"Are you laughing at me now?" Ryan asked.

She shrugged. "Maybe."

"What about this is so damn funny?" he demanded, although the teasing tone was still there.

"I don't know. You're this big, strong, firefighter who doesn't seem to get easily ruffled. And you're laying on the ground in ripped pants threatening to show me what you've got."

He snorted. "I...Jesus. You're going to get me into trouble."

"Trouble can be so much fun," Bella said with a grin.

Ryan shook his head. "Come over here and help me off the ground. I need to get to the bench."

Bella walked over and offered him her hand. She wondered for a second if he was going to tug her to the ground with him, but he just put his hand in hers and let her help him up. She wasn't really sure he needed the help, but touching him was definitely not a hardship so she did her best to help him.

He towered over her as they moved the last few feet to the bench together. As soon as his butt hit the bench, he yelped and jumped up.

"Holy fucking shit, that's cold."

Bella laughed again.

"You knew that, didn't you?" he asked.

She shrugged. "It was cold when I first sat down, but I forgot about it. Sorry. Don't you live here? Shouldn't you know it's cold? I mean, the ground's frozen you know."

He moved toward her slowly and grabbed her shoulders loosely. She wasn't sure what was happening, but she had to admit she was a big fan of anything that involved Ryan touching her. Or her touching him. Or them touching each other.

He moved his body closer to hers, and she enjoyed the nearness of him. She drew in a breath of cold air that smelled like him. She almost reached up to touch him, then he pushed her onto the bench.

"Oh, shit," she yelped, jumping up like he did. "I think it got colder since I've been sitting here. Dammit, that's cold."

Ryan chuckled. "Told you."

"You jerk," she said half-heartedly.

He laughed. "Hey, at least you have all of your pants. My bare thigh hit that bench. Fuck me. I think I have a freezer burn."

Bella snorted. "Freezer burn? Really?"

He shrugged. "Yeah. What do you call it?"

She shook her head. "An ice burn. Freezer burn is what happens to food in the freezer when it's not air tight."

"Whatever, it's fucking cold. I don't care what it's called, I thought my nuts were going to fall off."

Bella stopped, her laugh trapped in her throat. "Um, are you...I mean, do you..."

"Am I naked under these pants? Is that what you want to know, Bella?"

Well, hell. So much for being cold.

5
______

RYAN WISHED HE COULD SEE HER FACE. THE MOON WAS OUT
but it wasn't bright enough to illuminate her face and tell
him if her cheeks turned red or if her eyes widened. But that
little gasp? Ryan definitely enjoyed that.

He forced himself to chuckle and shake his head. "No,
I'm not naked under my pants. Briefs, since you asked."

"I didn't ask," she practically shouted.

Ryan shrugged. "You might as well have. And for the
record, I live with my cousin and his girlfriend, so I keep
things covered up at all times. I wouldn't want her getting a
peek and switching beds at night."

"What?" Bella gasped.

Ryan chuckled. She was too much fun to play with. And
he hadn't enjoyed himself that much in a long time. "I'm just
kidding. Sara adores Leo. And I'm not that kind of guy."

"What kind of guy are you?"

Ryan smiled into the darkness. She was flirting back.
Damn, that felt good. "I'm the kind of guy who knows how
to treat a woman. And knows how to treat another man's

woman. I don't steal and I don't share, and I expect the same from the women I get involved with."

"Are we involved?" she breathed.

The question surprised him. It shouldn't have, but it did. He was talking to her like she mattered and acting like she was someone important. And he barely knew anything about her.

"Why did you come here, Bella?"

She shifted, shrugging as she moved slightly away from him. "I don't know."

"You don't know?"

She shook her head. "No. I guess I thought it was going to be different. I thought...I wanted a connection."

"And you don't think we have a connection?"

She looked up at him. Her eyebrows knitted together in the middle then eased and she grinned. The brilliance of it had his lips curling up in response.

"Not even a little connection?"

She laughed softly. "Maybe a little."

"Then I guess we are involved. Maybe a little."

She grinned and looked out at the water. "I bet it's beautiful here in the summer, isn't it?"

Ryan leaned against the bench, his heavy coat blocking the cold from his back, and nodded. "It really is. We have a few boats that run adventures from our dock, and the vines are in full bloom. It's stunning."

"Have you always lived here?"

Ryan nodded. "I have, and I don't plan to leave. I love it here."

Bella nodded but she didn't say anything.

"What about you? Are you going back home sometime?"

She shrugged. "Probably not. My mom isn't there anymore, so I'm not really sure I want to be there. She was the reason I stuck around as long as I did. A lot of my friends got out as soon as we graduated high school. Some people stayed, but my mom was my best friend. Without her..."

Ryan nodded in understanding. "When my dad died, I wasn't sure I'd ever breathe again. It's a pain you can't understand unless you've been through it, but it's a pain I wouldn't wish on anyone. Losing a parent is something almost everyone will go through, but it sucks."

Bella laughed. "Yeah, it really does."

They were silent for a few minutes, just sitting quietly together. Ryan drew in a deep breath and blew it out slowly.

"Sounds like you're breathing," Bella said with a smile.

Ryan grinned at her. "It feels easier with you."

Bella let her hair fall in her face, blocking his view of her. He tucked the shoulder-length strands behind her ear and slid his finger down her jaw. She shivered and ran her tongue over her bottom lip.

Ryan wanted to give her a chance. He wanted to ask her. But he couldn't sit there and not want her. He leaned forward and captured her lip between his, drawing her to him. She didn't fight him. She willingly climbed onto his lap and wrapped her arms around his neck. She willingly pressed her body to his. She willingly slid her tongue into his mouth.

And he fucking loved it.

Too many women were afraid to ask for what they wanted. Bella was telling him with her body. She pushed closer until he could feel the heat of her against his growing erection.

He ached to feel her, to touch her skin. He went slow, sliding his hands up and down her thighs so she would get used to his touch. Then he went higher, cupping her ass and pulling her over his cock. She moaned and arched into him. The warmth of her body beckoned him, and he slid his hands up her back.

She screamed and jumped off him.

Ryan held his hands up and sucked in a breath. "I'm sorry, Bella. I wasn't trying to do something you weren't comfortable with."

"Your hands are cold as fuck," she gasped.

It took a few seconds for her words to penetrate the lust and guilt fog. Once they did, he breathed a laugh and shook his head. "I thought you were going to punch me. I thought I hurt you or scared you."

"You did scare me, but just because you're cold. Up until you touched me, I was rather enjoying myself."

Ryan grinned. "You and me both."

Instead of walking back to him and crawling on his lap again, she took a step toward the inn. "I should probably go."

"Really?"

She nodded. "Yeah. I think it's better if we don't do this outside."

"But inside is okay?"

That time he could see the blush on her cheeks. He smirked and she rolled her eyes. "You're horrible."

He shook his head. "Actually, I'm very, very good, Bella."

She chuckled and started walking. "Good night, Ryan."

"Good night, Bella."

He watched her until she disappeared behind the inn, then leaned back against the bench again. He listened to the water and wondered what it was about Bella that made life something he wanted to be a part of again.

~

RYAN HADN'T BEEN able to get the idea of looking into Perry out of his head. When Matt first mentioned it, he considered the idea then dismissed it. But the longer it went on, the more Ryan wanted to find out the truth and get the proof his father insisted was out there somewhere.

Ryan waited until he was sure Henry's wife, Cynthia, was gone, then went to the home they grew up in. Henry and Cynthia reconnected right after Victor died and moved into the family home when Henry and Ryan's mom decided she wanted to be with her sister and mother instead of in a big house all by herself. Henry and Cynthia made the house their own, but they didn't get rid of anything.

Henry opened the door in bare feet with sweatpants and a tee on. He grinned at Ryan and stepped back so he could walk inside out of the bitter cold that settled in overnight.

"Want some coffee?" Henry asked.

Ryan nodded. "Yeah, sounds good."

Henry poured Ryan a cup from the waiting coffee pot and slid it across the island. Almost all the homes on Amavita had large islands in the middle of the kitchen. Most were built around the same time and had similar features, but they'd all been upgraded and remodeled over the years to make them feel different.

"Everything okay?" Henry asked when Ryan didn't immediately tell him why he was there.

Ryan and Henry weren't close growing up. The more than seven years between them didn't help, but they were also into their own things. As adults, they had a lot more in common and became friends who knew each other as well as two people could. It didn't surprise Ryan at all that Henry could see something was bothering him.

"I want to find the proof Dad was looking for. That Perry stole from us," Ryan finally admitted.

Henry drew in a breath and leaned back. He crossed his arms over his chest and shook his head slowly. Ryan sipped his coffee and waited, knowing his brother would need to process the idea for a minute before he said anything. Henry didn't leap, but he was a reasonable person who worshipped their dad the same way Ryan did. Losing him was a hit to both of them, but Henry fell in love with Cynthia and found comfort and relief in her. Ryan was still alone in his grief.

"Where do you think you'll find proof?" Henry asked.

Ryan shrugged. "I don't know, but I was going to start here. Dad took notes on everything. I thought there might be something in one of his old books. Even if it's just something to give us a direction."

"Eventually, you're going to have to get onto Perry's property."

Ryan nodded. "I know. I haven't figured that one out yet. But I have some brothers in blue and might be able to talk one of them into it, especially if I can find something in Dad's stuff."

Henry nodded slowly. He finished his coffee and rinsed it then set it in the dishwasher and turned to Ryan again. "Let's go look."

Ryan followed his brother down the hall to their parents bedroom. Henry never felt comfortable moving into the bedroom their parents shared for so many years. Cynthia agreed, so the room stayed the way it was when their mother moved out. She insisted they use it, but Henry confided that having sex in their parents' old bed was a mood killer. Even the thought of it had him shriveling. Ryan chuckled, but he understood completely.

Henry turned on the light and moved to the windows to pull back the curtains. The room was clean and neat and obviously used, but it was still the same as ever.

The brothers worked side-by-side for an hour. Ryan went through their father's nightstand and read notes he kept not long before he died. Henry searched the bookshelf for more notes. By the end of the hour, neither of them found anything helpful.

"Dammit," Ryan said, sinking to the bed. "I really thought we'd find something."

Henry sat next to him and nodded. "I hoped we would, too. Dad was positive Perry stole from us. He built a vine-yard way too quickly and with too many similarities for Dad to have been wrong. Even if he misplaced something, there was no doubt in my mind he was right."

"Did you ever wonder if Dad was wrong? If Perry didn't really steal anything, just Dad thought he did and it was misplaced?"

Henry turned to look at Ryan, his brows drawn together in anger. "No. Do you really think that? Is that why you came looking in here? Because you thought you would find the manual Dad insisted Perry stole?"

Ryan shook his head, struggling to remain calm. "I didn't want to find anything like that, but I've wondered. All these years and nothing was ever found out. It was Dad's word against Perry's."

"And you don't believe Dad?" Henry asked, pushing off the bed to pace across the room.

Ryan stood and sighed. "I didn't say that. I just said..."

"That you aren't sure," their mother said from the doorway. Josephine Wilson wasn't a tall woman, but she was the kind of woman who took up space. She was round with chubby cheeks and an easy smile for everyone. But she wasn't smiling as she looked at her sons.

"Ma," Ryan started.

Jo held up her hand. "Your father wondered the same

thing for years. He thought he was going crazy when the manual first went missing. He couldn't figure out where he'd put it. He hated the idea of Perry having taken something from him, but he insisted no one else could have. Even before Perry opened Perry Mount, your father was sure he was the one who stole from us." She sighed and moved farther into the room. "Your father wasn't perfect. Neither am I, and neither are you two. We're all flawed, but that's doesn't mean he was wrong. I think we never found any proof because Perry either destroyed the proof or he was smart enough to hide it somewhere people wouldn't see it. If I stole something, I wouldn't flaunt it. I would hide it."

"I'm sorry, Ma," Ryan said, feeling like a scolded child.

Jo shrugged. "You don't need to be sorry. It's reasonable to wonder. Your father and I talked about it constantly. He was always second guessing himself, even after we'd retired. He was worried about you boys. What if Perry tried to get something else? What if he tried to destroy what we built? What if he ruined Amavita Estates? Your father loved this place, and he trusted and cared about others with his whole self. He reminded me of my father in many ways. Willing to take someone under his wing and help them learn without a thought to who they were. They both believed everyone deserved a fair shot, and everyone deserved more than a few second chances. With Perry, your father was hurt. He trusted the man and was cheated by him. He would have given everything to Perry if he'd been honest, and we could have built a relationship with Perry Mount, but instead he lied and cheated and stole from us. That's why your father never let go of what happened."

"I'm sorry," Ryan said again.

Jo nodded and stretched out her arms for him to step into them. Ryan took the embrace from his mother, wondering if she needed it as much as he did. Henry moved behind him and the three of them held on to each other for a long moment, missing the man who completed their family.

"I wish your father was still here, and I wish he had found the proof he believed was there, but proof wouldn't really change anything. He knew what happened," Jo said sadly.

Ryan pulled back and nodded. "I just feel like Dad could rest if we found something."

"Is this about you or your dad?" Jo asked.

Ryan shrugged. "Maybe a little of both."

"I think you boys should look into it. Go through Dad's stuff and check his old notes. If there is anything to find, you will find it. And if not, maybe we can let him rest."

The message was clear. She didn't like them digging things up, but she would support Ryan's need for answers. But if they didn't find the answers he hoped to find, she wanted him to let it go.

Ryan wasn't sure how he was going to let it go, which meant he had one option. To find the proof.

"Not that we're not happy to see you, Ma, but what are you doing here?" Henry asked, breaking into Ryan's determined thoughts.

Ryan turned to their mom and waited for her to say something.

"Can't I come visit my sons?"

"How did you know I was going to be here?" Ryan asked.

She shrugged. "Fine, I didn't. I was talking to Marie and Ma and thinking about getting rid of some of your dad's things. I wanted to come check it out. See if I could handle letting go of his stuff."

Pain hit Ryan so hard he had to sit on the bed. He looked

around the room and wasn't sure he'd ever be able to walk in there if it changed. Change was bad enough, but getting rid of things?

"You can't," Ryan said immediately. "You can't get rid of Dad."

Jo shook her head. "He's already gone, honey. I hate it, too, but he's gone. All this is just stuff."

"But it was *his* stuff," Ryan said.

Jo nodded. "I know, but I feel like I need to move on. Like I need to start to let go. I moved out of here right after your dad died because I couldn't stand to be in this house without him. It's been two years. I miss him every day, but this room is a shrine. No one enjoys it. Henry and Cynthia should be able to enjoy this room. Use it. Make it theirs."

Ryan swung his gaze to his brother and growled. "Did you put her up to this? Did you tell her she had to erase Dad? Is that what this is?"

Henry shook his head, but before he could open his mouth, Jo said, "Henry didn't know anything about this, Ry. This is all me. And I'm not saying I'm doing anything yet, but this room just sits here. I don't remember your dad because of his things. I remember your dad because I loved him and still love him. I remember him when you smile or when you share your love with Cynthia. This room is just a place where his old things sit."

"It's not...but it's..." Ryan sighed. "I can't believe you would do this."

Ryan glared at his mother and brother then stormed out of the room and the house. Henry called out to him, but he ignored his brother and kept going. He didn't want to hear it was time to let go of his father. He wasn't ready. And he wasn't sure he ever would be.

6

———

Bella scrolled through her phone absently. She wanted to make a call, but she knew there would be no answer. That was the hardest part. Knowing no matter what she did, she'd never talk to her mother again. She'd never tell her about Ryan or about meeting her dad or about anything else that ever happened in her life.

Bella tossed the phone onto the bed. She'd been in Bereton two weeks, and in all that time, she hadn't made friends with anyone. She hadn't called any of her former coworkers or so-called friends. And they hadn't called her. It was like no one noticed, or cared, that she left town.

She thought about calling her mom's former partner, but Julia made it clear the last time they spoke that she wasn't a big fan of Bella's. Julia said she wasn't going to keep paying Bella unless she actually did good work. She didn't think she was that bad, but Julia told her about all the times her mother saved her ass and redid her work.

Bella never knew.

More and more she was learning things about her

mother. On one hand, she was so mad at her for hiding her father from her, but on the other, she was her mother, her best friend, and her biggest supporter. It was the times she thought about that when Bella wasn't sure how she was going to make it through the day.

Bella laid back on her bed and wondered what she was going to do with her life. She'd been thinking about it a lot and hadn't come up with anything. It was sad really. She was going to be thirty in less than three years, and she had no more going for her than she had when she was graduating high school.

A knock on her door brought her out of her pity party. It was a shitty party anyway, and she was definitely ready to leave. She plastered on a smile and opened the door.

Albert shifted his weight and grinned at her. He looked as comfortable as she felt. "Um, hi, Bella. I don't want to interrupt anything. I was wondering if you...I mean what you're doing today."

Bella shrugged. "I don't have any plans. I don't know anyone, so I don't really have a life."

Albert grinned and Bella was surprised again how much his smile looked like hers. Her own lips curled up seeing his smile.

"Well, I was going to go walking around the vineyard. I like to be out there, and it's quiet and peaceful right now. I wondered if you wanted to join me. And maybe I could teach you about making wine."

He was cute. He clearly had no clue how to talk to her, or what to say, and the shy, nerdy thing was endearing. Especially since she expected a first class asshole.

Bella nodded. "That sounds good. What do I need to wear?"

"Oh, what you're in is fine. I mean, you need a jacket, too, but we won't get dirty or anything."

"Sounds good. Thanks, Albert."

He nodded and turned away, still grinning.

Bella breathed a laugh and followed him. She put on her boots and winter coat, then let him lead her from the house at the back of the property into the vines that surrounded it.

When she first arrived there, she felt connected to the place. It was like she was meant to be there. She'd always known there was more to her, and seeing her father and living on his property felt like maybe that was it. Maybe she really was meant for more than just screwing up everything around her.

Albert walked a while before he stopped suddenly. Bella almost crashed into him, stopping herself just before she collided with his back. He drew in a deep breath and held it, then turned to her. "Do you smell that?"

Bella sniffed the air and shrugged. "I smell dirt, I think."

Albert nodded. "It's good dirt. And lake water. And crisp, winter air. All that is why I bought this piece of land. We're up on the hill so we are a little insulated from the cold water off the lake. We can grow different grapes up here than they can. It's what makes Perry Mount Vineyards so successful."

"Really?" Bella asked. She was more than a little surprised. Perry Mount had been fairly quiet since she'd been there, but the few times she'd gone to Amavita, it was busy.

Albert nodded. "Yes. They draw in customers with gimmicks like parties and using the restaurant, but when people come here, it's because of the wine. They know they're going to get a great glass of wine."

"But isn't it good to diversify your offerings? To give

people more than one reason to come here so they can get different things? I always buy my wine at the liquor store. Coming to a vineyard, especially when it's only open a few hours a day, is kind of a pain."

Albert huffed and turned toward the large building off to the south. Bella wasn't sure why he was annoyed with her, but it was clear by his fast pace and the way he ignored her that he definitely was.

When he finally made it to the building, Bella raced to catch up to him. He held the door open for her, waiting until she got there with a look that said she needed to move faster.

"Sorry," Bella said softly. "I wasn't trying to tell you how to run your business. Obviously you know a lot more than I do."

Albert sighed again and closed his eyes. "I'm sorry, too. I shouldn't take it out on you that I'm frustrated. I tried to start up a restaurant, but it was too much for me to handle so much on my own. I considered a partner, but giving up control of everything was hard to fathom. Everything you said was true, but it frustrates me that across the street they can do everything because there's a million of them running the place. Everyone has a job, and I'm just me."

Bella bit her lip to avoid offering more advice. She didn't know how to run a business. She wasn't an expert in anything. She just nodded and gave him what she hoped was an understanding smile.

Albert smiled back and nodded deeper into the building. "Let's stop talking about that family and talk about the best wine on Cayuga Lake. Want to try some?"

Bella nodded eagerly. "I wouldn't pass that up."

Albert chuckled and led the way. He stopped outside an office and pulled out a key. He unlocked the door and let us inside. "This is my office. I don't let many people in here, but I always have some samples of wine. What do you usually drink?"

"White. A little sweet."

Albert grabbed a bottle from the fridge and twisted the top off. He poured it into a glass and handed it over.

Bella swirled the wine the way she'd seen people do in restaurants. She didn't really know what she was doing or why, but she wanted to impress her father. She wanted him to like her and think she was smart.

"When you swirl the wine," Albert said, "you are introducing air into it. You're letting the wine breathe and you're checking for how well it holds up. If you hold it up to the light, you'll see what we call legs running down the side. That's a good sign. Of course, I know this wine is amazing."

Bella laughed with him then brought the glass to her lips. She could smell the fruity scent of the wine, and when it hit her tongue, the cool, refreshing sweetness exploded in her mouth.

"Wow," she breathed. "That's amazing."

Albert grinned proudly. For the first time since she met him, she saw what her mother saw in him. He was older than her mother, by a good bit if she had to guess, but he had a charm about him that would have been easy to get sucked into. On top of his nerdy exterior, he was smart and enjoyed what he did. If he showed any of that to her mother, it was no doubt she fell for him.

"I knew you would like that one. This is a little drier, but it's still good."

He opened another tiny bottle of wine and poured it into her glass. He was right, it was drier, but it was still excellent wine.

"This is the last one we'll try today. I don't want you feeling sick," Albert said.

Bella nodded. She didn't think about the alcohol getting into her head. That was the last thing she needed.

"The first one was my favorite," Bella said after she tried them all. "I'd definitely take a bottle of that home."

"You can have as many as you'd like," Albert said quickly. "You don't have to pay for them."

"Thanks," Bella said. "But I'll pay. I mean, this is what you do. My mom was always really careful about that. She said you should get paid for the work you do, even by family and friends."

Albert shrugged. "I guess your mother and I would disagree on something else then."

Bella wanted to defend her mother, but the words were stuck in her throat. She always thought it was cold that her mother didn't even offer a discount to her closest friends. She was excellent at what she did, but Bella thought they should treat friends like friends and clients like clients. She was always outvoted.

"For what it's worth, I agree with you," Bella said softly.

Albert grinned at her. He cleaned up the office and led them back out, locking the door behind them. He showed her the equipment they use to press the grapes and all the kettles and barrels where the grapes fermented into wine. His joy and excitement were clear with every word. He truly loved what he did the way her mother loved working with numbers.

Bella wanted that. She wanted to know she was made for something. That she couldn't go another day without having that passion in her life.

She just didn't know what would bring it to her world. Or if she'd ever know.

"DO YOU WANT TO HAVE LUNCH?" Albert asked as they walked back to the house.

Bella considered saying no, but she was enjoying her time with him. He was interesting and had a way of explaining everything without making her feel stupid. And she was there to get to know him.

"Yeah, that sounds good."

His grin told her exactly how much her agreement meant.

Bella followed him into the kitchen and washed her hands after he did. He went to the fridge and stared into it. She stood behind him and peered at the mostly empty space.

"We can go out, too. There's a restaurant across the street," Bella offered.

Albert slid her a glare over his shoulder. It was so icy, Bella shivered. He closed the fridge and turned to face her. "Have you been to Amavita Estates?"

Bella quickly shook her head, lying easily even though she wasn't sure why. "No. I just saw a sign at the road."

"I'm not welcome on their property, and I imagine if they knew you were my daughter, they'd feel the same about you."

"Why?" Bella blurted.

Albert drew in a breath and released it slowly. The pain in his eyes surprised her, but it was gone so quickly, she wondered if she imagined it.

"They think I stole from them. It's all lies, but they think I did."

"Really?" Bella asked, more than a little surprised.

"They're sore losers who think they should be the only

vineyard in this part of the lake. When I opened this place, they were mad. Every other vineyard in the area came over and offered help and advice, but Victor said he hoped I fell flat on my face."

"What?" Bella blurted. The vitriol in his voice told her how much Albert hated Victor. The only one she'd met was Ryan, but she couldn't imagine the rest of his family being so cruel.

"He used to manage the grapes, the growing. I worked for him for a summer, and he accused me of lying to get a job and stealing from him when I left. None of it is true."

"They must have seasonal workers all the time," Bella defender her father.

Albert nodded. "They do. Everyone in the area does. At least, everyone who picks grapes by hand. But Victor was upset with me. He never forgave me, and when he died two years ago, I hoped the family would let it go. I think it only fueled some of them. Especially his sons."

Bella couldn't breathe. Ryan's father died two years ago. It couldn't be a coincidence. "His sons?"

Albert nodded again. "Henry and Ryan. They believed their father, and they make sure I know it every time they see me."

"When do they see you?" Bella asked. If he didn't go there, and they didn't go to his vineyard, where did they see each other?

Albert's ears turned red. "Just around. It's a small town."

Bella nodded, but something was off. She learned to lie at a very young age and doing so came naturally to her. Her mother told her she could have been a politician with how easily she switched her story to suit the person she was talking to. For Bella, it meant she had a natural ability to tell when others were trying to bullshit her. And Albert was definitely trying to bullshit her. There was a lot more to the story.

"That really sucks," Bella said, letting his lie go. She'd never learn the truth if she called him on his first lie.

Albert nodded again and shuffled to the pantry. He rubbed his belly, something she noticed he did when he was anxious. He grabbed something and turned to her. "How about we make nachos? I have ground beef in the freezer and we can add some jalapeños and tomatoes and cheese and have an easy lunch?"

Bella nodded even though she wasn't a big fan of spicy food. She loved the Italian food at The Drunken Grape, but she was going to have to avoid that for a while.

Albert put the frozen pack of beef in a pan and put a lid over it to keep the heat in. Bella spread tortilla chips on a baking sheet to bake everything once they assembled it all.

Albert was quiet while he cooked. He added spices and browned the meat, then drained it before adding in the chopped tomatoes and sliced jalapeños. He stirred it all together and spooned it evenly over the chips, topping the whole thing with shredded cheese before sliding it into the oven.

Albert poured himself a glass of water and one for Bella. While they waited for the nachos to finish, he cleaned up the kitchen and made everything look perfect again.

"I'll get to the store today," he said with a sheepish grin. "I need to do better about that, especially with you here. Living alone, I tend to eat whatever I have, but with a woman in the house, I'll be better."

Bella nodded. "I can shop, too."

"You're my guest. I can't ask you to do that."

Bella shrugged. "I don't mind. My mom taught me to cook when I was young, and we were always careful with money, so I'm used to shopping on a budget."

Albert nodded. "I don't know if I said it, but I'm sorry about your mom."

The pain hit Bella. Talking about her mom was normal. She always talked about her mom. But his apology reminded her that she would never again talk to her mom. She sucked in a breath and nodded, forcing a smile.

"You two were close, weren't you?" Albert asked softly.

Bella nodded. "She was my best friend."

"She was a sweet woman. She was much younger than me, and I never understood what she saw in me, but maybe that's why we didn't last. Maybe she didn't see much good in me."

Bella didn't know what to say. The truth was her mother never spoke highly of Albert, except to share his knowledge. She always told Bella he was smart, but other than that, she wasn't a fan of his.

"I'm guessing you agree," Albert said with a sad smile. "It amazes me how much you look like her."

Bella shook her head. "Mom didn't tell me much about you. I asked all the time when I was young, and she told me how smart you were. She said she cared a lot for you, but she said you didn't want me. I gave up asking when she told me you were dead."

His angry glare appeared and vanished in the same second. He pressed his lips together and retrieved the nachos from the oven. When he faced her again, his smile was forced and fake. "Shall we eat?"

Bella nodded and forced her own fake smile. They filled their plates and talked about absolutely nothing while they ate. The weather, the town, and the weekend coming. Bella thought they were making progress and getting closer, but it was one step forward and four leaps back with Albert. Maybe her mom wasn't so off in her assessment of him. Maybe he was cold and distant, and maybe she was better off without him in her life.

7

____

72 years ago

CARMELO SCOURED THE STREETS THE NEXT DAY WHEN HE went into town. She was there somewhere, he just didn't know where. Tina Vincenzo had played in his dreams the night before, the woman who stirred something in him when she ran smack into him on the street in broad daylight.

His first impression of her was concern, but once he knew she wasn't injured, he appreciated the woman. She was full of lush curves and legs that could inspire a man. He'd known his share of women, but none like her with an innocence he knew wasn't fake and a genuine interest in him.

He thought about asking around to see if anyone knew who she was, but he thought better of it. The small towns where they lived were full of gossips and he wasn't interested in it getting back to anyone that he was asking after a woman who belonged to someone else.

Carmelo threw the bag of sugar over his shoulder and

headed back the way he came. When they had to run errands in town, the vineyard sent one truck and all the men had a job to minimize the time they were gone. Since Carmelo was the youngest one on the crew, they always gave him the hardest job. Heavy lifting or dealing with shopkeepers with young daughters they were trying to marry off.

For the most part, Carmelo didn't mind. Carrying supplies helped keep him in shape, and many of the daughters were more than happy to sneak out at night and meet up with him, not that their fathers knew. He had a pretty good life, even though he didn't come from one of the wealthier families in the area. He made his own way, and he planned to work his way up and make a name for himself. One day, he'd have his own vineyard.

Carmelo set the sack of sugar down outside the sweet shop and went inside. Regina was behind the counter as she usually was. He plastered on a smile and sauntered up to her, winking when he caught her gaze.

Regina's cheeks pinked, but she didn't turn away. Regina was one of the women Carmelo met up with regularly. He worried she was getting attached, but she assured him she knew there was nothing more between them and that she was going to marry someone else. Carmelo didn't get involved in the inner workings of Andalo, and who was marrying whom, as long as no one was marking him as their territory.

"Hey, Carmelo," Regina said with a wide grin. "You here for your regular order?"

Carmelo nodded even though they both knew why he was there. If the shop was quiet, they would sneak into the back and have a little fun while her father was out on deliveries.

"No one's here," Regina said suggestively.

Carmelo grinned and moved toward the edge of the counter. Before he got there, the bell over the door chimed and alerted them to company.

Carmelo stifled his groan and sighed. He wasn't sure he would have time to wait until customers cleared out, but if they were quick...

"A dozen cookies, Regina. And some of those pastries. Ma said she can't get enough of them."

Carmelo turned. He knew that voice. He'd only heard it once, but he knew it as well as he knew his own. "Tina?"

She turned to him with shock in her wide, brown eyes. A slow grin curled her lips. Not seductive, but one of pure joy. "Carmelo. I wondered if I was going to see you again."

Carmelo moved closer to her. "I'm just happy it's not on your bottom this time."

Tina laughed with abandon. Her head tipped back to expose her succulent neck and the upper swell of her breasts. The blue plaid dress she wore fell all wrong on her, but he grew hard at the curves that pressed against the fabric. Her long, slender fingers reached out and wrapped around his arm. She shook her head.

"Thankfully, I'm upright today."

"Is that all?" Regina asked in a tone that told them she was impatient and ready for Tina to leave.

Tina let go of Carmelo's arm and faced Regina again, flashing her a smile. There was a small gap between her front teeth, and a bead of sweat ran down her neck, disappearing between her breasts.

"Some muffins, too. Half a dozen of them."

"I'm not sure you should be eating those," Regina said under her breath but loudly enough that Tina and Carmelo heard her.

Tina clamped her mouth shut and chewed on her lip.

She didn't look at Carmelo, and didn't say anything to Regina as she boxed up the muffins.

Tina was eyeing the cannolis in the case also, but when Regina asked if there was anything else she wanted, she shook her head.

Once she paid, Tina raced out of there and turned the same way Carmelo was heading. He spun to face Regina and glared at her.

"Are you ready? I made sure I got rid of her."

"Why did you treat her like that?"

Regina rolled her eyes. "Are you here to lecture me or here to go in the back? Because you don't get to tell me how to run my father's business."

"What did it help to make her feel badly?"

"She doesn't matter. She's a chubby girl who thinks she can flirt with you. She needed to know to keep her hands off."

Carmelo's eyebrows shot up. "Is that your way of saying you think I'm yours? Because that's not the way this works."

"We've been together for almost a year. And you don't go out with other women. I know. I've asked around. Made sure everyone knows you're mine," Regina said.

Carmelo backed up, shaking his head. "No. I'm not yours. I never was, and I never will be again. We're over."

"What? Why? Is this because I told the fat girl she needs to lay off the muffins?"

Carmelo saw red. Tina was ten times more beautiful than Regina, and she ran out of there thinking she wasn't enough for him, and Regina thought she was.

"You don't need to talk to people like that. And we're over because we were never anything."

"You don't mean that," Regina said, her voice low and deadly. "You love me."

Carmelo snorted and shook his head, backing closer to the door. "No, Regina. I don't. I never have, and I never will. We're done."

She was still screaming when he walked out and snagged his sugar sack and took off down the street.

He wasn't sure where Tina went, but he ran anyway, hoping he'd catch a glimpse of her. At the first turn, he went right. At the second turn, he went left. Then he spotted her. She was up ahead, shoulders slumped as she carried her bag from the sweet shop home.

Carmelo ran faster, knowing she'd duck in somewhere or hide if he called out to her. When he finally caught up to her, he dragged in a deep breath. "You're fast."

She jumped at his words and nearly dropped her bag. "What? Why are you here?"

"Regina wasn't nice to you. I wanted to make sure you were okay."

She stopped and looked him over, then closed her eyes and shook her head. "I see. Yes, you can report back that I'm fine. And that I'll send my brother from now on."

Carmelo's brows pulled together. "Why?"

Tina rolled her eyes. "Because she doesn't want me around you. She doesn't want anyone around you. I didn't realize you were the same man she's told everyone in town to stay away from."

"I'm not hers. I don't belong to her. And I've just ended things with her."

Tina shrugged and continued walking. "That's up to you."

Carmelo raced to catch up with her again. "She's not my girlfriend."

Tina just shrugged. "Not my business."

"No, but I want you to know I didn't know how she was

with people. I didn't mean for her to treat you that way." Carmelo put his hand on her arm to stop her. That same jolt he felt before sparked through him.

Tina looked down to where his hand rested then up to his face. He thought she was going to say something about their connection, but instead she asked, "And what if the person in there next time you visit is a young girl who looks like me? One with a little extra weight around her middle or who developed early? One who cares what beautiful people think about her? One who can't shake off the bitchy mean girl? Are you going to chase her out of the store or are you going to just thank Regina for running off the distraction and go in the back?"

Carmelo wasn't sure what to say. She was right. It wasn't the first time Regina had run someone off, and she wasn't usually nice about it. But he let it happen because he was thinking with his cock instead of his head.

"You're right," Carmelo said to her retreating back. "You're right, I should have stopped her long before this. Regina isn't a nice woman, and I wasn't nice by standing by while she treated others poorly."

Tina nodded. "Yep."

"I told her not to speak to you that way, and I ended things with her."

"And you think she's going to stop?"

Carmelo shook his head. "No, I'm sure she won't."

"Our actions have consequences. Something I'm learning right now. It's not fun, but it's the way the world works."

Carmelo leaned down to capture her gaze and saw a sadness there that ripped him in two. "What happened, Tina?"

She looked up and shook her head. "It's nothing."

"It's something, and I'd like to know what it is."

She shook her head again, then asked, "Why do you need that much sugar?"

Carmelo wanted to press her, but she clearly didn't want to talk about it. She was still talking to him, so he let it go and explained how they use sugar to sweeten some of the wines at the vineyard where he worked.

"Aren't the grapes sweet enough?" she asked.

He shrugged. "Not always. This year everything is a little drier than we'd like. Harvest is coming, and we're trying to get prepared."

"What do you do at the vineyard?"

"Whatever needs to be done. The vintner likes me so I work with him a lot. I'm in the fields every day, too. I can fix equipment and drive just about anything."

"You sound like a good guy to have around."

"I'd like to think so."

She smiled and ducked her chin, a blush creeping up her cheeks.

"Do you have a boyfriend, Tina?"

She shook her head.

"Why in the world not?"

She shrugged. "I haven't picked one yet."

He laughed at her answer. It sounded accurate. She could have her pick of any man in town if she wanted. He watched the way others followed her with their eyes, and how oblivious she was to all the attention. He wasn't the only man who'd noticed her feminine curves and wanted them for himself.

"Am I in the running?" Carmelo asked.

She grinned slyly. "Well, until an hour ago, you were off limits. I'm pretty sure I'd end up with poison baked in our muffins if I considered you for the job."

"I'll be your personal taste tester. Make sure everything is safe for you. Peel your grapes and feed you."

She laughed, the sound going straight through him once more. She had no clue how much she captivated him. He wanted to wrap her in his arms and take her away, never to let another man have a chance with her.

"I don't think you have to worry about anything like that. That's what siblings are for."

Carmelo barked a laugh at her joke. He'd left behind siblings when he moved north to get a job on the vineyard. His parents didn't like him leaving, but he wasn't far away. His parents couldn't afford to feed him, and he was old enough to work, so he left and committed to sending money home every chance he had. But he also understood the contemptuous relationship common between siblings. He wanted to help his parents, but helping his siblings was a byproduct.

"They're lucky to have you."

She smiled, but it didn't meet her stunning brown eyes.

"There's that look again. A beautiful woman like you shouldn't be so worried about things."

She smiled up at him. "Thank you."

He cupped her chin and stepped closer to her, letting the sack of sugar slide to the floor. He leaned down, the need to know what her lips taste like erasing all other thoughts or cares.

She slicked her tongue over her pink lips and drew in a shaky breath. He leaned closer and closer, giving her more than enough time to argue. He expected her to push him off or tell him no or slap him, but she just let her eyes slip closed and waited.

Her sweet breath danced over his cheeks, and he drew one last breath, savoring the moment.

Then a horn blasted. She jumped back, her chin falling from his grasp as she moved away from him quickly. He turned to see who interrupted them and found his coworkers piled into the truck ready to go back to work.

"Tina," he tried, but she didn't stop her retreat before she turned and ran the other way.

With a sigh, Carmelo hefted the sugar into the truck then leapt over the tailgate and stared at Tina's rapidly vanishing figure.

"You got lucky," Joey said with a nod.

Carmelo shook his head. "I wish. You guys showed up too soon."

Joey shook his head. "No, you got lucky. If we were a few seconds later, you'd have been in a world of hurt."

Carmelo glared at his best friend and partner. Joey was the one who vouched for him when he showed up at the vineyard even though they'd never met. Carmelo promised Joey he wouldn't regret the decision, and after almost two years, Joey knew Carmelo was a man of his word.

"What are you talking about?"

"She's off-limits. Don't even think about touching her again."

Carmelo's gaze tracked back to Tina. She was no longer visible, but he could still feel her presence. He wanted her back in his arms, and the idea of not touching her again was more painful than losing any woman ever had been.

"Do you know her?"

Joey nodded and swiped his straw hat off his head and wiped his face with the rag underneath. "Everyone knows Tina Vincenzo. You should, too."

"What are you talking about? Why should I know her? Who is she?"

Joey sighed and shook his head. "She's the oldest of the

Vincenzo's. And she's going to marry the boss's son. She's off-limits, unless you plan to leave the country. She's not yours, Carmelo, and she never will be."

Carmelo fell back. He stared after the woman he almost kissed. She was a girl the last time he saw her, although it was less than a year ago, so she wasn't. He just didn't remember her.

And now that he did, he knew what everyone in the truck knew the moment they drove up.

He was never going to have her because he wasn't anywhere near good enough for her.

8

Present Day

RYAN STOOD OUTSIDE THE APARTMENT DOOR AND TOOK A breath. He hadn't seen his mother since the day she caught him and Henry going through their dad's old things. Usually he heard from his mom daily, but it had been four days. It was past time for a visit.

He raised his hand and knocked on the door, waiting patiently. Andie told him his mom was inside, so it was a matter of waiting for her to answer his knock and hopefully agree to have lunch with him.

"Well, this is a surprise," Nonna said, opening the door instead of Jo. "What do I owe this honor to?"

Ryan floundered. He didn't want to upset the other woman who mattered more to him than anything, but he had fences to mend with his mom, not his grandmother.

"I was hoping to take Mom to lunch. Is she here?"

Nonna nodded and moved back so Ryan could walk into the room. "She is. We were about to grab something. Do you want to join us?"

It wasn't what Ryan planned, but maybe having Nonna there wasn't such a bad thing. If anyone knew the history of Amavita and could shed some light on what happened, it was her.

"That would be great."

"What would be great?" Jo said, walking out of the bedroom and meeting Ryan's eyes. Her dark hair was streaked with more gray every year, but she still looked the same as when Ryan graduated high school. She wore a pair of jeans and a purple top with a square neck and the necklace Victor gave her the last Christmas he was alive.

"Ryan's going to join us for lunch," Nonna answered for him.

Ryan held his mother's gaze, hoping she would nod. When she finally did, he felt like he took his first breath in days. Everything would be okay.

Ryan smiled and let Nonna hold his arm as they walked through the inn to the back where the restaurant was. As a kid, Ryan loved playing there. He would run up and down the stairs with his brother and cousins. They would play hide and seek all throughout the space. He lived and breathed Amavita Estates his whole life, and through all of it were his grandmother and parents. His aunts and uncles were there, too, but being one of the youngest cousins, the rest of them had their hands full by the time Ryan arrived. Nonna was never too busy for him, though, and neither were his parents.

"Let's sit by the window," Nonna said. "Then I can look out at the water while you two argue."

"We're not arguing, Ma," Jo said with a sigh.

"Could've fooled me. You barely said hello to your son, and he didn't do any better."

Ryan knew Nonna was right, and that nothing ever got

by her. He let Nonna lead him to the table she wanted to sit at, and Ryan said, "I wanted to find proof about Perry. Mom heard me ask Henry if he thought there was a chance Dad was wrong."

"That's not why I'm upset with you," Jo said.

"It's not?"

Jo shook her head, her dark hair spilling over her shoulders.

"Why are you mad at me?"

"I don't like that you thought about it, or that you doubted your father. You know who he was, and if his own flesh and blood isn't going to believe him, then why would anyone else. But what really bothered me was that you were doing all this behind my back. I thought you would have come to me about it. Instead, you went to your brother and started digging through my room."

"I'm sorry, Ma," Ryan said, feeling about a foot tall. "I should have asked you if it was okay to go through Dad's stuff. I just didn't want to give you any false hope."

Jo shook her head. "It doesn't matter if you find anything or not. I know the truth. I told you that."

"She's right," Nonna said. "Your father wasn't the kind of man who made accusations lightly. There was never a doubt in my mind that he knew exactly what happened. If he just wondered, he would have kept it to himself. Instead, he made sure all of us knew what Perry did."

"But what about everyone else? All the people who bought into Perry's innocence. Who doubted Dad?"

Jo shrugged. "I'm sure some of them won't believe even without any sort of proof. I don't want you going down the same rabbit hole your father went down. It's been twenty years. I don't know if it's worth it anymore."

Ryan wanted to agree with his mother, but something

kept telling him he needed to know. He had to help his father rest.

Ryan almost groaned when Amy walked over to take their orders. "Hey, everyone. Can I start you with something to drink or are you ready for your orders?"

"We can order, honey," Nonna said. "I'll start with Riesling, a big glass, not the little ones. Then I want a Caesar salad and lasagna for lunch. What dessert does Zach have today?"

Amy scribbled the order then flipped her book to the front. "Today he has tiramisu, cannolis, chocolate cheesecake, and cookies with ice cream."

"Tiramisu, please. After we're done with lunch, please."

Amy nodded and looked at Jo. "For you?"

"I'd like the house salad with balsamic, chicken parmesan, and I'll skip dessert."

"To drink?"

"Oh, just water for me."

Nonna snorted. She thought water was for peasants. Jesus drank wine, so she did, too.

"How about you, Ry? No date today. Same order as usual?"

Ryan nodded, not knowing what Amy thought his usual was and not really caring. Zach would make sure he got something amazing, whether he knew it was for Ryan or not. Everything that left the kitchen was worth salivating over.

"Anything else I can do for you?" Amy asked not to subtly.

"No, but you might need to dump a pitcher of water on your head if you don't cool off," Nonna said, drawing Amy's attention off Ryan.

Amy flushed and ran off, racing into the kitchen to hide. Ryan almost felt sorry for her. Almost.

"You brought a date here?" Nonna asked. "How have we not heard about this already?"

Ryan rolled his eyes. Definitely not feeling sorry for Amy anymore. "I didn't bring a date here. She came here for lunch, and I joined her. It wasn't a date. It was two people sitting at the same table and eating a meal."

"Sounds like a date to me," Nonna said with a scoff.

"So, we're on a date, Nonna?" Ryan countered.

Nonna snorted. "You couldn't handle a woman like me."

Ryan chuckled. "That's for sure. You'd wring me out and hang me up wet."

"Damn right."

"Can we please talk about something else," Jo asked, shuddering. "I don't need to think about either my mother or my son having sex."

"Who said anything about sex?" Nonna asked innocently. Too innocently.

"Ma, if you're talking, it's either about wine or sex."

Nonna nodded slowly. "Fair point."

"Who was the date with?" Jo asked Ryan.

Ryan choked on his water, not expecting the inquisition from his mother. From Nonna? Definitely. From his mother? Not quite.

"Her name is Bella, and she's visiting family in town. She's only here for a few weeks."

"Who is she visiting?" Nonna asked.

Ryan shrugged. "I don't know. I didn't ask."

"You aren't curious?" Jo asked.

Ryan shook his head. "Not really. It doesn't matter all that much."

"Well, what is she like?"

Ryan thought back to the way she felt on his lap and her body pressed against his and had to choke back a groan. Nonna raised her eyebrow but let it go. "She's funny. And she's crazy smart. And she's gorgeous."

"And you just randomly sat down and ate lunch with this woman?" Jo asked.

Ryan shook his head. "No, I met her before that. She…uh…she was at the dock the night of Dad's party."

"What?" Jo asked.

Ryan shrugged. "It wasn't a big deal. I told her she wasn't supposed to be there, and she left. She isn't a guest, and I guess she's staying with someone who lives close because she walked."

"And you didn't think a stranger on our property was something to worry about?" Nonna asked.

"I…" He paused and shook his head. "She was just looking at the water. She wasn't doing anything else. I don't know why, but I trust her."

"You trust a complete stranger?" Jo asked.

Ryan shrugged. "Yeah, I do. I know it sounds crazy, but she wasn't here for any reason other than to look at the water. I believe her."

Jo nodded. "It's not crazy, Ryan. It's how your father knew Perry was guilty. It's intuition or faith or conviction. It doesn't matter what you want to call it. It's inside you, and you don't have to defend it. Not to me."

Ryan held his mother's gaze and saw the truth in her eyes. She understood. She didn't have to agree, but she understood and she trusted him enough to trust her.

"Why don't you invite her to meet the family this weekend?" Jo suggested.

Ryan scoffed and shook his head. "Um, no."

"Why not?" Nonna asked.

Ryan smirked. "Because you two only want to meet her so you can grill her. I barely know this woman. I'm not letting you chase her away."

"So, you do like her," Nonna said, not asked.

Ryan sighed. Busted.

"You should definitely introduce her if you like her, Ry," Jo said.

Ryan shook his head. "It's too soon, Ma. Maybe in a few months."

"I thought you said she was only here a little while."

Dammit. He was hoping she forgot about that part. "Well, then it's not a big deal, right?"

"Invite her over. Even if it's just lunch with us. We'd like to meet her."

"I'm not settling down, Ma. Not like everyone else," Ryan argued.

Jo shook her head. "I never assumed you were."

Her words and the sparkle in her eyes told two very different stories. Ryan huffed a laugh and accepted his fate. They'd hound him forever until he introduced them to Bella. He'd hoped to keep her to himself for a while. He should have known better than to think that could happen.

Bella needed to get out. She felt like she'd been cooped up in Albert's house since she arrived. The only time she left was to walk over to Amavita Estates, and she wasn't sure she should be doing that anymore. Not knowing the problems between Ryan's family and her father.

She should have some loyalty to him, but she'd spent her life hating the man for abandoning her and not wanting. Just because none of that was true didn't mean those feelings went away overnight.

While Albert was out of the house, Bella snuck out like a grounded teenager. She considered leaving a note, but she didn't know what to write, so she just left.

Instead of turning toward Amavita, she went the opposite direction into Bereton. She hadn't explored the tiny town yet, and it seemed like a good day to get outside and walk around. There was snow on the ground, but it wasn't snowing at the moment, so she could walk and get some fresh air, and hopefully clear her head.

Bella found a parking lot that wasn't attached to a business and slid into a spot. She looked for a place to pay, but it was a free lot provided by the town so people could explore and enjoy their time without worrying about a clock. Only in a small town.

Bella zipped her knee-length coat up to defend against the cold. She pulled up her faux-fur lined hood, but even the light breeze knocked it back. She gave up and tugged on her gloves, wishing she'd brought a hat.

Main Street was lined with small shops and restaurants that smelled amazing as she walked by them. She'd already eaten lunch, but she was seriously tempted to kill time until dinner and pick a local place to try.

She was almost to the end of the street when she spotted a clothing store. The mannequins in the window looked warm and cozy, so Bella let herself in hoping she could find a new hat and some better gloves.

"Hi!" a voice said as soon as the door closed. "Welcome to Renewed Chic. I'm Sadie. Is there anything I can help you with today?"

Bella finally found the woman the voice was attached to and returned her bright and friendly smile. "Hi, Sadie. I'm actually looked for gloves and a hat. Your mannequins look really warm."

Sadie chuckled, the sound warm. "That's compliments of the owner. Blake is pregnant and about to pop. She's nesting, which means she's rearranging the store and redesigning the windows almost every week."

Bella laughed. "Well, it worked this week. I wanted to feel like they look."

"Don't we all," Sadie said. "Come on. Let me show you our accessories."

Bella followed Sadie toward the back, letting her eyes wander as they went deeper into the store. The pieces inside were just as beautiful as the pieces on the mannequins out front. Bella saw at least a dozen things she wanted.

"We have a lot of options," Sadie explained. "And, of course, some are warmer than others. Neutrals are over here."

Bella looked down at her beige coat and tan gloves. Her jeans and brown boots were the only thing visible beneath. She scowled at herself and shook her head. "I think I need some color."

Sadie wore a bright red wrap dress and black leggings with red leaves on them. Her red booties and black jewelry made her look like she was ready for Valentine's Day a month early, but it was fashionable and bright for the dreary winter.

"What color are you thinking?" Sadie asked, turning to the brighter accessories.

Bella loved how everything was laid out by color so she could shop based on what she was looking for. "Pink," Bella said definitively. "I really like pink."

Sadie grinned and led the way to the pinks, reds, and maroons. She grabbed a pair of light pink gloves and handed them to Bella. "These are really warm. And there's a matching hat."

Bella tugged them on, loving the feel of the fuzzy fabric on the inside. They were soft and warm even inside the store. The hat had the same furry detail as her jacket and would look perfect with it.

"I really like these. Obviously, I wasn't prepared for this weather."

"Every year seems to get colder, doesn't it? Last winter was brutal," Sadie said conversationally.

Bella shook her head. "I didn't live here last winter."

"Oh, well, you're lucky you missed it. This year shouldn't be so bad."

Bella nodded absently. Last winter she was with her mom. She was warm and cozy in the house she grew up in. She had no cares in the world and loved her life.

Now, everything had changed. She was all alone, except for a man she barely knew. She had no job, no home, and no friends.

"Are you okay?" Sadie asked softly.

Bella nodded. "Yep. I'll take the gloves and the hat, and this set, too."

Bella handed everything over to Sadie and swiped her card through the machine. She accepted the bag with a smile neither of them believed, then ran out of there as quickly as she could.

She never should have gone to Bereton. She never should have left home. She should have figured out how to move on, gotten her job back, and rebuilt her life right there in Binghamton.

She was heading back to her car, then she would go back to Albert's and pack up and leave. She couldn't handle being in a strange town with all strange people and feeling like she was just floating, unattached but not free. She was living off a man she didn't know.

Bella was almost to her car when she heard her name. Since she didn't know anyone, she ignored it and kept walking. But she heard it again and it was getting closer.

She finally stopped and turned toward the voice. Her smile was genuine but not as big as the other times she saw Ryan. He was the one bright light about Bereton. At least, he was before she found out the truth about their families.

"Hey, Bella. I thought that was you," Ryan said, his grin wide.

She wanted to sink into him and let him take away everything, but she couldn't. She had to figure out who she was, and she wasn't going to jerk him around while she did it.

"Hey. I was just heading out."

He stopped her from turning away from him. His dark brown pulled together as he leaned down and caught her gaze. "Heading out to go to where you're staying, or heading out of town and not coming back?"

He was far too astute, and she really didn't want to answer his question.

9

———

RYAN TOOK IN THE LOOK IN BELLA'S EYES AND KNEW SHE WAS getting ready to lie to him. What he didn't know was why. He liked her, but he didn't know her well enough to know what was going on with her life. Clearly, there was a lot.

"I just need to head back," she finally said. It was vague, probably so he couldn't say she was lying.

"Head back where?" Ryan asked, pushing her to clarify.

She looked up at him and the answer was in her eyes. "I shouldn't be here. I never should have come."

"Why not?"

Bella shook her head. "He's not who I thought he was. Who I guess I hoped he was."

"Who?"

"My father. I came here to meet him."

"Wow," Ryan breathed. "I didn't know."

Bella shrugged. "I didn't want you to know. I...my mom told me he didn't want me. She said she told him about me and he wasn't interested in being a father. When I kept pushing, she finally told me he was dead, but after..." Bella drew a breath. "After she died, I found out he wasn't dead, and I came here to meet him. I planned to tell him off, but he welcomed me in and apologized and wanted to get to know me. I thought...it doesn't matter what I thought. I was wrong about him. He's not a good man."

"Did he hurt you, Bella?"

She finally took a breath and shook her head.

"Let me buy you dinner. We can talk about your dad, and anything else you want to talk about."

She looked up at him with pain in her eyes. She shook her head again. "I don't think that's such a good idea."

"Why not?"

"Because my father is Albert Perry."

Ryan's lungs were instantly tight. He took a step back. She obviously knew the history between her father and his family or she wouldn't be telling him they shouldn't spend time together.

"Is that why you were on Amavita? To steal for him?"

Bella shook her head slowly, holding his gaze. "No. I didn't know anything about Albert or your father until he told me about it a few days ago. I'm sorry, Ryan."

She stepped around him and walked by. Ryan was numb, frozen in place. A part of him wanted to stop her, but she was the daughter of the only person his family truly disliked. The man who made a fool of Ryan's father and had him questioning everything.

But instead of defending her father, she was walking away. She was leaving town because she knew what he did, and she wasn't willing to be a part of it.

"Bella, wait," Ryan said, jogging to catch up to her. She didn't slow down, but she didn't run from him either. Ryan passed her and stopped in front of her, holding up his hands so she would stop, too.

She finally looked up at him, those ice blue eyes striking him all over again. "Just let me go, Ryan."

He shook his head. "Let me buy you dinner. Please."

"Why? I don't know anything."

He nodded. "I know. And I also know you're not like him. If you were, you wouldn't have cared enough to tell me who your father is, or why you're ready to pack up and leave town when we're just starting to get to know each other."

Bella shook her head. "We can't, Ryan. I don't know the whole story, but Albert told me enough to know you and me aren't a good idea."

Ryan shrugged. "I thought we were a very good idea the other day. And if you know Perry's part of the story, then you should let me tell you our side. And I'll pay for it, literally, so we aren't freezing our asses off during a conversation for once. Unless you just really like freezing me to death."

He finally got a small chuckle out of her. She drew a breath and nodded, and he felt like he won something. A few hours of time with Bella, a chance to talk to her, maybe even kiss her again, was definitely a victory.

Ryan put his hand on her back and guided her to the closest restaurant, just in case she decided to run. He figured if they were already inside, she'd be less likely to ditch him.

Dines in the Vines was warm and cozy and had a family feel to it that always put him at ease. Aside from eating at The Drunken Grape, Dine in the Vines was Ryan's favorite restaurant in town.

The hostess showed them to a table for two in the front, close to the window. Ryan helped Bella out of her coat then removed his own and took his seat across from her. She chewed on her lip and looked around. Uncomfortable didn't even begin to describe her.

"Welcome. Can I start you off with a glass of wine or something from the bar?" the waiter asked with a smile.

Ryan gestured for Bella to answer first. "Wine please. Sweet."

"We have a great selection of local wines if you'd like something from the area," the waiter coached her.

Ryan would have been happy if his words didn't make Bella look even more uncomfortable. "She'll take a glass of your house white. And I'll have the Amavita Estates merlot."

The waiter nodded and wrote down the orders. "Would you like a few minutes with the menus or do you want to put in some appetizers now?"

"A few minutes, please," Ryan told him.

The waiter nodded and brushed his floppy hair back, then disappeared quietly.

"If you really don't want to be here with me, I'm not going to force you," Ryan said softly.

"It's not you."

Ryan cocked an eyebrow at her and smirked. "You could have fooled me. I'm the only one here, and you're acting like I dragged you in here against your will."

Bella offered him a small smile. "I'm sorry. I'm just thrown by all this. I promise, I didn't know anything about what happened when I went to your family's property. I wouldn't do anything. I was only at the lake and walking down the road. I didn't go through anything or go inside, except for lunch that one day. I wouldn't do anything like that."

Ryan nodded and drew in a breath. He held Bella's gaze and smiled. "I know, Bella. I trust you."

Her shoulders eased just enough that he could see her neck again, and she picked up her menu. Ryan grabbed his and scanned the menu, even though he knew what he was getting.

When the waiter returned, they ordered dinner and appetizers, with a promise of dessert. The waiter's dark eyes sparkled at the hope of a good tip coming his way, and he walked off with a grin.

Ryan raised his glass and waited for Bella to do the same. "To connections. Beviamo."

Bella clinked her glass softly against his and took a sip of her wine. Her eyes widened then slid closed as she savored the light, crisp flavor of the wine. Ryan knew it was another local vineyard, another family run establishment that had been friends with his family for years. They made good wine, not great, but consistent, which was important when it was the house wine in a restaurant.

"Good?" Ryan asked.

Bella nodded. "Very. But I'm not super picky about wine. As long as it tastes good, I'm happy."

"That's how it should be. Some people are very particular about wine, and that's okay, but most wine drinkers are casual drinkers. The taste is what really matters."

"Is this yours?" Bella asked.

Ryan shook his head. "No. It is local, but it's not ours or Perry's."

Bella nodded, looking pleased he'd given her a neutral option in the battle around her.

"What did you think of Bereton?" Ryan asked, hoping it was an easy enough question.

"What do you mean?" Bella asked.

"You were shopping, right? You shoved a bag from Renewed Chic into your gigantic purse."

Bella grinned and nodded. "Yeah, I wanted to get out for a little while. I didn't bring a lot of stuff when I came here, and I haven't gone back home to get more. Shopping was easier, and it was a good excuse to get away from Albert."

Ryan tried to hide his scowl, but apparently failed.

"He's not that bad," Bella said softly.

Ryan sucked in a breath full of sauce and spices and wine mixed with frustration and desire. "I'll have to take your word for it."

Bella sighed. "This wasn't a good idea. You really don't want to be here with me, and I feel like I'm betraying both of you. I'm just going to go."

"Bella, please sit," Ryan said quietly, hoping the plea in his voice would soak in and make her think twice about walking away from him.

She stared at him for a long moment, then sank into her seat again. She tilted her chin up and met his gaze, letting him see how hard it was for her to sit there.

"I don't remember him from when I was younger. I was about seven when he worked with my father. At the time, I was oblivious to everything, just enjoying my life and running around with my cousin, Leo. He and I are the youngest, and we always wanted to be with the older boys. All that really mattered to us every summer was spending as many hours outside as we possibly could. It wasn't until I was older that I really understood what happened."

Bella leaned forward like she was anxious to hear the story. She already knew, but she was giving Ryan a chance to tell his family's side of it, which he appreciated.

"Everything I know is from my dad, but I believe him. He was a good man, and Perry...The summer he worked for my dad, it was clear he was smart. He understood things and picked everything up quickly. It was a good year, and by the end of the summer, my dad wanted to offer him a permanent job on Amavita Estates. Perry didn't accept and disappeared. My dad was upset, but he figured Perry had a good reason. We learned what that reason was the next year when Perry launched Perry Mount Vineyards right across the street."

Bella sucked in a breath but didn't interrupt.

"My dad was hurt because he had no idea. The previous owners were friends of the family and said they would let us know if they were ever interested in selling, but Perry snatched the prime location right out from under us, after he learned everything he could from my dad and stole his manual."

Ryan practically spit the words. He didn't have to remember what happened to be angry because of it. Perry hurt Ryan's father, made Victor feel like a fool for years, and walked around like he never did anything wrong. They caught him on Amavita property and dealt with his threats of stealing their chef. He was a thorn in their sides from the day he opened the doors to Perry Mount Vineyards.

He wasn't going to sugarcoat things for Bella. She wanted a relationship with her father, but she needed to know the kind of man she was dealing with. If she expected care and affection from him, she was going to be disappointed. He wasn't that kind of person, and it was better if she knew it before she got her hopes up.

"I'm sorry, Ryan," Bella said. Her eyes burned with regret and pain. "I wish none of that happened."

"You didn't do it," Ryan said.

Bella shook her head. "No, but I thought he was a good man. He welcomed me in without a second thought. He gave me a room and fed me. He was nice to me, even if he's a little stiff. I just never imagined that's the kind of person he was. Not once I met him. The way you describe him is more like the man my mother warned me about. The one she told me was dead, probably so I didn't go looking for him."

"I'm sorry, Bella. The man your mom knew sounds like he hasn't changed."

She nodded sadly and drained her wine glass.

Ryan was too late. She already had her hopes up.

BELLA WANTED to explain everything to Ryan and make him understand, but she didn't understand it all. And she had no right to defend her biological father to a man she barely knew. She couldn't possibly decide which one was right, or which to believe. Ryan's story was all what he'd heard, and Albert's painted himself as being wrongfully accused. There was no way to prove either side. And she wasn't in a position to try.

Bella sat back and tried to figure out what to do. She knew two people in town, and they hated each other. Two men she wanted to get to know better.

When the waiter offered her another glass of wine, Bella accepted it and drank it quickly even though she was starting to feel the effects of the alcohol. By the time their food arrived, she was starving and on her way to being drunk.

Ryan watched her carefully as she jumped headfirst into her dinner. The bread was soft and warm. Her dinner smelled like heaven. Her company was definitely the best part, though. Ryan chatted with her about the town, telling her about the people who lived there and suggesting other places she should visit. When Bella admitted she loved to read, Ryan told her his sister-in-law's mother was the librarian.

"Wait, what? Your sister-in-law's mother? Did I get that right?" Bella asked.

Ryan nodded with a smile. "Yep. Vivian is amazing. She has a lot of programs for seniors and she loves books. If they don't have something, she's happy to track it down for you."

"What about ebooks? I mostly read those. A lot of libraries don't have a good selection."

Ryan shook his head. "From what Cynthia says, there's a great selection. You should check it out tomorrow."

"Maybe I'll go tonight," Bella said, slurring her words. "I need to walk off this wine."

Ryan shook his head again. "The library is closed this late."

Bella's heart sank. She wasn't sure how she was going to get back to Albert's. She never should have had so much to drink. She really knew better, but she'd been dealt more than enough blows in the last few months. Learning about Albert was just one more hit, and she didn't think she could take more.

"I'll drive you home," Ryan said quietly.

"What about my car? I can't leave it out all night." Bella was more than a little panicked. Her car was the only thing she really had left. She couldn't risk it being stolen or vandalized.

"I'll make sure it gets back to you. You can't drive, though. It's not safe."

Bella nodded. "But first, dessert."

Ryan laughed, and Bella felt like she won the lottery. Seeing his genuine smile and having him take care of her when she was a mess made her feel like maybe, just maybe, everything was going to be okay.

They ordered cheesecake and cannolis and shared them. Bella lifted one of the cannolis to her lips and took a bite, the tart taste mixing with the sweetness and the crunch from the shell. She groaned in approval and let her eyes slide closed. When she opened them again, Ryan was staring at her.

"What?" she asked, her mouth full and crumbs spilling from the edge of her dessert.

Ryan shook his head and speared a bite of cheesecake.

Bella wiped her mouth and set the cannoli down. She brushed her hands over the plate and wiped her mouth again. "Do I have food in my hair or something?"

Ryan shook his head again.

"Why are you looking at me like that?"

He looked up at her and his hard eyes lit with desire. "Because you made the same sound when you kissed me."

Bella's cheeks burned, and she ducked her head. Ryan reached across the table and drew her chin up so she'd look at him again.

"I like that sound, Bella," Ryan told her roughly. "I just wish it were under different circumstances."

Bella's lips curled up at the edge. She nodded to the waiter, drawing him over to the table.

"Everything okay?"

Bella nodded. "Very much so. But we need a box for the desserts, please."

"Just one?" he asked.

Bella nodded again. "Just one."

Ryan lifted an eyebrow at her as the waiter walked away.

Bella grinned. "Don't worry. I'll share."

Ryan groaned and slapped his card on the table. He was just as eager to get out of there as Bella was.

10

RYAN COULD BARELY WAIT LONG ENOUGH FOR THE SERVER TO get them a box and run his card before ushering Bella out of there. He was vaguely aware of the fact that she'd been drinking, but she didn't stumble and didn't act like she was at all affected by the alcohol.

When they got outside, the slap of cold air was enough to make him stop. It didn't matter if she was drunk. She had two, maybe three, glasses of wine. He'd slept with women who'd been drinking before, but only when they were women he'd slept with before and they talked about sex before drinks were involved. He didn't like the idea of Bella or any woman feeling pressured.

Bella snuggled against his side and slid her hand up his chest. He grabbed her hand and pulled her to the side of the sidewalk, out of the flow of the light traffic walking around. She grinned up at him but sobered quickly when she saw his face.

"You changed your mind," she stated. No question, just acceptance. "I get it." She took a step back and turned to walk away.

"Bella, don't," Ryan said quietly.

She stopped. Her shoulders slumped then rose with her breath. When she turned back to Ryan, there was a fire in her eyes, but it wasn't one born from desire.

"I understand, Ryan. You changed your mind about being with me. Whether it's because of who my father is, or how little we know about each other, or...what I look like..." She shook her head. "It doesn't matter. You're done, so I'm done."

Ryan took a step toward her before she could walk off. He was close enough to feel her surprise shudder through him. To her credit, she didn't shy away from him and looked up at him with steel in her spine and flames in her gaze.

"First of all, I didn't change my mind. This—" he gestured between them "—has nothing to do with your father. It also has nothing to do with how little you think we know each other, but I promise you, it has a hell of a lot to do with what you look like. I think you mean that differently than I do, but let me be clear here, Bella, you're fucking beautiful. I haven't seen nearly enough of you, and one day I plan to look, taste, and touch my fill of you."

She shivered at his words, and he pressed closer.

"Me stopping you only has to do with one thing. You."

Her eyebrow went up in question.

"You had something to drink. You were clearly upset when we ran into each other. There's a big part of me that worried I'm taking advantage of you. That I'm out here ready to bury myself in you, and you're feeling like I'm pushing you into something. Or that you're not all that interested but the alcohol is telling you it's a good idea. Or—"

Before he could say another word, she threw her arms around his neck and dragged his lips down to hers. She pressed her tongue past his surprised lips and slicked it along his.

Ryan groaned and wrapped an arm around her waist, dragging her body against his. They were on a mostly deserted street, but they were still in public, and all of a sudden, he wasn't sure he could wait to have her until they were alone.

Bella kissed him like she couldn't do anything else. He returned every last drop of her desire with his own, needing her and wanting her and wondering why it was this woman, a woman he should hate on principle, that he had to have more than he needed air for his lungs.

Ryan managed to pull back long enough to start them moving in the direction of his truck. Bella hung on him, her desire making him feel drunk. He'd never had a woman who turned him inside out the way she did.

They finally reached his truck, and he opened the door for Bella. She stopped and looked up at him, her eyes lit with worry.

"Now you've changed your mind."

She shook her head immediately. "No. Not even a little bit. But I can't take you back to Albert's. I haven't...I don't know...I..."

"You're coming home with me," Ryan said with a growl. He wasn't about to step foot in Albert's house, and he needed Bella in his bed.

"Don't you live with your cousin?" she asked.

Ryan nodded. "They won't bother us. Besides, it's better than your father."

Bella hesitated for a second then nodded and climbed in. Ryan shut the door behind her and jogged around to his side. He had the truck started and was on his way home before he took another breath.

The roads were dark, but Ryan could have gotten them there blindfolded. He parked in front of his house and said a silent prayer that there weren't any lights visible from the outside. Both Leo and Sara's vehicles were there, but with any luck, they were already in bed.

Ryan went to open his door, but Bella didn't move. She stared at the house and chewed on her lip when she looked at the other cars. "Are you sure about this?"

"Yes," Ryan said firmly. "But if you're not, I'll drive you...home."

Bella looked at him again. "Your cousin is going to hate me. He's going to tell you we can't be together."

"My cousin has no say in who I sleep with. He's not my keeper, and he doesn't judge me."

"He'll judge me."

"He doesn't know who you are."

Bella's eyes widened than a breath shook her. "You didn't tell him about us."

Ryan shook his head and tilted her chin up to meet his gaze. "He knows you exist. He doesn't know everything because he doesn't need to. Everyone knows we had lunch, and my mother and grandmother know about us meeting at the lake—"

"You told your mother about us kissing?" Bella gasped.

Ryan shook his head again. "No. I told her we first met there. The rest is for you and me only."

"What about who my father is?" Bella asked softly.

Ryan smiled at her. "Considering I've only spoken to you since you told me, my family doesn't know who your father is."

"They're going to hate me when they find out."

"I don't hate you, Bella," Ryan said honestly. "I think

you're beautiful and smart and funny, and I think anyone who can't see that doesn't deserve to know that."

She drew in a breath and looked at the house again. "Let's go in."

"Are you sure?" Ryan asked.

Bella nodded.

"Really, really sure? Because once I get you in my bed, I'm going to be much less of a gentleman. I'll stop anytime you tell me to, but I'm not going to want to when I have you spread out on my bed, wet and ready for me."

Bella gasped. "Let's go. Now."

Ryan chuckled as Bella scrambled to get out of the truck. She met him at the front and they stumbled to the front door together, kissing and laughing. Ryan unlocked the door and let them in, both of them whispering and trying not to make any noise.

They had their coats and boots off and were kissing their way through the kitchen when one of the lamps in the living room clicked on. Ryan pushed Bella behind him and squinted into the sudden light.

"Hey, Ryan," Sara said with a grin. "Who's your friend?"

Ryan forced a smile. "Sara, this is Bella. Bella, that's Sara and my cousin, Leo."

Bella smiled at them, but Ryan could feel her tension.

"How do you two know each other?" Sara asked.

"We're old friends," Ryan said, remembering Bella's words from The Drunken Grape.

Bella grinned up at him, some of her tension fading.

"That must be why you look familiar," Leo said. "I'm sure we've met if you're old friends."

Bella nodded, but it was forced and the tension was back.

"Well, we're going to my room. I'll see you guys later," Ryan said.

"Nice meeting you, Bella," Sara called after them.

"You, too," Bella replied.

Ryan half-dragged Bella away from his cousin before Leo figured out why she looked familiar. Ryan and Leo were close growing up, and even though Leo didn't know everyone Ryan did, Bereton was a small town, and it wouldn't be long before Leo figured out that Ryan was lying about Bella being an old friend and started asking more questions.

In his room, Ryan closed and locked the door, with his eyes on Bella. She flinched at the sound of the lock, and Ryan wanted to go back to the living room and choke his cousin.

"He knows who I am," Bella said. "He's going to be so mad."

"Let me worry about Leo. For right now, all you need to worry about is if you want to stay here with me right now or if you want me to take you home."

Bella looked up at him. She held his gaze and slowly shook her head. "I don't want to leave, Ryan. I know that's selfish, but I'm not drunk and I'm not spiraling. I just want you."

BELLA WAITED while Ryan processed her words. She wasn't sure if he believed her until he sighed and the edges of his lips curled up in a smile of pure male satisfaction.

She moved toward him the same moment he moved toward her, meeting him in the middle. His arms slid around her and his lips came down on hers, and all she could think about was getting closer to him. She pushed her hands under his shirt and dragged her nails up his back.

He broke their kiss with a hiss and reached back to yank his shirt over his head. Bella appreciated the new access and took full advantage, skimming her hands then her lips over his smooth chest. Her tongue darted out and flicked his nipple, and he groaned.

She could tell her was letting her take the lead and direct things where she wanted them, but she was interested in seeing what he wanted. She was already half out of her mind with desire, and she was anxious for him to feel the same.

Ryan's hand on her back startled her into pulling back. He captured her lips like he expected the reaction and dragged her deeper into him. His hand lifted her shirt as it grazed her skin and made her head spin more than the wine had. She let him pull her shirt up and over her head and fought the urge to cover herself when she saw the heated look in his eyes.

"Jesus, you're gorgeous. How did I let you stay wrapped up in those heavy coats for so long?"

Bella giggled at the lust-heavy tone.

"Tell me you're okay with this, Bella. Tell me you want this. I need to know."

"I want this, Ryan. I want you. Don't stop."

He barely waited for the words to leave her lips before he was pressed his body and lips to hers. He tilted her head back with a gentle tug on her hair and brushed his tongue along the seam of her lips. She opened eagerly for him, as ready to keep moving as he was.

He backed them up to his bed and crawled over her when she laid down. Ryan sat back on his heels and stared at her, his eyes roaming her exposed top half.

Bella's skin heated, a mixture of desire and self-doubt. While he looked at her, she devoured his body with her eyes. From his broad shoulders lined with muscles to his chest sprinkled with dark hair that trailed straight down and disappeared beneath the waist of his jeans where his erection bulged against his zipper. Bella licked her lips and pulled the bottom one between her teeth, wondering if she'd get a chance to taste him.

"Where did your mind just go?" Ryan asked softly, his voice low and husky.

Bella looked up at him and felt her cheeks warm. "I was wondering if I'd have a chance to taste you."

His dark eyebrows shot up, and a sexy smile gave her the answer she was hoping for. "What time do you need to be home?"

Bella shrugged. "I'm not a child. I'm twenty-seven. I don't have a curfew."

"Then I'd say we have time for anything and everything you want to do, Bella."

Bella nearly came at the erotic sound of his words. Anything. Everything. She had a very active imagination and enough experience with men to know she could definitely spend all night with Ryan and still want more.

"I want to taste you," Bella said, feeling more and more bold with her words the longer she spent with Ryan. He wasn't judging her, and he wasn't telling her what she should or shouldn't say. Her last boyfriend, if she called him that, told her men didn't like pushy women. Really, he didn't like a woman who knew what she wanted in bed. Not that it was unreasonable for her to ask for an orgasm, but he never seemed to be able to deliver. Whether it was laziness or a lack of caring, she usually had to finish herself off after sex, which pissed both of them off.

Bella didn't expect much from Ryan, but if he was going to ask, she'd tell him.

Ryan leaned over her, both of them still clothed from the waist down, and kissed her, stroking up against her. She gasped, granting him access to her mouth, which he used to continue to drive her crazy.

When he pulled back far too quickly, he kissed his way down her neck to her chest. "I want to taste you, too, Bella. Are you going to let me?"

Bella nodded and struggled to catch her breath. Ryan slid his tongue beneath the edge of the cup of her bra, just far enough away from her nipple that she groaned. He smiled against her skin and pulled the cup to the side with his teeth, capturing her nipple between his lips.

Bella's hands went into his silky hair as she arched up. He opened his mouth and took more of her breast into his mouth, grazing his tongue over her nipple. She groaned and a breath shuddered through her.

Ryan eased his body to the side and unbuttoned her jeans as he tortured her. The sound of her zipper sliding slowly down echoed in the room, the only sound besides their breathing.

"Take off your bra," Ryan commanded and he slid down, dragging her jeans and panties with him.

Bella did as he directed, tossing her bra somewhere over the edge of the bed once she was completely naked. She ached between her thighs, ready for him. Her fingers twitched with the need to slide them between her legs and make herself come. She hadn't been so turned on in far too long, and if the look in Ryan's eyes was anything to go on, she wasn't going to be disappointed when he was done.

He pressed her ankles apart and slid his rough hands up

the inside of her legs, pressing her legs farther and farther apart as his hands moved closer and closer to her core.

She twitched at the feel of his hands on her inner thighs. She ached to close her thighs and rub them together. She needed relief, and if he didn't make a move soon, she would.

Ryan leaned over her, diving into her lips like a starving man. He kissed her like he was a man dying for a woman's touch. She held on to him, needing the same connection. His tongue slicked over hers, both of them grasping at each other as they tried to get closer.

Ryan finally pulled back, gasping for breath. He didn't pause before sliding his lips down her body, stopping to circle first one nipple then the other with his tongue. Bella's greedy body cried out at the loss of him until he nudged her thighs wider with his shoulders.

He blew a soft breath on her, the cold air making her squeeze her channel. One finger traced her seam before sinking slowly inside her.

"Oh, Bella, you're so tight. I can't wait to stretch you out."

Bella groaned.

"How do you want to come the first time? Because I really want to taste you, but your greedy pussy is sucking my finger in." He pulsed his finger in and bent it as he slowly dragged it back out. "Both, Bella?"

"All of it. Please. Oh, God, Ryan."

"I love the way my name sounds on your beautiful lips. I can't wait to see how they look wrapped around my cock." He groaned. "I guess you like that idea."

Bella nodded. Every inch of her twitched at the erotic image of Ryan in her mouth. She wanted that, but the feel of him inside her was too much. She was dizzy with desire and aching to come.

"Oh, fuck, Bella. I can't wait to taste you. I need to right now."

He didn't wait for her to agree, just dove in and licked her from her entrance up to her clit. Her hips jerked in response, pressing closer to him for more. He teased her with a swipe of his tongue over her clit, and she almost cried. She was already so close. And she hadn't laid a hand on herself.

He added a second finger to her channel and sucked her clit into his mouth for barely a second. Long enough to tell her he was torturing her and drawing out her orgasm. Not because he couldn't figure it out, but because he wanted her to feel it for days.

His fingers pumped in and out of her slowly, ramping up her body and stretching her out. With each stroke out, he brushed against her channel and made her twitch. Then he added a third finger and everything changed.

The slow, steady strokes were replaced by hard thrusts that tightened every muscle in her body. Every few thrusts, he withdrew completely and teased her entrance with his fingers, coating her with her own juices until she was sure she was soaking his bed.

His tongue danced down and licked her come then returned to her clit, flicking at it in rhythm with the thrusts that drove her mad. Bella wasn't sure how much longer she was going to last, only that when she finally came, it was either going to be the best orgasm of her life or a massive disappointment.

She was hoping for the former.

11

———

RYAN COULDN'T GET ENOUGH OF BELLA. LISTENING TO HER quiet moans was hard enough, but tasting her and feeling her channel grip his fingers made him impatient for more from her.

Ryan pressed his tongue flat against her clit and dragged his fingers inside her. He could tell she was close, and he wanted her to wait just a few more seconds. In truth, he needed those seconds. He was desperate for more, but he wasn't ready to move on from licking her yet.

"Ryan," she whimpered.

That was what he was waiting for. Hearing his name on her lips sent him over the edge. He thrust in hard again, spreading her out as he entered her with his fingers, and sucked on her clit, and she came instantly.

Her entire body tensed, then her orgasm shook through her, tightening her channel as she drew his fingers in deeper. He didn't let up, thrusting harder and deeper into her as she moaned his name and flung her arms around. Her orgasm never stopped, sending her from one right into another while he drank her up.

"No more, please. Stop. I can't take it anymore," she begged.

Ryan reluctantly pulled back from her, kissing the inside of her thighs then slowly removing his fingers from her. Her entire body shook, tightening around him and trying to draw him back in as she begged him to leave.

"I've never come like that," she gasped.

He couldn't help the cocky grin that curled his come-soaked lips. He licked them, loving her taste on him, then wiped his face on his hand because he liked kissing her lips just as much.

"Come here," she said as he rose above her.

He didn't hesitate to cover her body with his and plunge his tongue into her mouth. She didn't recoil at her own taste on his tongue. Her nails ran down his back, then up again and into his hair. He groaned at the feel of her touching him. His cock throbbed in his jeans, ready to be let out for his own fun.

"I want a taste of you now," Bella said, pulling back from their kiss and pushing on his chest.

Ryan thought about resisting, but Bella shoved him again and he let her push carry him onto his back. He was an even bigger fan when she crawled on top of him and pressed her perfect breasts to his chest and kissed him again.

She smiled against his lips and wiggled her butt, making him groan when she rubbed herself on his erection. Bella winked as she slid down his body, kissing, licking, and biting him as she moved.

Ryan watched as she kneeled on the bed between his legs. She unbuttoned his jeans and pulled the zipper down, the reached inside to stroke him. His hips lifted to meet her hand, thrusting his cock into her grasp.

"Me, too," she said quietly.

Ryan reached down to push his jeans and briefs off so he could watch her hand stroke him. She didn't stop the entire time, her little hand squeezing as she lifted up then loosening as she stretched to hold the base of his cock.

"I love your pink nails," Ryan growled.

"What do you think about my pink tongue?" she asked, then she stuck out her tongue and swiped it up his length.

He groaned and swore, tightening his fingers in the sheets to keep from reaching for her. "I fucking love your tongue."

She smiled and wrapped her lips around him.

"Fuck me, I love that, too."

She hummed her agreement and sucked him deeper into her mouth. Ryan wanted to watch her, but it felt too fucking good. His eyes slid closed, leaving him in darkness to feel. Her lips, her tongue, her teeth. He held himself still, but his cock ached to thrust deep into her mouth.

"Fuck, Bella. That feels so damn good. Too good. I'm not going to last much longer."

She hummed again, withdrawing only long enough to run her tongue along the underside of his cock then sucked him back into her mouth.

"Jesus, Bella. I need to be inside you when I come. I want to feel that tight pussy wrapped around me when I blow," he groaned.

She shivered and moaned, then let him fall from her mouth. She crawled over him and plunged her tongue deep into his mouth.

They lined up perfectly as they kissed, and her wet heat called to him. It would be easy to thrust into her, but Ryan never had sex without a condom. He held her hips still when she tried to line them up, and she pulled back.

"I thought you wanted to be inside me," she said, her face scrunched in confusion.

"Condom, Bell."

Her cheeks reddened, and she shook her head. She moved off him, and Ryan reached for the box on condoms in his top drawer. He rolled one on and put his hands on her hips again, guiding her over him.

"I can still taste you," Ryan whispered, closing his eyes. "I need to feel you."

"Ryan," she moaned, already sounding like she was on the edge of another orgasm.

"Go slow, Bell. Let your body take me in," he coached her. Just the tip of him sank inside her tight body. He urged her to lift and slide down again, and inch by inch they worked together until he was sweating and buried deep inside her.

Bella shuddered and leaned forward, resting her hands on Ryan's chest.

"You okay?" he asked.

"I might come again," she said.

"I sure as fuck hope so," Ryan growled. "I plan to."

Bella laughed and leaned back. She lifted slightly, then sank down again. Ryan waited, letting her set the pace that worked best for her. He skimmed his hands up her legs and kept going, sliding them up over her belly to cup her breasts. He rasped his thumbs over her nipples, and she hissed then increased her pace.

Ryan bit down on his tongue to keep himself from taking over. She felt good, tight and wet and perfect. He thrust up into her as she sank down, and they both groaned.

"Oh, yes," Bella moaned long and low. "More."

Ryan held onto her breasts as his anchor and met her

stroke for stroke. She squeezed around him and everything tightened, his body readying to explode.

She whimpered, her face falling, and she tried to change positions. She leaned back, then forward, but the orgasm she was chasing was still out of reach.

Ryan grabbed her hips and stilled her for long enough to get her to stretch out over him, then he rolled them so he was on top. Her sweaty hair clung to her neck, but it only took one stroke for that frustrated look to disappear.

Ryan kept his body close, dragging himself against her clit with each thrust inside her. He lifted one leg and spread her out, sinking in even deeper, and she moaned.

"Ryan. Oh, God, yes. Ryan. I'm...I'm..." She didn't have to finish her thought, he felt her channel tighten around him, milking him as her orgasm took over.

Feeling her squeeze him like she did, her perfect, tight core drawing him in deeper with each rhythmic pulse, Ryan's control slipped. He leaned back, bringing him knees under him for added leverage, and plunged in harder, deeper, more. He chased his own orgasm, letting hers fuel him as his focus narrowed to Bella and the connection between them.

His balls tightened and his body begged for release, and he was happy to let go and let it happen. He slammed into Bella, and she screamed with him as they came together, their bodies linked and synced.

He jerked through his orgasm, emptying himself into her, then collapsed on top of her, knowing her needed to move. She wrapped her arms around him and slid her leg from his shoulder down to circle his waist. Ryan's breath pulsed through him in awkward pants, every cell of his body trying to catch up to what happened.

Perfection. That was the only way to describe it. He'd

slept with plenty of other women, and it had never been like that. Bella was different, and being with Bella was...he didn't think there was a word for it.

"Wow," she murmured after a minute.

Ryan finally found the strength to roll over, carrying her with him as he did. "Yeah," he replied. That seemed to cover it.

BELLA DIDN'T KNOW what to say. Her mom would have said she was falling in love, but her mom always thought it was love when it wasn't. For a woman who lied and walked away from the one man she should have tried to build a relationship with, she believed in love more than anyone Bella ever met.

But Bella wasn't like that. She struggled to accept love was real. Especially after finding out the one person she loved without question spent her entire life lying.

None of that mattered as Ryan slid out of bed and went into the bathroom right off his bedroom. The low snap of the rubber was followed by disposal then he washed his hands. Bella was vaguely aware of the fact that she should really get up and leave, but when Ryan slid into bed beside her and pulled the covers over them and tugged her close, she couldn't bring herself to move.

It wasn't long before sleep pulled at her and dragged Bella under. She kept telling herself to get up and walk home, but leaving Ryan to get back into the frigid night was less and less appealing by the second.

When Bella woke up again, it was still dark out. She forgot, for a minute, where she was. Ryan still held her, his heavy arm draped over her body even as he laid on his stomach.

The need to pee drove Bella from the bed, and once she was up, she knew she had to leave. She did her best to silently collect all her clothes, but once she was dressed, she realized Ryan was staring at her.

"Are you sneaking out?" he asked quietly, his voice deep and rough.

She opened and closed her mouth before nodding. "I figured that was for the best."

Ryan pushed out of bed, his cock semi-erect as he walked toward her. "Let me get dressed and I'll drive you home."

Bella shook her head. As a rule, she never spent the night with a man. Even the ones she dated, she went home or sent them home before they fell asleep. She didn't like sleepovers and didn't want to get too attached. She broke that rule with Ryan and needed the cold air to clear her head.

"I've walked back from here before," she admitted.

He breathed a laugh and nodded. "True. But now that I know where you live, why don't you let me drive you? Or just wait until morning and I can give you a ride to your car?"

Bella wasn't sure how she was going to get her car back, but she knew counting on Ryan wasn't a good idea. He was sexy and sweet and smart, and she was an idiot for getting involved with him. Not that she sought him out, but she let it happen.

She wasn't lying to him when she said she wanted him, but they weren't building something. They were still strangers, and that was all they'd ever be. Strangers who shared one amazing night.

"I want to see you again," Ryan said suddenly, as if he read her mind. "Just stay and we can talk in the morning."

Bella shook her head again. "That's probably not a good idea."

"Staying, talking, or seeing each other again?" Ryan asked.

"All of the above. This was amazing, but we both know your family will never be okay with who my father is. It's better if we just..."

"End things now?" Ryan finished for her.

Bella nodded. "I think that's for the best."

Ryan crossed his arms over his chest and nodded. He was still gloriously naked, tempting Bella to throw all caution to the wind and dive back into bed with him, but she knew better. She knew it didn't make sense. They'd never work, and she would get hurt. And she couldn't handle anymore pain.

Ryan didn't try to stop her again as she quietly left his room. She made it outside without seeing his cousin or Sara, and Bella was finally able to take a deep breath.

The sharp cold made her cough, but she relished the chill. She didn't know exactly where she was within the vineyard, but she could see the water. She let her eyes adjust to everything around her and thought she saw the big building where the restaurant was, and headed that direction.

Knowing the history of her father and the vineyard she was sneaking around on, she debated turning around and asking Ryan to escort her off the property so no one accused her of doing anything, but she couldn't face him again. Not so soon. Not when she knew she'd fall for him if she let herself.

She made it to the inn and turned toward the road,

trekking up the driveway and rushing across the street before any cars came. Her father's vineyard was dark with only the moon overhead to guide her. She snuck into the house and down the hall to her room, closing the door with a soft snick. Bella kicked off her boots and collapsed onto the bed, feeling more alone than ever.

BELLA DIDN'T SLEEP well the rest of the night and woke up feeling like crap. She still didn't really know who her father was, and she'd alienated the one person she felt like she was getting to know.

Bella changed into pajamas so Albert didn't see her in her clothes from the day before then headed to the kitchen in search of breakfast.

The house was quiet, something she was happy for. She fixed herself a cup of coffee and some toast to settle her stomach and sat at the island to eat and decide if she wanted to stick around longer or just go back to Binghamton.

She was still debating when Albert came inside. He smiled when he saw her. "I thought you might have left when you didn't come home last night. We haven't talked much since I told you about Amavita and their accusations against me."

Bella almost forgot about all of that. She didn't care for herself, but she cared if Albert did something to hurt Ryan's family. "I was processing."

He nodded and avoided her gaze while he stripped off his gloves and hat then toed off his boots and hung up his jacket.

When he made it to where she was sitting in the kitchen,

she asked, "Did you do it? Did you take something from them that you weren't supposed to?"

Albert looked at her and shook his head. "No."

Bella drew in a breath and nodded. She believed him, but believing him meant Ryan was wrong, and she knew Ryan thought his dad was right, too.

"Can you give me a ride into town sometime today?"

Albert nodded. "Sure. Is something wrong with your car? I have a great mechanic who can take a look. Or you can just take one of my vehicles."

Bella shook her head. "No, I left my car in town yesterday. I just need to get it back."

Albert's brows tugged together, and he shook his head. "Your car is outside, Bella. It was there when I got up this morning."

"What?" Albert pointed, and Bella turned. Her car was parked right outside, next to Albert's truck. She huffed a laugh.

"You didn't drive it here?" Albert asked.

Bella shook her head.

"Then how did it get here?"

"A friend dropped it off for me."

Albert must have heard something in her tone because he grinned. "You should invite him over so I can meet him."

Bella sobered at the thought of Ryan walking into Albert's house and the two of them fighting. She shook her head. "We're not that close yet. But I should thank him. Excuse me."

Bella went to her room and grabbed her phone. Ryan put his number in her phone the day before. She pulled up his contact and thumbed out a text.

> Thank you for my car. And for yesterday.

She didn't have to wait long for his response.

> I told you I'd take care of it. Are you feeling better?

> ???

> You're texting me. I thought that might mean you'd changed your mind about seeing me again.

Bella couldn't help but smile. She needed to add smart to the long list of adjectives she used to describe him.

> That depends.

> On?

> On how long I have to wait to see you again.

> I can be there in five.

> LOL. How about tonight?

> As long as you don't change your mind by then.

> I won't.

> See you tonight, Bella.

She smiled and put her phone down. It would all be okay. She wouldn't fall for him, but she could have fun while she was in town. And when she decided what she was going to do next, she'd have some good memories and great orgasms to remember Bereton.

12

---

72 years ago

TINA WENT INTO TOWN THE NEXT DAY HOPING TO SEE Carmelo again. After they talked and almost kissed, she hoped he would come find her, but it was like he disappeared.

Unfortunately, her parents doubled down on their efforts to marry her off. Her father brought up friends that he wanted her to meet, and her mother told her she needed to listen to her father. She hated every minute of it, but she suffered through it.

Her father invited another friend over that night with his wife and son. Tina knew Mark from school. He'd been a year older than her and was a jerk. He made fun of her friend because her boobs weren't big enough. Tina had no interest in him, but she pasted on a smile and spent the night telling him how funny he was while secretly wishing she could stab him in the eye with her fork.

She snuck away for a little while and Mark ended up following her outside. Tina rolled her eyes when he walked up behind her and told her he was happy they finally had a chance to get to know each other.

"We're not getting to know each other," Tina argued.

"We could," Mark replied with a leer. His gaze scanned her body, making her feel like she was a piece of meat instead of a woman he should be trying his hardest to impress. "My father tells me your father wants you married within the next few months. The fastest way to make that happen is to get you pregnant. We could start now."

He moved closer and pressed himself against her. Her skin crawled, and she pushed him off. "I don't think so."

"Why not? If you're desperate to get married, you're desperate to have kids."

Tina scoffed. "I'm not desperate for either. This is all my father's doing."

"Being in good with a man like your father will do wonders for my family."

He came closer again, and this time, Tina slapped him. The echo of the sound vibrated through her stinging hand.

Mark took a step back and glared at her. "What do you think you're doing?"

Tina held her sore hand. "I'm making sure you know I'm not going to be someone you can force yourself on. I recommend you leave. Now."

Mark was not interested in taking no for an answer. He went at her again, dodging her attempts to fend him off. Tina screamed, and he put a hand over her mouth. He grabbed her breast and squeezed. "You have been giving me looks all night. Don't start acting like you don't want me now that we're finally alone."

Tina opened her mouth and clamped down on his finger, biting as hard as she could. Mark screamed and pulled his hand back, jumping up and down like a kid who needed to pee.

"You bitch. What was that for?"

"You have no right to touch me," Tina spat.

"What are you talking about?" her father said from the shadows. "He touched you?"

Tina didn't want to say anything to her father, but he obviously heard her.

"She's lying," Mark immediately argued. "She came on to me, then she bit me when I tried to kiss her."

Her father moved closer, his eyes hard and directed at Tina. "I'm sorry for her behavior. Where did she bite you, son?"

"She bit my hand," Mark said, showing the red skin to Peter.

He took Mark's hand and examined the bite. "That's a rough one. The only thing I can't figure out is how she bit your hand if you were trying to kiss her."

Mark opened and closed his mouth, fumbling for an excuse. If Tina wasn't still shaking, she might have found it funny.

"What it seems like to me is that you came out here to pressure my daughter into something she wasn't comfortable with. Just because I'm interested in her getting married doesn't mean I'm going to promise her to a man who will force himself on her. I highly recommend you and your father leave my property immediately, and don't plan to return. And if I ever see you near any of my children again, I will make sure it's the last time you touch anyone. Ever."

Mark scrambled away, running into the house and thanking Maribel before telling his parents they needed to leave right away.

Tina waited until they were definitely gone to sink onto

the bench and take a deep, shuddering breath. She was on the verge of tears and not sure she could keep them back when her mother sat down next to her.

"Where's Papa?"

Maribel brushed the hair back from Tina's face and smiled. "He asked me to check on you. He doesn't deal well with certain things."

Tina nodded.

"Are you okay?"

Tina shrugged.

"He had no right to touch you. He has no right ever unless you say it's okay. And that's true whether he's a stranger or your husband."

"I'm not marrying that man," Tina spat, shocked her mother would even say that.

Maribel shook her head. "No, I don't want you to, but the man you do marry needs to respect you."

"Is Papa still going to put me through all this?"

Her mother stood and looked down at her. Gone was the sympathetic, understanding woman of a moment ago. "We've given you time to choose your own husband, and you've refused. You're old enough to be married."

Tina knew enough not to argue. None of her arguments made a difference so far, and continuing to say the same things wouldn't get her anywhere. She simply nodded and waited for her mother to leave her alone.

Once she returned to the house, Tina pushed off the bench and walked down the steps into the olive grove that stretched out far and wide around her home. They didn't own the grove, but they were friends with the owners and Tina knew she could wander all she wanted. She'd always seen the place as a haven for her. Her home, the place she felt the most safe and comfortable. Since she turned eighteen, it was beginning to feel like a prison. One she couldn't escape from.

Tina walked the land, knowing her parents wouldn't worry. She often wandered off, and they only worried if she was supposed to be somewhere, like meeting her next husband candidate.

She sighed. She didn't like any of the men her father wanted her to consider for marriage. She'd known all of them her whole life. Most of them were jerks, but a few just weren't right. She felt like they were her brothers, not men she had any interest in kissing, let alone doing anything else.

Tina always wanted to be free. She had dreams of taking over the family bakery, but her father made it seem as though he didn't see her. He was grooming her younger brother to take over. Andres would be successful, but he didn't love the place the way Tina did. It would be purely a business for him, whereas Tina would run it with her heart.

It didn't matter either way because she didn't get a say in it. And when she made it to the road on the far side of the olive grove, she stopped. She never got a say in anything. Her entire life, she had to follow the rules laid out by her parents. It was only when she was out by herself, alone at night, that she was allowed to pick.

Tina looked across the road. She'd never left the safety of the grove, always choosing to turn around when she made it that far. It was safe, but Tina didn't want safe. For one night, she wanted to be free, even if it was an illusion.

She stepped onto the dirt road and drew in a shaky breath. She blew it out and smiled. Then crossed the street.

She kept walking, not thinking about where she was going. She knew her town well and had no fear of getting lost. She just wanted to explore.

CARMELO HAD TO BE DREAMING. He didn't think he was, but that was the only explanation for Tina Vincenzo to show up in front of his eyes. He'd been thinking about her, and there she was.

"Hello," he said to the apparition.

She jumped and turned to him. "Carmelo? What are you doing here?"

He smiled at his fantasy. "I guess I'm waiting for you. I was just thinking about you, and now you are here."

She smiled that sweet, innocent smile that reminded him how young she was. And that she wasn't his. But possession didn't apply when she wasn't real.

"I am here. I needed to get away from my family. My father especially. He's trying to marry me off, and I don't like the men he's chosen."

"Why not?" Carmelo asked. It didn't matter if she was real or not, she was there, and she was talking to him.

She shrugged, and Carmelo fell into step next to her. "My father wants me to marry someone with a family he knows. He keeps bringing men over, but they're all men I grew up with. I have no interest in them. Tonight was the worst, though."

"What happened tonight?"

Tina sucked in a shaky breath and wrapped her arms around herself. She stopped and looked up at him. "I feel safe with you. Why is that?"

Carmelo shrugged. "I don't know, but I'm happy to hear it."

The edge of her lip turned up.

"What happened tonight, Tina?" he asked again.

She turned and started walking again. Away from her home. "He thought he had a right to touch me."

"Who did?" Carmelo demanded, his voice steel and his fists ready to teach a lesson someone desperately needed.

"It doesn't matter. My father heard him and told him to leave. Thankfully, he's off the list, but I still have to marry one of them."

"I was told you're going to marry Antonio Costello."

Tina laughed. Then she laughed some more. Carmelo stood and watched her and finally realized the woman in front of him was as real as he was. He didn't make her up, and she was actually talking to him. And laughing at him.

"Does that mean you are not marrying him?"

Tina shook her head and stood upright again. "No. I've known Antonio my whole life. He's like my brother."

Carmelo filed the information away for later and asked, "Why do you have to get married now?"

She shrugged. "I just turned eighteen, so I guess it's time for me to not be a burden to my father any longer."

"Children should never be a burden."

"I agree," she said softly.

They walked together silently for a few minutes, neither of them breaking the companionable quiet between them. The streets were quiet, and it felt like they were the only two people in the world.

"Thank you for talking to me," Tina said softly.

Carmelo nodded. "I'm happy I was here."

"Me, too." She chewed on her lip then boldly met his gaze. "Can I kiss you?"

Carmelo's brows went up, and he took a step back. He'd been with women who asked for what they wanted, but never one like Tina. He assumed she was a virgin, and she certainly didn't have much experience with men. Yet, she was putting herself out there.

"Never mind," she said quickly, moving away from him.

Carmelo took two steps and caught up to her, grabbing her hand and spinning her to face him. She gasped, her other hand landing on his chest. She looked down at where her hand was and tried to pull back, but he pressed his other hand over hers.

"You don't have to do this," she said firmly.

"What if I want to, Tina? Can I kiss you?"

She stared into his eyes for a long moment, so long that he wondered if she'd changed her mind. Then she lifted on her tiptoes and pressed her lips to his.

Carmelo stilled under her clumsy kiss, learning the feel of her before he slid his hand up her throat and buried it in her hair. He tilted her head opposite his and slid his tongue over her lips. She gasped and let him in, and he pressed their joined hands to her back.

She stilled, then sighed and sank into him. Her entire body melted against his. Carmelo let his body take over, pressing against her. She moaned softly, but he eased back.

"Why are you stopping?" Tina asked.

"Because I like you, Tina."

"If you liked me, you wouldn't stop."

Carmelo shook his head and tucked her hair behind her ear. "Trust me, I like you. Some women want sex only, and some want love. You, Tina Vincenzo, you want love. And I'm not sure I can give that to you. I'm not the kind of man your father would bring home for you. I work in the fields. I'm not wealthy. I have nothing to my name. And you deserve the world."

Tina stepped closer to him and shook her head. "I just want to feel safe. I want to know someone is going to listen to me. I don't care about money or status or family names. I care about not having the life my mother has. A life where someone else dictates my every move. A life where my children can choose what they want to do, no matter what parts are in their pants. And yes, I want love, but why is that a bad thing?"

Carmelo drew in a breath and inhaled her right along with the air. She was a challenge, and not because she was easy to resist, but the opposite. She said all the right things. Things that made him question how he lived his life.

"That was my first real kiss, Carmelo. My father expects me to marry someone, but I've never been touched by a man, or even a boy. I'm not ready for marriage. I don't want to marry those boys. I want to meet someone and fall wildly in love and have a bunch of kids."

"And you know none of the men your father has set up for you will be men you fall wildly in love with?"

She took a deep breath, her chest rising and falling slowly. She reached for his hand and pressed his palm over her chest. "Do you feel that? My heart racing?"

He nodded.

"It's never done that before. Not for any of the boys I've ever known. It's only done that when I'm around you. I can't promise you I'll never fall wildly in love with someone else, but I can tell you none of the men I've ever met have made me feel half as wild as you do."

Carmelo didn't stop to think, he just acted. He stepped toward her as he slid his hand up her throat and around to the back of her neck to pull her closer. She opened for him immediately, their racing hearts pounding in rhythm as they kissed.

Her hands wandered up and down his back, then his chest. She touched him as he kissed her, making it harder and harder to resist her. When her tentative touch grazed his bare skin, he groaned and plunged his tongue deeper into her mouth.

She returned his aggressive kiss and grew bolder with her hands, sliding them up his back and around to tease his nipples. He ached to touch her the same way, but if she'd never been kissed, she'd never been touched either.

"Touch me, Carmelo," she whispered between kisses. "I want to feel your hands on me."

He couldn't resist her another second. He cupped her breasts through her shirt and teased her gently. She squirmed in his arms, pressing herself to him. He groaned, needing to get closer to her.

Carmelo had no idea how long they stayed like that, their bodies sealed together, and their lips tasting each other's. It could have been a minute or an hour. All he knew was he wanted it to last a lifetime.

They finally eased back, both of them aware that she needed to return home before her father sent someone to look for her.

"I'm sorry," Tina said softly.

"I understand," Carmelo told her.

"Um, can we meet again?"

Carmelo nodded. "I'll be here every night. If you can come, I'll be waiting for you."

Tina's nose wrinkled up. "You'd do that?"

Carmelo nodded again. "I think I'd do anything for you, Tina."

Tina reached up on her toes and kissed him softly on the lips again. "Thank you."

Carmelo wrapped her in his arms once more and inhaled her deeply. He didn't want to let her go, but he would and he did. "I'll see you soon, Tina."

She nodded and turned to walk back toward her home. She paused before she turned the corner and looked back. Carmelo waved. She waved back and blew him a kiss then disappeared around the corner.

Carmelo smiled and put his hand over his heart. He'd never felt that way before either. Maybe love wasn't so far out of the question.

13

Present Day

THE RINGING OF THE ALARM WOKE RYAN FROM A HELL OF A dream about Bella. She was wrapped around him, her wet, warm body drawing him in deeper and deeper until he felt like he was a part of her.

But the damn alarm interrupted him before he got to the good stuff. Which meant he was rushing from the bunks to pull on his turnout gear with a hard-on that wasn't willing to go away.

Thankfully, the only other guy in the fire station wasn't paying any attention, trying to get himself into his gear without falling over. It had only been an hour since they got back from the last call. Reggie didn't want to go home in the middle of the night and risk waking his kids, so he crashed at the fire station with Ryan.

They jumped in the truck and headed out, keeping the siren off so they didn't wake up everyone in Bereton in the middle of the night.

When Reggie pulled up to the house, Ryan nearly

groaned. Half the house was engulfed. The houses on the street were close together, which meant they were going to have to evacuate the homes next door, and soak them if they couldn't get the fire put out quickly.

Ryan and Reggie worked to hook up their hoses while they waited for the others to show up. They just barely got ready when three other vehicles pulled up and the men jumped out, dressed and ready to fight with them.

"Edwards and Mack, you two on the hose. Hit the south side of the house where the flames are the worst. Thomas, Wilson, you're with me. We're going in the front. The call said there is someone home, and since no one out here is claiming this as their house, we have to assume someone is still inside."

Ryan nodded and pulled on his mask. He was the third one in the house, checking to make sure nothing was missed on their way through.

"No movement. Bedroom looks like where the fire started. Going in," Reggie said.

Ryan and Thomas followed him in, one going left, one right, and Ryan heading straight into the middle of the room. He scanned the area, keeping both men in his line of sight so they didn't miss anything.

"Bathroom," Thomas said through the radio. "Going in."

Ryan kept looking at the room, checking that the bed was empty. He didn't see anyone, and turned to leave the room.

"Got someone," Thomas shouted. "Unconscious, but there's a pulse. I need help."

"On my way," Reggie said. "Wilson, lead the way. Stay close."

Ryan scanned the room and waited for them to come up

behind him. When he heard the command, he started for the door.

They were able to get outside the house with the woman. Reggie and Thomas carried her to the waiting ambulance, but she didn't wake up. The ambulance drove off, lights flashing in the dark night, and the firefighters returned to the task of saving the woman's house.

The house was small, but the fire burned quickly with the dry air of winter. No snow was coming, and the snow on the ground melted without helping to suppress the fire at all.

Ryan took turns with the other men holding the hose and adding a second line when the house next door lit up. They were able to put that fire out quickly, but by the time the first fire was out, the house was gone.

Ryan and the others sank against the truck to rest and watch the house. They didn't want embers to light up and restart the fire.

"That was a bad one," Reggie said.

"Any idea what caused it?" Edwards asked.

Reggie shook his head. "No way for us to know. We just put them out."

"Any word on the lady you guys carried out?" Mack asked.

All heads swung to Reggie. He shook his head slowly. "She didn't make it. Her pulse was weak, and she inhaled too much smoke. She was DOA."

"Shit," Thomas swore.

Ryan closed his eyes and said a prayer for the woman. He didn't know where everyone in Bereton lived, but it was a small enough town that he had no doubt he knew the woman.

"Anyone know who she was?" Edwards asked.

"Ms. Loveland," Reggie told us. "She was a teacher forever ago. I had her growing up. Retired for a few decades now."

"Family?" Thomas asked.

Reggie shook his head. "Never married as far as I know. Did your family know her?" he asked Ryan.

Ryan nodded. "My Aunt Marie was a friend of hers. I'll talk to her in the morning."

The others nodded and fell silent.

Losing someone was always hard for Ryan. He knew it was part of the job, but he hated it. Especially when it was someone he knew. Ms. Loveland had been at more picnics than Ryan could count. She and Aunt Marie were friends, but he was fairly sure the entire family knew her.

The guys waited for the requisite time, then started to pack up the truck. It was still the middle of the night, but the cold bed back at the fire station didn't hold any appeal for Ryan. What did appeal to him was a warm bed with Bella in it.

Ryan rode with Reggie back to the station then packed up his stuff and headed out. He parked at his house and stared up at it. He could go inside and crawl into his bed, or he could walk over to Perry's and get Bella to let him in so he could hold her.

It didn't take long for him to turn toward town and start walking. He felt like a thief sneaking onto Perry Mount property, but he wasn't there for any reason other than to see Bella.

Not wanting to scare her, he stopped near the end of the driveway and sent her a text asking if he could see her. If she didn't reply, he'd just walk back home and not worry about it.

Ryan tried to get the image of Ms. Loveland out of his

head. He wanted answers and knew Aunt Marie would, too, but he didn't have them yet.

He was about to give up on Bella and go home when his phone buzzed in his hand.

Are you okay?

Not really. Wanted to see you.

Where are you?

Outside.

Outside here?

Yep. It's kind of cold.

The front door opened, and Bella stepped outside. "What are you doing here?"

Ryan jogged to her, feeling better just seeing her. "It was a rough night."

She took one look at him and wrapped her arms around his neck. "Come with me," she whispered, dragging him into the house.

Ryan followed her as quietly as he could with his boots on. He'd never been inside Perry's house. He didn't know what to expect, but it was neat and comfortable from what he could see in the dark.

Bella pulled him into a bedroom and closed and locked the door behind them. She didn't turn on the light, but she kept a hold of him and pulled him to the bed. She sat on the edge and tugged him down with her. "Are you okay?"

Ryan shook his head. "Not really. We lost someone tonight."

Bella sighed and closed her eyes. "I'm so sorry, Ryan. Someone you knew?"

He nodded.

She squeezed his hand then slid off the bed onto her knees. She tugged at his laces until she got his boots untied and pulled them off, leaving them on the floor next to the double bed. She stood and climbed onto the bed and pulled him down with her, covering them both up with the covers.

Ryan took his first deep breath since he heard Ms. Loveland didn't make it and let himself sink into Bella. He pressed his nose to her neck and breathed her in, the now familiar scent of her making him hard instantly.

His dream from so long ago came rushing back to him with the need that pulsed through him hours ago. "Bella," he breathed.

She tilted her chin up and kissed him. When he pressed his tongue to her lips, she welcomed him in and stroked her tongue along his. She slid her hand between them and cupped him through his clothes, knowing what he needed with him having to say the words.

Ryan's hands were rough and clumsy when he reached for her. It wasn't long before she was pushing him onto his back and taking over, straddling him and making him crazy before either of them had any clothes off.

"What do you need, Ryan?"

"You," he admitted.

She grabbed the hem of her shirt and stripped it off, then leaned over him and sealed their lips together. He palmed her heavy breasts and teased her nipples, letting himself feel instead of think.

Bella kissed her way down his body, pulling his shirt up to expose his abs. She slid her tongue over his muscles and nudged his shirt out of the way until he reached back and pulled it all the way off. Then she worked her way down, undoing his pants and helping him get them off.

"Did you bring a condom?" she asked a second before she wrapped her pretty pink lips around his cock.

"Fuck me," Ryan growled. "I have one, yeah. I...Jesus, Bella. I didn't plan this."

She withdrew from him and licked down his cock to his balls. She sucked one then the other into her mouth and he had to recite the alphabet to keep from embarrassing himself.

"I know you didn't," she said when she stood and stripped her pajama bottoms off. "And if you did, that would be okay, too."

He grabbed his jeans and dug his wallet out, thankful he tucked a condom in there a few days earlier. They'd slept together a few times already, but always in his bed where condoms were easy to come by. He didn't know what made him think to put a condom in his wallet, but he was glad he did.

Bella took the condom from him and opened the package. She rolled it down his length, stroking him again before she released his throbbing cock. She crawled onto the bed again, positioning herself over him.

"You didn't come yet," Ryan growled as she started to lower onto him. "You need to come first."

Bella shook her head and kept shifting, up and down, taking him in deeper with each shallow stroke. "I just want to feel you inside me."

"Bella," Ryan groaned. "I feel like an ass."

She shook her head. "There's no reason for you to feel that way."

Her body drew him in deeper, and he gritted his teeth. Without a warmup, she was even tighter than usual. Every short thrust was making him crazy. Ryan wasn't sure he would last long enough to make it all the way inside her.

"You feel so fucking good," she whispered. She spread her thighs and he sank in farther.

Ryan groaned again, his hands going to her hips. "Fuck me, Bella. You feel amazing."

"So do you, Ryan. So good," she moaned and shifted. Her eyes fluttered closed and her channel squeezed his cock.

Ryan slid his hand from her hip and pressed his thumb against her clit. She clamped down on him and shuddered.

"Ryan," she whispered.

She didn't need to say anything else. He slid his thumb down until it slicked through her wetness, then dragged it back up to touch her again. She rose up on her knees and sank down again. He timed his strokes with hers, plunging up when she went down and pressing tight to her clit at the same moment.

Ryan held back as long as he could, gritting his teeth and focusing only on Bella. With each stroke, her beautiful breasts drew his attention and thickened his already painfully hard cock. But she wasn't ready. She wasn't there yet. And he couldn't come until she did.

"Bella, stop. Oh, fuck, stop, Bella," he groaned.

She froze mid-stroke, her face going from near bliss to shuddered fear. She started to move off the bed, but he held her hips.

"Slide up, Bell. Let me taste you."

The bliss returned when she realized what he wanted from her. She crawled up his body and settled on top of his face.

Ryan groaned and dove in. She was wet and ready, her come already seeping from her. He pressed her back so she would lean forward. She held on to the headboard, and he thrust his tongue into her.

Bella groaned and sank down onto him. He fucked her with his tongue until she leaned forward, struggling to keep herself upright.

Ryan moved up and captured her clit. Her moan was quiet but unmistakable. Ryan licked and sucked and teased her clit until she rocked her hips over his face.

"Oh, God, yes, Ryan. I'm so close."

He teased her entrance with his fingers, and she rocked her hips faster. He teased her like that for a minute, then plunged his fingers deep into her and sucked hard on her clit, and she went flying. She pulsed all around him her entire body tightening and releasing with her orgasm.

Then she collapsed, barely supporting her own weight.

Ryan wiggled out from beneath her and kissed his way up her back. When he reached her ear, he whispered, "Lay down, Bell. I'm not done with you yet."

"More," was all she said, but she did as he asked.

With Bella stretched out beneath him, Ryan positioned himself at her entrance and watched her. The sleepy, satisfied grin had him wanting to go slow, but the aching in his cock said he wouldn't last.

"Fuck me hard, Ryan. Please," she said without opening her eyes.

And he did. He thrust into her so hard she gasped. Her legs wrapped around his back and drew him in deeper with each hard stroke. Thank God the bed was sturdy and didn't shift with their movements, or Ryan would have stopped, and he didn't think he could handle stopping.

His thrusts were relentless and demanding. He needed her. He had to have every inch of her. And she was giving it to him. Her hands slid over his body as he fucked her hard and deep. And when his orgasm demanded to be released, she fell into her own with him, quietly crying his name as she came.

Ryan fell onto Bella, all his energy drained from the night and from Bella. He wasn't sure he would be able to move for hours, and he knew he didn't want to. She wrapped her arms around him and held him, letting him take even more from her.

Ryan softened and knew he had to move before he made a mess on her bed. He pulled back and removed the condom, then looked around for a tissue. Boxes and boxes surrounded them.

"What is this room?"

"I think it's an office or storage or something. He said it's his guest room, but I don't think he's ever had guests. He said he would move everything out of here, but I told him not to worry about it."

"I...Wow," Ryan said. He forced himself to look away from the boxes. If there was any evidence Perry had stolen from his father, it was probably in the same room he was in, but he couldn't ask Bella. It wasn't fair to put her in the middle, and it wasn't right, even if the room she'd spent every night in for the last three weeks held the proof he needed.

Ryan crawled off the bed and found tissues on the desk. He wrapped up the condom and threw it in the trash under the desk. The boxes behind him called to him, and he knew he had to get out of the room before he asked her about them.

"I should go."

Bella slid out of bed and pulled on her clothes. Ryan dressed silently, hating that he showed up, fucked her, and was leaving, but if Perry found him there, in that room, there was no telling what he would do.

"Are you okay?" Bella asked when they got to the front door.

Ryan nodded. "I'm better now. I'm sorry I showed up and jumped you."

Bella grinned. "I didn't mind a bit."

He kissed her softly and stepped back so she could unlock the front door. He kissed her once more, then stepped out into the cold. "I'll talk to you tomorrow?"

Bella nodded. "Let me know you're home safe."

He nodded and turned to walk away. The door closed quietly behind him, and Ryan walked home, wondering the entire way if Bella's room contained the one thing his family had searched years to find.

14

———

Spending time with Ryan was definitely messing with Bella's head. She liked him, a lot, and when they were together, she started thinking about things she had no business thinking about. Like falling in love and bringing the two families together.

Definitely things she had no business thinking about.

But that was the reason she was standing in front of the small mirror in the tiny bedroom she was starting to think of as her own and wearing a black dress and boots.

"Are you almost ready?" Albert asked, pausing outside her door. His eyes scanned her, then returned to her face with a blank expression.

Bella learned that meant he didn't really see her. There were times he looked at her and knew he was paying attention, but most of the time, he looked without seeing. For her, it was fine, but every time he did it, she wondered if her mother felt the same.

"Yes," Bella answered, pasting on a smile for him.

He nodded and continued toward the rest of the house. They hadn't spoken as much in the last few days. Bella wondered if he heard her sneak Ryan in, but he never said anything. He never said much about anything. She was starting to wonder if she was overstaying her welcome, but she wasn't ready to leave yet.

She was not going to examine why.

Bella grabbed her coat from the front and followed Albert out of the house. He was in the truck with it running by the time she got there, and he started moving before she buckled her seatbelt.

The drive to the church was quiet. Bella hadn't been in a church in years, but she wasn't going to tell Albert she wouldn't go. It obviously upset him when he found out Ms. Loveland died. The entire town seemed to feel it if the stuffed parking lot and overflowing church were any indication.

The service was nice. The priest obviously knew her well and spoke fondly of her. It made Bella wish she'd met the woman.

At the end of the funeral, another woman stood and nodded at Father Richard. He smiled at her, and she faced the crowd.

"As you all know, Millie was a wonderful woman with an unmatched love for this town and the people in it. I was lucky to call her a friend, as were we all. My family would like to invite everyone back to Amavita Estates for a meal to celebrate the life of Millie Loveland. Since she didn't have family, we are her family," the woman said, gesturing to the room.

"Who is that?" Bella whispered to Albert.

He jumped as though he'd forgotten she was there, and looked at her. "Marie Richliano. The oldest of the sisters."

Bella nodded. Ryan's aunt Marie. He mentioned her, but Bella hadn't met her. "Are we going?"

Albert paused then shook his head. "I'm not welcome."

"She just said everyone is welcome."

"She didn't mean it."

"I think we should go. It's important to you to be here. You should go say goodbye, even if it's just for a minute."

Bella didn't want to think too hard about why she was pushing. Was it the possibility of seeing Ryan? Or maybe the hope that she could reunite the families? Or was she just watching out for Albert? She wasn't sure.

When he nodded, Bella smiled. They filed out of the church with everyone else and followed the massive crowd through Bereton out to Amavita Estates.

Albert parked near the edge. Bella noted it was a spot where he wouldn't get blocked in and could leave whenever he wanted. She hoped it didn't come to that.

He fidgeted with his keys until the got inside. Albert looked around the entire time, his eyes scanning the rooms as they walked from the front of the inn to the back where the restaurant was.

"It smells good," Bella commented.

Albert nodded, but he was barely paying any attention to her.

They made it to the front of the line and grabbed plates, filling them with food that made her stomach growl. She followed Albert to a small table in the back corner. There were only two chairs, and Albert chose the one that faced away from the crowd.

"Are you okay?" Bella asked after a long, silent minute.

Albert looked up at her, again looking surprised she was there, and nodded. He focused on his plate, eating quickly and ignoring everyone around them.

Bella didn't know many people in town, so she people-watched as she ate. The room was overflowing with people who came to share stories and celebrate the life of a woman who was clearly loved.

Bella thought back to her mother's funeral. The service was nice, but it was simple. Her mom didn't plan for her funeral, so Bella was forced to make decisions on her own. And since she didn't have a lot of money to use for the funeral, her budget guided most of her choices.

It would have been nice to have a reception like the one they were having for Mrs. Loveland. A chance for family and friends to gather and grieve in a different way. Instead, Bella was alone in her grief.

She pushed her food around on her plate and thought about her mom. She would have hated Bella looking for Albert. She would have been so mad. But she would have loved Ryan's family. Aunt Marie was playing hostess, greeting people at every table. There were other women making their way around the tables, checking in on people and ensuring everyone had enough food.

"Are you ready to go?" Albert asked, eyeing her plate.

Bella glanced down and realized she'd eaten everything. She nodded and stood. She pulled on her coat while Albert grabbed both their plates.

"I'll meet you outside," Albert mumbled as he walked away.

Bella nodded, wondering why he was in such a hurry.

Bella buttoned her coat and tied the sash around her waist, then slung her purse over her shoulder. She worked her way through the crowd, smiling at people she didn't know, until she was out of the bulk of the room and free to get to the front door.

"Hey, I know you," a voice said from right next to her. "You're a friend of Ryan's, right?"

Bella turned and saw Ryan's cousin, the one who worked at the front desk. She nodded. "I'm Bella."

"Andie. Nice to meet you. Did you know Ms. Loveland?"

Bella shook her head. "No. I'm sorry for your loss, though."

Andie nodded. "Thanks. She was a great teacher, but I've gotten to know her a little since I finished school, and she was a wonderful person, too. If you didn't know her, why did you come? Oh, sorry. I should have known."

Andie looked around the room while Bella struggled to figure out what she thought she knew.

"Oh, there he is," Andie said, pointing toward the front door. "Dammit. What the hell is he doing here?"

"Who?" Bella asked, following Andie's gaze and finally seeing exactly who.

"Albert Perry owns the vineyard across the street. He knows he's not supposed to be on our property. Ryan and Henry are going to kill him. Excuse me." Andie rushed toward them.

Bella stood still for a moment, then followed Andie.

"...no right," Henry was saying. "We're going to have to file a restraining order if you don't stay off our property."

"I was here for the celebration. Your Aunt Marie invited me, along with everyone else," Albert defended himself. He stood facing down Ryan and Henry with a hard expression. His hands were clenched at his sides, and he leaned forward, as if ready to attack.

"You know that invitation didn't extend to you," Henry spat.

Albert sneered. "She didn't say everyone except me, so how was I to know?"

"This isn't the place for this," Andie said, moving between the men.

All three men looked chagrined and glanced around. When they noticed Bella, all three had different expressions. Ryan's was joy, then fear. Albert's was relief. And Henry's was surprise.

Before any of them could say anything, Leo walked up. "I think it's best if you go," he said to Albert. He turned to Bella with a smile, then realization lit his gaze. "You're his daughter," Leo said, not asking. "That's why you looked so familiar." He turned to his cousin. "How did you not know you were sleeping with Perry's daughter?"

Ryan opened his mouth to answer, but Albert spoke first. "What the hell is he talking about?"

"I can explain," Bella said.

"You're not a friend of Ryan's?" Andie asked.

"I am. And he knew who my father was. I told him."

"What the hell are they talking about?" Henry asked. Ryan's brother. That was not the way Bella hoped to be introduced to him.

"Ryan and Bella have been sleeping together for weeks. I knew she looked familiar when I met her, but I didn't realize why until I saw her next to him."

Henry spun toward his brother and barked, "You thought it was smart to bring another liar into our house? Onto our property?"

"She's not a liar," Ryan said, getting in his brother's face. "You don't know the first thing about her."

"I'm guessing neither do you. If it wasn't a big enough red flag that she was on our property without permission, she's his daughter. What made you think getting involved with her was a good idea?"

"You don't get to judge my life. Ever. I make my own decisions."

"You brought her here. To our property. You, of all

people, should know what that man is capable of, and you didn't even once think that maybe he sent her here on a spy mission?" Henry faced Albert. "What was the plan this time? Get her to steal our recipes? Steal our equipment?"

Albert's eyes were wide with anger. Bella knew everyone would find out who she was related to, but she didn't think it would happen the way it was, in public with everyone yelling.

"I didn't know anything about this. And I never stole anything from your vineyard," Albert hissed.

"What the hell is going on?" another man asked, joining the group of them. "What the fuck are you doing here? Get the hell off our property."

"Did you know our cousin was screwing his daughter?" Leo asked.

The new guy's gaze swung to Ryan. Ryan closed his eyes and breathed, and Bella knew it was time for her to go. She didn't want to hear another word, from any of them. She moved around the group, ignoring the calls of her name, and walked outside into the cold afternoon. The air was clean and pure. The sun shined brightly, mocking her. She started walking fast, desperate to get as far away from all of them as possible.

Her phone buzzed, but she ignored it. She kept walking until she made it to the house. She seriously thought about packing up and leaving, but she just wanted to get away. She got in her car and pulled out, leaving it all behind. She'd consider going back later, but until she had some time to process, she wasn't making anyone any promises. Even herself.

RYAN STARTED to go after Bella, but Perry's angry words stopped him.

"You're the one she snuck into my house, aren't you?"

Ryan turned and glared at the man. He'd hated Albert Perry most of his life. He'd been seven when Perry stole from his father and embarrassed him by opening a competing vineyard right across the street. Ryan grew up hearing how horrible the man was. But he'd never been on the receiving end of Perry's distaste.

"You have no right being in my home," Perry snarled.

"I was Bella's guest, not yours."

"It's my damn house!"

"And she lives there."

"I don't want you to ever set foot in my home again. In that room, or any other room in my home. If you do, I promise you won't have to worry about a restraining order against me because I'll have one against you," Perry growled. He turned and walked away without another word, leaving Ryan to face his family.

"You're fucking Perry's daughter," Zach said. He joined them at the end of the conversation right before Bella walked away, but he was clearly up to speed.

"And he brought her to our home," Leo spat.

"And went into his. Did you find any evidence?" Henry asked.

"Evidence?" Leo and Zach repeated.

"Ryan's been looking into Perry again. He wants to find the proof Dad never found. Is that why you're sleeping with her?" Henry asked.

Ryan didn't think, just acted when he grabbed his brother by the collar and shoved him against the wall. All he saw was red, followed by the undeniable need to beat the living shit out of his older brother, something he'd never done in his life.

"Ryan!" Andie shrieked.

Her voice got through the fog of anger that consumed him, and he let go of Henry.

Henry brushed his hands down the front of his shirt, smoothing away the wrinkles Ryan created. He glared at Ryan, then stormed back to the celebration.

Some fucking party.

"Is that why you started seeing Bella?" Leo asked. "Because you really seemed like you were into her."

Ryan didn't look at them. He couldn't. Bella was Perry's daughter. She was a woman he shouldn't want. She wasn't even sticking around. There was no way he could choose her over his family.

Except he was.

"He likes her," Zach supplied. "He likes her a lot. He might even be in love with her."

"I'm not in love with her," Ryan finally said. "I barely know her. And she's Perry's daughter."

"I didn't even know he had a daughter," Leo said.

Ryan shook his head. "He didn't either. Her mom died a few months ago. She looked him up, hoping to find distant family. Her mom told her he was dead, and that he never wanted her. She came here to rip him a new one, and he told her he never knew she existed and welcomed her into his home."

Leo and Zach wore matching expressions of shock.

"The son of a bitch has a heart. Who knew?" Zach said. "I gotta get back to the kitchen."

Ryan watched his cousin walk away, then turned to Leo. Leo was his best friend, and the only one who'd met Bella. They didn't spend a lot of time together because she was worried about him figuring out who she was, but he'd spoken to her more than the others.

"Why didn't you tell me who she was?" Leo asked.

Ryan drew in a breath. "She was afraid you would react exactly like you did. She thought everyone would hate her simply because Perry's her father."

"Why? I mean, she didn't grow up with him, and if she's not close to him or like him, then what difference would it make?"

"She didn't know who we were when she got here. I met her the night of Dad's service. She was down at the docks and just watching the water. We talked, and she made me forget for a minute that he was gone. We met down there a few more times, then we ran into each other in Bereton. She'd just found out about Perry and Dad, and she felt like she had to pick sides. We were getting to know each other, but she was here to meet her father. She felt like she was trapped between us. But she told me as soon as she found out what happened. She didn't lie to me or keep it from me."

"And you're sure she's telling you the truth? You're sure she's not just a really good actress?"

Ryan thought about it for a minute. He'd asked himself the same question long ago. Could she be lying to him. Could she be reeling him in to get information. He nodded. "I trust her. Maybe I'll regret it, but I think she's being honest."

"Well, Perry definitely looked surprised that you were the one in his house," Leo said with a laugh.

Ryan grinned, then realized what Perry said. "Was he surprised or pissed?"

Leo shrugged. "Probably both. Why? What difference does it make?"

Ryan grabbed Leo by the shoulders and shook him.

"The room Bella is staying in. It's full of boxes of files. All kinds of stuff that she said she thinks he's been storing for years."

"And you were in the room. Did you go through it?"

Ryan shook his head. "No. I didn't want to put Bella in the middle. I thought about it, but if Perry was pissed, was it because he thought I might have seen something?"

Leo drew in a breath. "I don't know, but I think it's a better bet that he's pissed about that than he's pissed that you're sleeping with the daughter he never knew he had."

Ryan nodded. "I need to get back into that room."

15

———

Bella hated being in a strange town and not knowing where to go when she was feeling alone and attacked. If her mom was still alive, they'd be curled up under a blanket and watching a sappy romantic comedy. But if her mom was still alive, Bella never would have met Albert or Ryan or any of the other people she was running away from.

Her phone didn't stop ringing, so she turned it off and dropped it into her enormous purse, hoping she would lose it before she lost all sense of self-preservation and checked her messages. As much as she wanted to talk to Ryan and Albert, she didn't want to talk to them until she figured out how she felt about the whole thing.

She really needed a friend.

No. She needed her mom. Her mom was her best friend. Always was, always would be. And it didn't matter that her mom was gone, she wanted to talk to her.

Bella drove through town and kept going. She ended up heading north, not really caring where it led. The entire time she drove, she talked.

"I really screwed things up, Mom. I don't even know

what I did, but I screwed up. I guess just my existence caused a problem this time. Then again, it's not the first time for that. I guess that's how you always felt about me. Just by existing I was causing you a problem."

Bella paused at a stop sign and decided to keep going straight.

"I wish I could ask you why you lied to me about my father. I really want to know. He doesn't seem like he's that bad of a guy. I mean, he's odd, but odd isn't mean or cruel. Then again, when I'm talking to him and I know he's not listening to me...Okay, fine. I guess a part of me understands. But he was my father. Why couldn't you at least tell him about me? Or tell me about him? Give me a chance to meet him and decide for myself if I wanted to have a relationship with him. Instead, you took that choice away from me. And you lied to me. That's what I have the hardest time accepting. You lied to me. I never thought you lied to me. I thought we were honest with each other about everything."

Bella wiped her face and slowed down as she passed through another tiny town. They lined the lakes and fought for the tourists that frequented the vineyards all along the water. But during the winter, the vineyards were as deserted as the towns. Nothing was growing, which meant very few people made it to the area.

"I don't know what to do, Mom," Bella said once she was through the town. "I like Ryan a lot, but Albert isn't a bad guy. They obviously both feel like they're right, and I don't think I can choose between them. I don't want to have to choose between them. I want them to get along."

Bella laughed to herself, remembering her mom's words from middle school.

"Not everyone is going to like you, and you're not going to like everyone. There's nothing wrong with that. Spending all your time trying to be friends with people you don't click with and ignoring the people you do is not going to make you happier. Move on and focus on the people who matter the most."

Bella laughed again, then sighed.

"Who matters most here? The father I never knew, or the man who makes me feel like I'm not alone?"

Bella drove in silence for a minute, hoping she'd get an answer. When none came, Bella admitted to herself that she couldn't run away from any more problems.

She picked up her phone and called her mom's partner. Julia was the only person Bella knew wouldn't lie to her. Julia would be harsh and honest, which was exactly what Bella needed.

"Bella?" Julia asked when she answered the phone.

"Hey, Julia," Bella said, drawing in a deep breath and preparing herself.

"Bella. Holy crap. Where are you? Are you okay?"

"I'm fine. I went to visit my father," Bella said.

"Your father? I thought he was dead," Julia said, sounding annoyed.

"I did, too. I wanted to see if I had other family around. I didn't expect to actually find him."

"Are you sure it's him, Bella? That it's not some random person pretending?"

"I went to him, Julia. I found him. He didn't know who I was. He was just as surprised as I was when I showed up on his doorstep. He never knew about me."

Julia gasped. "Melanie said she told him. She said he never wanted a kid. That he told her to get rid of you."

"She told me the same thing," Bella said. "It wasn't true. None of it. He never knew."

Julia blew out a breath, and Bella waited. There was

more. There was always more with Julia. "Are you sure about this? Did you do a DNA test or something?"

Bella shook her head. "No. He didn't ask for one, and Julia...he owns a vineyard. If anyone should be worried about a random relative showing up out of the blue, it's him, not me."

"He owns a vineyard?"

"Yeah. He owns a vineyard and is a nice guy. He's quiet and keeps to himself. I like him, Julia. And I know he's telling me the truth."

"That means your mom lied to you your whole life. She lied to me, too."

Bella sighed. Julia had a habit of turning things around so everything was about her.

"Wow, Bella. You must be so confused. I'm so sorry."

Bella sputtered. She wasn't sure what to say.

"Bella? Are you still there?"

"Yeah, um, sorry. I just was surprised that you asked."

Julia snorted. "Why? Because I always argue with you? Do you know why I do that?"

Bella shook her head, then remembered Julia couldn't see her. "Uh, no, I don't."

"Your mom never challenged you. Maybe it was because you were an only child, or maybe because she lied to you forever, but she let you be the center of attention for everything that ever happened. You needed someone who would push you to think about others."

Bella opened her mouth to argue and realized Julia was right. Her mom always let Bella throw tantrums and get away with things she never should have. Bella milked it, too, getting everything she could out of her mother and never standing on her own two feet. She thought she had time to learn.

"I'm sorry," Bella said after a minute. "I wasn't a very good person."

"You can't blame yourself," Julia said. "Not entirely."

"Thanks, Jules," Bella sneered.

Julia just laughed. "Well, it's true. But right now, this is about you. Are you okay? It had to be a blow."

Bella nodded to herself. "It was. It still is. I came here to tell him off and to make sure he knew I thought he was a complete ass, but he welcomed me into his home. He told me he was sorry he wasn't a part of my life before. He wished he'd known me. Then he asked me to stay for a while so we could get to know each other."

"Wow. That's amazing. He's not, um..."

"Ew, Julia, gross. No, he's not a dirty old man who's hitting on me."

"And you're okay?"

Bella nodded. "Yeah, I'm okay."

"Then tell me what's wrong."

Bella took a breath and told Julia everything. From meeting Ryan to finding out about the feud between his family and Albert to Ryan's family finding out who she was and Albert realizing she was involved with Ryan. She ended with the way they were all fighting and how Bella left.

Bella took a breath and waited for Julia to say something.

"Holy shit, Bella. What did you get yourself into?"

"I know. Only me, right? I'm a screw up and I never do anything right. It's why you fired me."

Julia laughed. "True, but I also fired you because I was sick of you thinking you could do no wrong. You needed to grow up, Bella."

"And I've just proven I haven't grown up at all."

Julia laughed again. "No, Bella, that's not true. The fact

that you've stopped and are trying to figure out what to do tells me you have grown up. You're not just running away from everything or letting someone else figure it out for you. You're trying to decide to fix things."

"Well, yeah. I can't just leave. And I care about them."

"You always cared, Bella. That was never something anyone questioned. Your mom knew she was the center of your world. She worried about it sometimes. She thought she was keeping you from figuring out your true potential. She was planning to fire you, Bella. Force you to find your own way. She knew you could do more than what you always did. She wanted to see you figure out who you were."

Bella's eyes welled with tears and her throat closed up. The tears she thought she'd cried all of slid down her cheeks and soaked her collar.

"Bella?"

"Yeah?"

"She loved you. I love you. She told me to watch out for you if anything ever happened to her. Ever since we became friends, she asked me to watch over you. But now? I don't think I'm doing a very good job of that."

Bella laughed. "I make it hard."

Julia chuckled. "No, honey. It's always been easy to love you. It's just hard not to kill you."

Bella laughed with Julia and felt marginally better.

"Bella, you're an amazing woman. Losing your mom was...impossible, but you're doing the right thing. You're looking for other options. So, tell me more about this feud and we'll come up with a few ideas to make it all better."

Bella took a deep breath and wished she was sitting at Julia's table with her, but a call would have to do.

WHEN BELLA MADE it back to Albert's that night, she wasn't sure what he was going to say. She wondered if he'd even let her in the door. But she was going to tell him everything, like she and Julia talked about, and she would let him decide how they would proceed.

She knocked on the door instead of simply letting herself in. She waited, blowing on her cold hands, until he opened the door.

"Why did you knock?" he asked when he saw it was her on the step. "Did you lose your keys? Where are your keys?"

"I wasn't sure if I was still welcome here," Bella answered honestly.

Albert nodded, then stepped back so she could walk in. He stood a few feet away while she removed her coat and hung it up, then put her purse on top of it and grabbed her phone.

"Why him?"

"Ryan?"

Albert nodded.

"I saw something in him the night we met. And every time we've talked since then that same thing was there. He's kind and funny and I like him, Albert."

"When did you realized his father accused me of something horrible?"

Bella lifted her chin and met his gaze. "When you told me."

"And you were already involved with him at that point?"

She nodded.

"When did you tell him you're my daughter?"

"A few days later. I ran into him in town. He bought me dinner and I told him."

"What did he say?"

Bella shrugged. "He told me his side of things."

"Did you defend me?"

Bella shook her head. "It isn't that I don't believe you, but I have no proof either way. Arguing with Ryan...I'm in the middle of two men I care about. Two men I don't know very well."

"And you snuck him into my home. How could you do that?"

Bella's cheeks heated. It wasn't like she thought Albert would assume she was a virgin, but rubbing his nose in it with the son of his enemy was a bad call. "I'm sorry I did that. He was having a bad night and came over. We didn't plan for that to happen."

"But you still brought him into my home knowing how his family feels about me, and how I feel about them."

Bella shook her head. "Actually, I don't know how you feel about them. There are times you seem indifferent, and times you seem frustrated. I don't know if you hate them or wish they still cared about you."

Albert's brows jumped up and his lips pinched. He drew in a breath, and his cheeks pinked. Then he left the room.

Bella wanted to follow him and press for answers, but it wouldn't do any good. If he wasn't willing to talk to her, it didn't matter how many times she asked him the question.

Bella's stomach growled, and she headed to the kitchen. Albert cooked dinner and left her a plate in the fridge, like had become his custom. Bella made an effort to be home to eat with him, but when she wasn't, he always saved her food.

She heated up the meal and thought about what she knew about him. Most of it came from the stories her mother told her growing up. He was smart, but selfish and didn't care about anyone else. He was the kind of man who only looked out for himself. The man she'd gotten to know didn't seem like the same person. He was kind and considerate. Yes, he got lost in his own world at times, but he'd been living alone his whole life, as far as Bella knew.

But she didn't know. The microwave beeped, and Bella grabbed the plate, then headed to the living room. She dug her phone out of her pocket and typed in Albert's name. Just like before, the first results were all about Perry Mount Vineyards. Instead of clicking on the results on page one and reading all about the man who created the vineyard, Bella kept looking.

Her food grew cold as she scanned through one after the other article about Albert Perry. Not all of them were the same man, but many of them were. There was a report in the local newspaper stating Victor Wilson accused Albert of theft. The police supposedly looked into it, but they never found anything.

There were more stories about Albert going back as far as college. He was crazy smart and won awards. He was interviewed in one article about wanting to start his own vineyard one day.

All the articles she read showed him as an ordinary man. No family was ever mentioned, but Albert was successful and private.

Bella didn't learn anything else about the man, except that no one knew anything about him. He obviously liked it that way as even the recent articles about him focused on the vineyard instead of on him.

Bella sighed and carried her plate back to the kitchen. She reheated her dinner and ate it quickly. She changed tactics and searched Ryan's family. There was a wealth of information on them, local and national thanks to his cousin, Dillon's, relationship with Kate Maddox.

Bella read articles about Ryan's family and their vineyard until she started to fall asleep. She put her plate in the dishwasher and decided she would reach out to Ryan and try to talk to Albert again in the morning.

Bella padded down the hall to her room and closed the door behind her. She was halfway to the bed before she realized everything in her room was different. All the boxes that were in the room since she arrived were gone. Everything. Box after box vanished in an afternoon.

And there was only one reason she could think of that would make Albert do it.

He had something to hide.

16

72 years ago

CARMELO WAS HUNGRY AND TIRED AND ANNOYED. ALL HE wanted was a good meal, a warm bed, and a woman to share it with. Preferably Tina.

He hadn't been able to get her out of his mind. They'd seen each other a few times since the first night they met out. Each time they kissed and touched each other, but their clothes stayed on. Tina confessed she'd never been with a man, and Carmelo ached to respect her. But it wasn't easy when she tasted like heaven and kissed like a sinner.

Carmelo headed into the house to get some dinner, and groaned when he saw Antonio in there talking to the group.

"All of you, you're lucky that you work here. My father is a good man, and he's paying you better than you deserve."

Antonio was a jackass who thought he ruled the world. He had big plans for the vineyard, and he made sure all the workers knew he thought they were easily replaceable. They probably were, but none of them enjoyed the reminder.

Antonio seemed to take particular pleasure in taunting

them with all the things he planned to change once he took over. And he seemed to really enjoy making sure Carmelo knew he wasn't a fan of his.

"Carmelo! How are you?" Antonio said, full of smiles.

"Very good, sir. How are you?"

"I'm doing great. I have a date coming up. A beautiful woman. I'm going to need a special wine to really impress her family. I need to know the best thing you have for me."

Carmelo nodded. It wasn't the first time Antonio came down and asked for a good wine, something that would impress a woman's family. He was always looking to schmooze local girls and get them to drop their panties for him.

Carmelo wasn't much better, but he was up front with the women he'd been with. They knew he was only interested in a roll in the sheets, not anything long term. Not until he met Tina.

"Of course, sir. I have just the thing," Carmelo said.

Antonio nodded. "Good. Not the same thing you gave me last time, though. Something better."

Carmelo nodded. "Of course."

"This girl...her family won't settle for anything less than perfect. She's special."

Carmelo thought of Tina and Joey telling him that she was supposed to marry Antonio. He couldn't help but wonder if Antonio was talking about her, but he didn't have the guts to ask. If he found out Tina was truly promised to Antonio, he would have no choice but to stop seeing her. She said it wasn't true, but Carmelo also knew her father wasn't honest with her about all of his plans. If he didn't know for sure, he could pretend for just a little while longer that she could truly be his one day.

"Good for you, sir. She sounds like a wonderful woman," Carmelo said, catering to his arrogant boss.

"She is. Maybe one day you'll find a woman half as good as her. Someone more your station in life."

Carmelo nodded, silently seething at the sneer in the other man's eyes. Carmelo would give anything to shut him up, but he didn't have a leg to stand on. As far as their town was concerned, Antonio was better than Carmelo. It didn't matter that Antonio was a worthless human that spent his daddy's money and treated people like crap. Carmelo wasn't perfect, but he had to believe he was a better person than that.

When Antonio finally left, Joey turned to Carmelo and rolled his eyes. "If you'd stayed away just five more minutes, we all would have been spared."

"If I'd known he was here, I would have."

Joey shook his head. "I don't know what his issue is with you, but he clearly has it in for you."

Carmelo nodded. "Always has, but I've never known why."

Joey rolled his eyes again. "More importantly than Antonio, what about your girl? You going to see her tonight?"

Carmelo shrugged. "I sure hope so."

Joey shook his head. "Damn. You've seen her almost every night for a week. She must be someone special. Even Regina said she hasn't seen you. No one's seen you. This woman has you wrapped up tight."

Carmelo laughed softly. "Not exactly wrapped up tight. She's special, though. Not like any woman I've ever known."

Joey shook his head. "I need to find me a woman like that. One that makes me forget about everything else. One who makes me want to abandon all other women just to spend time with her."

Carmelo clapped his friend on the back and said, "I truly hope you find one like her one day. One who'll make you feel like the world spins only for her."

Joey clenched his shirt and grinned. "Find me, my love. Find me!"

Carmelo laughed and headed for the door. He had a bottle of wine to find for Antonio and a shower to take before he went to see Tina.

Tina smiled at herself in the mirror. She was ready. She'd never felt the way she did about Carmelo. She'd imagined her first time over the last few days, and she was finally ready for it. She wanted to share herself with Carmelo. Tonight.

Tina wanted to tell someone what was happening, but she knew no one would understand. Her sisters were too young, and her friends weren't interested in her relationship. Not unless he was a man who had something to offer. A man that would impress others.

Carmelo didn't have much to show for who he was, but he was the only man Tina had ever met that made her feel like she was special. She was important. She was someone worth impressing. Not her father or her mother, but her. Tina Vincenzo.

When Tina felt like her house was quiet enough, she snuck downstairs and left through the back door like she'd done most nights. She rushed through the grove and out to the street where she turned toward their meeting place. She could see Carmelo waiting for her before she made it. He stood and walked toward her, greeting her in the middle of the street.

"It's been far too long since I've had you in my arms," Carmelo said, sweeping her up.

Tina giggled and wrapped her arms around his neck. He held her close, bringing their bodies together. She always felt safe with him. Loved. Cared for.

"I missed you, too," Tina said, burying her face in his neck. "So much."

"What are we going to do tonight?" Carmelo asked. He took her hand in his and turned them toward town. Everything was closed for the night, but it was how they liked it best. The town was all theirs, with no one to judge them and no one to ask questions. They could dance in the street, kiss on a bench, or just wander and talk like they did most nights.

"I want to do something we've never done before," Tina said. Her cheeks heated as Carmelo looked closely at her. She wasn't sure if he knew what she meant or not, but she wasn't going to back down. She knew what she wanted, and she was fairly sure he wouldn't argue with her.

Carmelo nodded and squeezed her hand. He smiled and pulled her forward, running into the abandoned street. Tina laughed with him and ran, too. They crossed the street and snuck between two buildings, darting out to the street behind. They paused just long enough to make sure nothing was coming and kept going.

Tina laughed, and Carmelo looked back at her. He stopped abruptly, and she ran into him. He tilted her chin up and lowered his head, capturing her lips in the middle of the street. Moonlight shone around them, and Tina was sure she'd never love another man the way she loved Carmelo. He was everything she always hoped to find and never thought existed.

Watching her parents interact over the last few weeks,

she realized her mother didn't feel the same way about her father. There was respect, and care, but not love. Not adoration. Tina would do anything Carmelo wanted her to do, and she knew he'd never ask her to do something she wasn't comfortable with.

That was love. If she knew anything, she knew she was in love with Carmelo.

He kissed her until they pulled apart laughing, then he kept going, racing them through the streets until they came to a ridge.

Tina gasped. "Wow."

Carmelo nodded and wrapped his arms around her from behind, holding her close to his chest. They stood like that, just watching the lights in the distance, for a long moment.

Tina drew in a breath and turned in his arms to face him. She smiled up at him and whispered, "I love you."

"Thank, God," he replied, pulling her in for a hug. "I love you, too."

She chuckled. "You do?"

He pulled back and tucked her hair behind her ear. "You don't know how much I love you?"

She shook her head. "I've never had a boyfriend before. The boys at school were always so...silly, I guess. My friends dated, but I never even kissed any of those boys. Until I met you, I never understood the appeal of dating."

"Are you saying I'm the only one you had any interest in, so you had no choice but to fall for me?" Carmelo teased.

Tina shook her head. "No, just that I don't know how to recognize love. I know I love you because I would do anything for you."

"Me, too, Tina."

She smiled and reached up to kiss him again. He leaned

down and kissed her sweetly with gentle pecks of their lips together.

He deepened the kiss with a slick of his tongue over the seam of her lips. She opened for him, sliding her tongue along his and moaning softly when he pulled her tighter against his body. She felt the outline of his erection through his jeans and her pants and felt a rush of heat through her body.

"Carmelo," she said softly through their kiss.

"Yeah?"

"Carmelo, I want…"

He pulled back and looked closely at her. "Are you sure?"

She nodded.

"Then come with me. You deserve more than I can give you, but—"

She put her fingers over his lips. "No. I deserve you, Carmelo. That's all I want. Nothing else matters but you and me and our love."

"I'm going to marry you, Tina. I would do it right now if I could, but I promise you, I'm going to find a way to marry you."

She grinned and nodded. "I'd like that."

He yanked her in tight for another kiss, then rushed her away and showed her just how much he meant every word.

Present Day

RYAN HATED the idea of putting Bella in the middle. Since he found out who she was, he didn't want her to have to choose between the father she just met and him, but that was where she was. In the middle.

He tried reaching out to her multiple times after she ran off, but she turned off her phone. He stopped trying and sent her a text asking her to call him when she was ready to talk. That he was sorry for the way his family reacted, and that what was going on between them was between them.

It was two days before she reached out. Two days of avoiding his family and dodging questions about why he was involved with Perry's daughter. They couldn't see her as a woman, they only saw her as a threat. But none of them gave her a chance.

Her text was simple, when she finally answered him.

> Sorry I ran off. Had some things to figure out. Can we meet tonight?

> Yes

She didn't text anything else, and he didn't push her. He worried if he did, she would spook and not reply again. She was in control, and he was just along for the ride.

All day, Ryan waited. He tried to prepare himself for anything she would say. She was done. She was leaving. She didn't want to see him again. She was choosing her father. It could have been any or all of them. And he just had to wait until they met and she said whatever she wanted to say.

Ryan went down to the dock early. He didn't want to take the chance that she would show up and he wasn't there. She didn't specify a time, but he waited until it was dark because he was fairly sure she wouldn't show up and risk running into anyone in his family.

Ryan brought a blanket and a thermos full of hot chocolate. He debated bringing a flask, but he needed a clear head to have a conversation. No matter what she said, he wasn't willing to lose her.

No one was at the dock when Ryan got there, so he laid the blanket on the bench and sat on it, then sat and waited. And waited.

It was nearly midnight when he heard footsteps coming down the hill toward him. He was almost asleep, and was freezing his ass off, but Bella was there.

He shifted his weight so she would know he was there, and smiled up at her when she sat next to him on the blanket.

"Hey," she said softly.

"Hey." Ryan ached to reach for her, but he wasn't sure how she would feel about it. If she was there to end things, he didn't think she'd appreciate him touching her, but he didn't think he could let her walk away without touching her.

They sat silently for a long moment, listening to the quiet night. Ryan wasn't willing to speak first. He wanted to let her say her peace, then he'd beg her not to leave him.

"I called my mom's business partner," she said.

Ryan wasn't sure why it mattered, but he didn't care. She obviously wanted him to know for a reason. "What did she say?"

Bella chuckled. "She said I needed to stop running away from the messes I make. She also said she likes you."

Ryan breathed a laugh.

"I've let my mother fix my mistakes my whole life. She was always there, smoothing things over and making things better. She wanted to help me, but Julia said my mother was planning to fire me."

"Why would she do that?" Ryan asked. He couldn't

imagine his parents or the other aunts firing any of them. Family looked out for each other.

"Because she wanted me to learn how to take care of myself. I haven't been a very good person. I've always let my mother solve my problems. She knew it was a bad habit to be in, and she wanted better for me."

Ryan nodded, trying to understand everything Bella was telling him. While he got it, he didn't understand why it was relevant.

"Julia also said my mother made mistakes. She didn't believe me at first when I told her I found Albert, but she admitted it could be possible after everything else my mother did. I loved my mother, but she clearly wasn't perfect."

"No one is," Ryan said.

Bella nodded. "True. I wish I'd been a better daughter. I wish I'd tried harder to be a good person. I took all the bad things my mom did and made them my own. I didn't realize it, but I have a lot of regrets. Some of them aren't my own, like not knowing my father."

Ryan sighed heavily, finally understanding what she was trying to tell him.

"I know your family doesn't like him, and I even understand why, but he's my father. I can't turn my back on him completely."

Ryan nodded and tried not to yell. He knew it was coming, but it still hurt like hell to hear her say it. He took a breath and cleared his throat. "So, you're done with us."

Bella hesitated a minute, then shook her head. "No. I'm not ready to end things with you yet. But I understand if you're not willing to continue seeing me. Your family hates my father, and they don't want me around. It's not a good situation for our families. I get that. And I don't blame you a bit if you're done."

Ryan leaned forward and rested his forearms on his thighs. The relief coursing through him was overwhelming. He wanted to just reach over and pull her into his arms, but he needed to know one more thing.

"What do you want?"

Her sharp intake drew his attention. He turned his head to look at her, his chest aching at the fear in her eyes. He didn't like being vulnerable either, and he was asking her to bare herself.

"I want you, Bella. I want to be with you. My family isn't happy because they were surprised, but I know they'll give you a chance, but I don't want to be forcing you into something. If you're done, or you're not sure, you can walk away right now and I won't bother you, but I want you to stay. I want to get to know you better. I want to find out where this is going."

She sat still for a long moment. Long enough that Ryan held his breath and felt all hope slip away.

She shifted beside him, and Ryan turned just in time to catch Bella as she leapt at him. Her knees slid around his hips and she pressed her body to his, bringing her lips down to his. She forced her way into his mouth, and he welcomed her in.

Ryan groaned and slid his hands down her back to cup her ass. He pulled her closer and licked along her tongue, drawing a matching groan from her.

"Ryan," she breathed.

"Yeah?"

"Can we go to your house?"

"Hell yes."

17

Bella wanted to run the other direction the entire time they raced to Ryan's house. She wanted to ask him if Leo was home, then go back to Albert's if he said yes.

But more than that, she wanted to be with Ryan. After talking to Julia, she knew she wasn't ready to let go of either Ryan or Albert. And after two days of trying to figure out where Albert hid the files he emptied out of Bella's room, she knew she had to simply move on. She might never know if Albert really did steal from Ryan's dad, but there was enough doubt in her mind that Albert was hiding something from her. Something that had to do with Ryan's family.

Ryan let them into his house and tiptoed to his room. No one was up, but if he was being quiet, Leo and Sara were in the house.

Once they made it to his room, he closed the door and slid the lock into place, then pressed her against the door. They didn't bother to remove coats on their way in, so there was more of a barrier than Bella wanted between them, but it would be gone eventually.

Reading her mind, Ryan eased the first button on her coat open. His cold hand slid around her neck, cooling her overheated skin. She'd spent the last two nights replaying every time they were together, but even the best fantasies didn't come close to the real thing.

"God, I fucking missed you," he breathed against her ear. His tongue slid over the shell, then dipped inside, making her moan for reasons she was too far gone to think about.

"Me, too," Bella breathed. Exposing herself to Ryan was terrifying, but him saying the words she was thinking gave her courage to bare more than just her body to him. "This...us...I'm really happy you still wanted me."

Ryan pulled back and caught her gaze. He brushed his thumb over her cheek and nodded. "Me, too."

He leaned back in and kissed her gently, so slowly and sweetly that her heart throbbed.

When her mom died, Bella never thought she'd love someone again. She thought she was all alone in the world. Then she found Albert and Ryan. She was still working on Albert, but Ryan...her mom brought her to Ryan. She knew Bella needed someone in her life, and Ryan was the best person possible.

Ryan eased Bella's jacket from her shoulders and let it fall to the floor. Bella lowered the zipper on his jacket and pushed it off him, replacing the fabric with her hands, following the same path over his chest and down his arms until they circled her hips again.

He guided them to his bed and pulled her down on top of him. His hands burned a delicious path up and down her back, making her squirm for more of him. He pushed her shirt up with his large hands buried beneath the fabric and unhooked her bra. He slid his hands around and tugged her breasts from the cups, sliding his thumbs over her sensitive nipples.

"Ryan," she breathed.

He pushed her shirt up farther and captured one nipple with his teeth. She arched back, pressing herself against his face. He groaned and sucked more of her into his mouth, pressing her nipple to the roof of his mouth.

Bella grabbed her shirt and bra and pulled both off, leaving herself topless on his lap. He growled and pressed up into her, making her gasp. Bella ground herself on him, needing relief from the desire he stirred inside her.

Ryan switched to the other side and tried to swallow her other breast. Bella couldn't get enough of his form of torture. She rocked her hips and let her head fall back, enjoying Ryan. Just Ryan.

He released her breast with a pop and stripped his shirt off. Bella's greedy hands toured his chest, unable to get enough of the feel of him. His muscles jumped as her nails grazed over them. His skin pulled tight. His chest rose and fell with his rapid breaths.

Bella took her time, memorizing every inch of him. It didn't matter how many times she was with him, it felt new every one of them. As if each time she saw him, she learned something new.

"You feel so good," he breathed, his words barely loud enough for her to hear. "Don't leave me again."

"I won't," she said automatically.

He wrapped a hand in her hair and pulled her down to him, pressed him tongue into her mouth with no finesse. She slicked her tongue over his and drew it into her mouth, needing to taste him. She wanted to taste all of him.

Bella pulled back from their kiss and slid her tongue down his throat. She slid off his lap and kissed his chest, licking first one nipple, then the other. His hands pulled her hair back from her face to watch. She continued her path down until she met the waistband of his jeans.

Bella looked up at Ryan and pressed him back just far enough so she could unbutton and unzip his jeans. She reached in and wrapped her hands around him, and his eyes slid closed. Her mouth watered with the promise of tasting him. She eased her hand up and down, testing his size. She loved the feel of his heavy, hot cock in her hand. She loved it inside her. And she was excited to have her lips wrapped around him.

He lifted his hips and helped her shove his jeans and briefs down to his ankles. He kicked them away while she stared at him. She'd felt him inside her, but she'd never been eye to eye with him, and he was beautiful.

Men weren't supposed to be beautiful, and cocks definitely weren't, but his was. It was thick and heavy in her hand. The plump head leaked a drop every few seconds. She leaned forward and captured one, sliding her tongue over him.

Ryan groaned and his hands speared into her hair. His hips lifted and he thrust into her mouth, surprising her. Bella tried to pull back, and Ryan dropped his hands.

"Fuck, Bell. I'm sorry, honey. Are you okay?"

She nodded and took him into her mouth again. She felt the tension running through him as she eased her mouth over him, sliding up and down his cock. Bella slid her hands up his chest, dragging her nails down his chest. He groaned and his hands touched her hair, then pulled back immediately.

Bella grabbed his hands and placed them on her head. He pulled back again, but she grabbed his hands once more.

"I'll hurt you, Bell. I don't want to hurt you, Bell."

She pulled back and met his gaze. "You won't hurt me, Ryan. I want to feel how much I make you lose control. Touch me. Guide me."

She didn't wait for his response before she drew him back into her mouth, sucking him in deep then letting him slide almost all the way out before she sucked him back in again.

He groaned and thrust up into her mouth capturing her hair at the same time.

Bella relaxed every cell in her body and let him lead her. He pumped into her mouth, his fingers tightening in her hair with each stroke. Bella closed her eyes and breathed deep, drawing his scent into her. Musky and male and delicious. She wanted more.

She hummed her pleasure, and Ryan groaned. "Jesus, Bell. You feel so fucking good. I can't wait to sink into you. To taste you and stretch you out. To fill you up and make you mine."

She hummed her approval of his words, then squeaked when he yanked her off his cock. The next second, her mouth was full with his tongue, plunging in just as insisting as his cock was.

He fell back on the bed, pulling her over him. Her knees fell to either side of his waist, and he ground into her, making her crazy all over again.

"I need you, Bella. I need you now, baby."

"Yes, Ryan," she moaned.

She stood and pulled her pants and panties off while he rolled a condom on. He reached for her the same moment she started to return to him. They came together lips first, then the rest of their bodies met as she fell on top of him. She immediately pushed off, not wanting to crush him with her ample curves, but he slid his hands over her body with reverence and held her in place while they kissed.

She spread her thighs and straddled him. He lined himself up at her entrance and teased her, sliding in and out just enough for her to feel him. She moaned softly and leaned back to make him go in deeper. He gasped and thrust harder, sinking in.

Bella lifted up and sank down, meeting his strokes. His hands slid up her body and down, landing on her hips and guiding her rhythm. Slow, deep strokes made her blood boil, then fast, hard strokes threatened to send her over the edge.

"Ryan," she breathed, barely holding on.

"Let go, Bell. Let me feel you."

Every fibre of her being ached to let go, but exhaustion was winning. She couldn't keep up the pace much longer, and the need to keep going quickly outpaced the need to come.

Ryan grabbed her hips and rolled them, dropping her to her back and taking over. He thrust in hard, hitting her in just the right spot.

"Oh, God, Ryan," she moaned softly. "Yes."

He did it again and again, then hooked her leg over his hip and slid deeper, sending her over the edge and into bliss.

She moaned quietly and let herself feel everything. Her pulse raced and her blood roared. She wanted to cry out, but she tamped down the urge and pulled Ryan to her for a kiss, pouring all the emotion she felt into it.

Ryan pumped hard four more times, then stilled deep inside her and grunted through his release. He swelled and filled her, and Bella wrapped her leg around his hip, holding him close.

Ryan fell onto her, and rolled to the side, pulling her with him. He breathed heavily, his heart pounding hard enough for Bella to feel it. She held him, not wanting to let go, and sighed happily when he pulled her closer.

After a minute, he slid free and went to get rid of the condom, then climbed right back into bed and wrapped both arms tight around her like he wasn't willing to let her go any more than she was willing to let him go.

RYAN BREATHED in the scent of Bella's hair and thanked God she hadn't run off without telling him. When she disappeared, a part of him thought he'd never see her again. Having her in his bed felt like a fantasy after wondering where she was the last few days.

Bella sighed and snuggled closer to him. Ryan tightened his grip, afraid that if he let her go for a minute, she'd vanish. He understood why she ran when faced with his family, but he hoped she wouldn't do it again.

Her breathing evened out as Ryan laid there, and eventually, her entire body relaxed. Ryan drew in a deep breath, loving the fact that she was willing to let go with him. He kissed her bare shoulder, and tried not to whisper the words that threatened to escape.

It wasn't that he thought they'd send her running, even though he was sure they would. It was his fear that they weren't real. He'd grown up with an amazing example of love. He wondered as his brother and cousins found love if he ever would, but he never doubted that love was real.

Having Bella in his arms, her soft breath a whisper in his otherwise silent room, made him wonder if he really was in love with her or if he just wanted to be in love. Seeing everyone else so happy made a part of him ache for that same joy. But another part of him enjoyed his freedom. His life wasn't always predictable, and he told himself it was best that he didn't have anyone to answer to.

He wasn't sure if that was still true. If it was, then he'd have to admit that he might never find love. If it wasn't, was Bella going to get sick of coming in second place to the careers he loved?

His mind raced with unknowns until Bella stirred and rolled toward him. She was still asleep, but when she turned, she reached for him. He pulled her close again, and she settled against him, her head on his chest.

His heart thumped. Everything felt right with Bella there. Together, they would get through anything. And if that wasn't love, Ryan sure as hell didn't know what was.

He faded before much longer, and was surprised when Bella was still there in the morning, her head still on his chest, her arm across his stomach.

Ryan didn't want to wake her up, and he wasn't ready to move, so he closed his eyes again and went back to sleep.

He woke again when Bella trailed her fingers down his stomach and wrapped them around his cock. He sucked in a breath and released a groan, and she disappeared under the sheet. He didn't last long in his half-asleep morning haze, and she swallowed him before she slid up his body and kissed him. Then she settled next to him and went back to sleep without a word.

When they woke up for good, Bella was smiling and beautiful, her hair a mess from his hands and her body glowing from their night together.

"Good morning," she said.

"Morning. Have you been up long?"

She shook her head. "No. You look peaceful when you sleep."

"Does that mean I look stressed when I'm awake?"

Bella's smile slipped, and she shook her head again. "I'm sorry I'm causing stress for you."

He pulled her closer and kissed her gently. "You're not. I knew who you were as soon as you found out why it could be a concern. You never hid it from me. If my family can't handle it, that's on them."

"But you still don't like Albert."

Ryan sucked in a sharp breath. "I don't know him well enough to say that, but if he did steal from us, then no."

"If he did? I thought you said he did?"

Ryan nodded. "I believe he did. My dad believed he did. But we never found any proof. I'm not saying that means he didn't do it because he could have destroyed what he took, but we have no proof. The manual my dad said was taken has never shown up, and he tore the vineyard apart multiple times looking."

"Was that the only copy?"

Ryan shook his head. "No, but they were specifically for employees. They were controlled. And every copy that was available was kept in one building."

"So, is it possible someone else could have taken it?"

"Of course, and my dad wondered that until he died. But the other employees either kept working for us, or if they left, they didn't start their own vineyard."

Bella was silent for a long moment. She rested her head on Ryan's chest, her fingertips making small movements on his stomach. He wasn't sure why she was asking so many questions, but he decided he would tell her anything she wanted to know. Anything he knew. Even down to when he had his own doubts.

He hated wondering if his father was wrong. He knew his father believed with everything in him that Perry was the one who took the manual. Ryan had a hard time thinking his father was wrong, but he wondered if maybe he made a mistake opening up the old wound.

"Ryan, I need to tell you something," Bella said, sounding scared.

Ryan tilted her chin up toward him and tried to reassure her silently. She chewed on her lip and worry swam in her eyes. "Are you okay?"

She nodded. "I think your father may have been right."

Ryan sat up, dislodging Bella from his chest. "What do you mean?"

Bella sat and pulled the sheet up to cover her bare chest. "My mom always told me Albert was the kind of man who would do anything it took to get ahead. Anything to help himself. He was singularly focused on his own success. A part of me understands that, but I don't think she meant it in a good way. I think she meant he wasn't afraid to cheat to get ahead. I think he might have done that with your family."

"Why do you say that?" Ryan asked.

"The room I've been staying in? The one with all the boxes?"

Ryan nodded.

"After we were here the other day and he found out about us, he cleaned out the room."

"What do you mean, he cleaned out the room?"

"I went for a drive. I didn't go back there for hours. When I got back, it was late. When I went to bed, all the boxes were gone."

"Where did they go?" Ryan asked, his heart pounding.

Bella shrugged. "I don't know. But the only reason I can

think of that he would have moved the stuff out is because there's something in there that he was afraid of you seeing."

"Like the manual he took from my father."

Bella looked like she was going to be sick when she nodded. "That's what I was thinking, too."

18

____

BELLA KNEW TELLING RYAN WAS THE RIGHT THING TO DO, BUT that didn't make it easier to face her father when she got home later that morning. Albert was in the kitchen drinking coffee when Bella walked in. He scanned her quickly and scowled, but he didn't comment on her showing up in the same clothes she wore the day before.

"Good morning," Bella said softly.

"Morning," Albert replied.

It was stiff. Uncomfortable. Worse than when she showed up on his doorstep unannounced. She wanted to fix it, but she didn't know if it was possible. But she had to try. Albert and Ryan were both important to her. She'd smoothed things over with Ryan, but Albert was going to be much more difficult.

"What do you have going on today?" Bella asked.

"I have someone coming to bottle some of the white and I have paperwork to go through," Albert said absently.

"Oh."

"Why?"

Bella shrugged. "I was hoping we could spend some

time together. I know I hurt you getting involved with Ryan and not telling you about it, but that was never my intention. I was hoping we could talk some."

Albert drained the last of his coffee and went to the sink. He rinsed the mug then put it in the dishwasher. He leaned against the edge of the counter, his green sweater bunching at his side, and crossed his arms over his chest. He pressed his lips together and scrunched his eyebrows.

Bella waited for him to say something, giving him time to formulate whatever it was he wanted to say. She fought the urge to shuffle her feet or just leave the room. When he finally drew a breath, she braced for his words.

"Why did you tell him who I was but not tell me who he was?"

Bella rocked back on her heels and thought about it. She remembered Albert telling her about his disagreement with Ryan's family, and she could have told him right then that she was involved with Ryan, but she didn't.

"I understand that you didn't know who he was, but when I told you about his father accusing me of stealing, you could have said you were involved with him. And if you knew who he was, you never should have brought him into my home."

Bella nodded. "I know. And I'm sorry. It wasn't planned. He had a bad night. It was the night Ms. Loveland died. He was on the call, and it bothered him. He sent me a text, and I didn't think about it when he said he wanted to see me."

"You didn't think bringing the son of the man who tried to ruin me into my house was a bad idea?"

Bella shook her head. "No. I didn't. Because it doesn't matter who he is, if you have nothing to hide, then why do you care?"

Albert gasped and took a step back. As soon as the

words were out, Bella felt guilty for saying them, but she couldn't take them back.

"Did you steal from them? Did you do what they said?"

Albert shook his head. "I can't believe you're asking me this. You're the one who came here. You showed up on my doorstep. You're the one who wanted a relationship. I never knew you existed, and you come into my home and try to blow up my life. Are you even who you say you are? Are you actually my daughter?"

Bella sucked in a sharp breath, tears welling in her eyes. His words hurt, but she couldn't say she didn't deserve them. "I am your daughter. At least, I'm Melanie Chase's daughter, and she told me you were my father. I didn't know anything about you or the Richliano's until I came here. I'm sorry I'm causing trouble for you. I can leave if you'd like me to."

Albert stared at her for a long moment while Bella willed her tears to stay in her eyes. When he sighed and shook his head, she released the breath she didn't know she'd been holding.

"I don't want that family on my property. Please don't bring him here again."

Bella nodded. "I won't."

Albert nodded once then turned and left the room. A door down the hall closed a minute later, and Bella stood staring at the wall where he'd disappeared.

Ryan made Bella breakfast before she left his house, so she wasn't hungry. She'd hoped to spend time with Albert and figure out once and for all if he stole the manuals or not, but she was out of luck.

Maybe it was time for her to figure out what she was doing with her life.

Bella went into her room and closed the door quietly. She opened her computer and froze. She didn't know what to look for. Did she search for jobs in the Bereton area? Did she plan to go back to Binghamton? Did she find somewhere else entirely? What did she want to do with her life?

The biggest question was where did she want to be. She considered going home and asking Julia for her old job back, but it felt like a step backward. Julia fired her because her mom thought she could do more, but she had no idea what more was supposed to be.

What she did know was the idea of going back to Binghamton was not working for her. She loved it there, but being there without her mom, and being there without Ryan, held no appeal. The thought of leaving Bereton made her chest hurt. She wasn't ready to leave Ryan or Albert behind.

She typed in a search for jobs in Bereton or the surrounding areas. Not much popped up that matched her skills, but Bella knew she could do just about anything if she had a little training. Julia would give her a good recommendation. Bella just needed to decide what that would be.

She chewed her nail and was still scrolling when she heard the front door close. She picked her head up and listened. The house was quiet, but that didn't mean Albert had left.

She opened her bedroom door and went to the living area. No one was there. She went back down the hall and found his bedroom door open.

The boxes.

All the boxes from her room were stacked in his. She thought about searching them, but it felt too much like a violation of his privacy. She had to give him the benefit of the doubt, didn't she?

She went back to the front of the house and saw Albert talking to someone outside. He was pointing toward one of the buildings in the back and nodding. The guy climbed back into his truck and back down the path Albert indicated. Albert walked in front of him.

Must be the bottling truck.

Which means he'll be busy for a while.

Bella shook her head. She couldn't. It wasn't right.

But she didn't want to be associated with him if he was the kind of person who would steal from someone else.

Bella checked outside again and saw Albert disappear behind the vines, still following the truck. She chewed on her lip then shook her head and went down the hall into Albert's room.

There were twelve boxes total. Three stacks of four. She probably couldn't get through all of them in the time she had, so she needed to be smart.

She took the lids off all the boxes on the top, assuming if he was hiding something, it wasn't going to be in the top boxes where someone could easily find it. All she found were files that looked like old tax returns. Very old if the first page was correct.

She put the lids back on the boxes and moved to the first stack. Those boxes didn't hold anything overly interesting. The second stack was the same. Nothing in any of them to say he was guilty. She was about to move to the third stack of boxes when she heard the truck. She peeked out the window and saw it slowly driving toward her.

Albert was done with the bottling, and she had no way of knowing when he'd be back. She stacked the boxes quickly and took a picture of them. They all looked the same from the outside, but a few of them had corners pulled or marks on the edges. Nothing anyone would notice unless they were looking for the marks.

Bella was fairly sure she had the boxes back exactly how

they were when she found them. She took one last look then darted back to her room and closed the door again.

Less than five minutes later, Albert was inside again. He walked down the hall, then back outside. She was about to go out when she heard him come in again. In and out, back and forth. Bella listened from the other side of her door until she figured out what he was doing.

He was moving the boxes out of the house. Shit.

RYAN OPENED his door at lunch to his brother carrying a bag of food. Only because the food smelled good did Ryan step back and let Henry inside. Henry knew what he was doing. Smart man.

They unpacked the bag silently, setting food on the counter and working around each other to get beer, because water was not going to do for the conversation they were about to have. Hell, if Ryan had something harder than beer, they probably would have grabbed that.

Ryan carried his lunch and beer to the table and sat down with his back to the wall. Henry sat opposite him and tucked in, still not speaking.

Ryan took his first bite and closed his eyes. A part of him wanted to ask if Zach put a laxative in the food, but he didn't think his cousin would be so cruel. Not Zach. Andie maybe. Kristen definitely. But Zach? Ryan was fairly sure the food was safe.

"How long did you know?" Henry finally asked when they were halfway through lunch.

"Long enough," Ryan answered.

"Long enough. Is that long enough that you should have told us or long enough that you didn't care or long enough that it didn't matter? What the hell does long enough mean?"

"It means I care about her. It means she was torn up when she realized the connection between him and us."

"Had you already slept with her at that point?"

Ryan shook his head. He didn't want to offer up the finer points of his relationship to his brother, but he figured blindsiding him and the rest of the family with the truth about who Bella was meant he owed them a little of his discomfort.

"When?"

"That night."

"Fuck me, Ryan. Why her?"

Ryan opened his mouth to answer, but he closed it again. He didn't sleep with Bella because of who her father was, or who his was. He didn't sleep with her because of any reason that had anything to do with either of their families. He slept with her because he was attracted to her. Because on the night he met her, he wanted to talk to her more. Because she was different.

"It had nothing to do with Perry."

"It has everything to do with Perry, Ryan. She's his fucking daughter. She could be here to spy for him. She could be—"

"Don't. Don't say another damn word about her. I care about her. I will not sit here and have you tell me she's using me for her father. You don't know anything about her."

Henry leaned back with a huff. "You're right. I don't know anything about her. Because you didn't tell me. You knew how I would feel about this, about her. You knew how everyone would feel. She shouldn't be on our property. You and I both have caught Perry here. He's not supposed to step foot on our land, and he shows up and gets all cocky about it because Aunt Marie said something at Ms. Loveland's funeral. This is classic Perry. He's not innocent, and neither is she."

"So, what? I just have to end things with her because my big brother thinks she might be suspicious? Get the hell over yourself, Henry."

Henry pushed his plate away and grabbed his beer. He drained the rest of it and set it on the table with a hard clang. He glared at Ryan, and Ryan glared right back.

"I have no reason not to trust her. As soon as she knew about the connection between our families, she told me. She isn't keeping things from me. She's honest and kind and she cares."

"Shit. You're in love with her, aren't you?"

Ryan held his brother's gaze for a long moment, neither confirming nor denying the accusation. It should have been a happy moment. A moment to celebrate that Ryan finally found someone he wanted to spend more time with, maybe even the rest of his life. Instead, Henry was acting like Ryan was choosing to face off with a firing squad and thinking he would win.

"Jesus, Ryan. Why?"

"Can you tell me why you love Cynthia?"

"Hell, yeah. Because she's my best friend. She's kind and beautiful and she's the only person who's ever allowed me to be my entire true self. I know I don't have to watch what I say or do around her because she loves me for who I am, and I love her for who she is. We're a match. Can you honestly say the same about Perry's daughter?"

"Bella," Ryan said.

Henry rolled his eyes.

"We might not be the same place yet, but I think we

could get there. She makes me feel like I'm not alone in the world."

"Who said you're alone? You have all of us."

Ryan breathed a laugh. "Yeah, but you all have someone else. And I'm happy for you guys, but if it's between me and Cynthia, she's going to win. Same with everyone."

"So you're with Perry's daughter because you're lonely. That makes a lot more sense."

"No, dammit," Ryan barked, pushing away from the table. He carried his food to the kitchen and shoved it in the fridge, hoping he'd be hungry enough to finish eating later. "I'm not lonely, and I'm not with Bella for any reason other than I like her. I don't have to answer to you, and I don't appreciate the fact that you're making it seem like I should."

"You're the one who can't explain why you want the one woman on the planet who has a connection to our father's enemy. What do you think Dad would say? Do you think he would be happy that you're screwing Perry's kid?"

"I told you not to bring Dad into this," Ryan growled at his brother.

"Dad's already in this. Dad's in everything that has to do with Perry. Don't you remember just a few weeks ago you wanted to check out Perry again. Put a rest to the whole thing. What happened to that? You're done now that his daughter is warming your bed?"

"Fuck you, Henry."

Henry nodded slowly. "You're choosing a woman you've known a few weeks over your family. You won't listen to me, and you won't even think about what Dad would say. Have you asked Mom? What did she think about you getting involved with Perry's daughter?"

Ryan didn't answer because Henry was right. He fucking hated his brother for it, but he was right. Ryan didn't talk to his mom. He didn't want to think about his dad. He hid who Bella was from his entire family. He didn't want to have to give her up because he knew he would have to. He knew his family would react the way they did.

Henry just scoffed and shook his head. "I hope she's worth it, Ry, because if she's not, you're going to be left with a lifetime of regrets. Just promise me you won't tell her about any of our proprietary stuff. Don't share secrets with her. And don't give her access to anything. Don't even tell her what buildings are for what purpose. Not that Perry doesn't already know, but we don't need it."

Ryan didn't reply.

Henry sighed and put the cover back on his lunch. "I hope you know what you're doing," he said, then left, the door closing echoing in the house like a shot.

Ryan let his brother's parting words ring through his head. He hoped he knew what he was doing, too.

19

———

Bella looked at her phone when it rang and tilted her head. She didn't know anyone who called her. All her friends texted, not that she'd heard from them either.

She didn't recognize the number, but it was a local number, so she answered it.

"Hello?"

"Is this Bella?"

"Um, yes."

"Good. You're coming to lunch today."

"I'm sorry, who is this?" Bella asked. She knew the voice was familiar, but she couldn't place it.

"Just be at The Drunken Grape at eleven, Bella. I think you know where that is?"

"Yeah, um, yes. I...I do."

"Good. I'll see you then. And Bella?"

"Yeah?"

"Please don't bring your dad, honey."

"Oh, no, of course. I wouldn't."

"Good. See you soon, Bella."

The woman hung up the phone before Bella could say

goodbye. She stared at the black screen and wondered what in the hell just happened.

Then she realized it was already ten, and she hadn't taken a shower yet. Bella rushed into the bathroom and took a fast shower. She wrapped her hair up in a towel and another one around her body then frantically searched for clothes. She had no idea who she was meeting, but it was most likely someone related to Ryan. His mother maybe? Or his grandmother. Either one scared the shit out of her.

Bella was going for something conservative, but she had no idea what she should wear. She was going to be judged. And if she wasn't what they felt was good enough for Ryan, she would be pushed out of his life.

Bella tried on half the clothes she brought with her, wishing she'd taken the time to wash the other half. She eventually decided on a pair of dark wash jeans tucked into black booties and a black sweater that draped off one shoulder. She added a black tank underneath so it looked slightly more conservative. She debated changing again, but a glance at the time told her she needed to dry her hair and get out the door if she wanted to be on time.

She raced to her car with three minutes to go before she was due at the restaurant and rushed across the street.

Andie was at the front desk again when Bella walked in. The reception she gave Bella was much less friendly than the last time she was there. Andie still smiled, but it was clipped, just like her words.

"Hello again."

"Hi. Um, I know I'm not really welcome here, but I got a phone call from someone asking me to be here at eleven. Do you know who it might have been?"

Andie flinched but recovered quickly. Her smile faltered then she fixed it and scanned the reservation book.

She was still flipping through when soft footsteps sounded behind Bella. She ignored it knowing she wouldn't know who was there but was surprised when she heard her name.

"You are Bella, right?"

Bella smiled at the woman. She was familiar, but Bella was sure they hadn't met before. She guessed her age made her Ryan's grandmother. From her gray hair to her long dress and thick tights, she was clearly from a different generation, but her eyes told Bella that the woman had a hell of a sense of humor.

"Yes, I am," Bella said.

"Good. You're right on time. I like someone who respects the time of others. Let's get some lunch, honey. I'd like to get to know you," the woman said. She reached out and took Bella's arm, letting Bella walk by her side with her head held high through the lion's den.

Bella could feel the stares and glares of Ryan's family as she walked. She could tell their grandmother was well respected and loved by the rest of them, and if Bella managed to pass whatever test she had for her, she would be good to go.

Bella followed the woman to a seat in the corner where they could see the lake. Bella held out the woman's chair and waited until she was settled to follow suit.

"Ah, much better. Thank you, honey," the woman said.

"You're welcome." Bella smiled at her and picked up her menu. "Can I ask you a question?"

"Well, sure, honey. Of course."

"Um, sorry, but um, who are you?"

The woman chuckled and shook her head. "I'm sorry, Bella. I forget that you haven't been here forever. Everyone in Bereton and half the lake knows me by now. It's unusual for someone to not know who I am."

Bella just smiled, still wondering who the woman was.

"I'm Ryan's grandmother. Tina, but everyone calls me Nonna. Well, the kids do. Nonna means grandmother in Italian. You can call me Nonna or Tina, whatever you're comfortable with."

"Thank you, Tina."

Tina smiled and patted Bella's hand then turned and smiled at the person approaching. Bella wanted to groan. It was Amy, the same server she had when she ate lunch with Ryan weeks ago.

Amy smiled broadly at Tina, but her smile faltered when she looked at Bella. "Oh, um, hi. I didn't realize you were still around."

Bella gave her a tight-lipped grin and studied her menu.

"Amy, dear, can you bring us a bottle, please? And my regular order. Do you know what you would like to eat, Bella?" Tina asked kindly.

Bella looked up and said, "I'll try the drunken penne." It was the first thing she saw and she barely read the description, but it sounded delicious.

"That's my new favorite, too," Tina said conspiratorially. "It's delicious." She turned back to Amy and said, "Bring us some bread, too. And house salads. And we might do dessert when we're done."

Amy scribbled everything on her pad, nodding as Tina spoke. "Anything else?"

Tina shook her head. "You'll bring more water with the wine, right?"

"Of course."

"Good. Thank you, dear. Now, let me get to know Ryan's new girlfriend."

Amy pressed her lips into a thin line and glared at Bella. Bella wanted to sooth the other woman's ruffled feathers, but she had no response.

Amy finally left, and Tina said, "Well, that shut her up for a minute."

"Excuse me?"

Tina rolled her eyes. "She's had her eye on Ryan since she started working here. Thought she could stake some sort of claim on him since she's an employee, but Ryan was never interested in her. She clearly isn't happy that I'm having lunch with you."

"Is she going to spit in my food?" Bella blurted.

Tina snorted. "Not if she wants to keep her job."

Bella held the other woman's gaze for a long moment. Tina was one of those people who laughed and enjoyed life but who didn't forgive easily if you made her mad. Bella could definitely respect that.

"So, tell me about yourself, Bella. All I know is all my grandchildren are having a fit that you're Albert's daughter. I know there's more to you than that."

Bella nodded. "I hope so. I didn't know about Albert until recently. My mom told me my birth father was dead."

"Why would she do that?"

Bella shrugged. "I wish I knew. My mom died last summer."

"Oh, I'm so sorry, honey. You're an only child, aren't you?"

Bella nodded.

"That's even harder. No wonder you came looking for Albert. You wanted a connection, someone to help you feel less alone in the world."

Bella's eyes swam with tears as she nodded. It felt good

to hear someone else say what she'd been thinking for months. It was validation she didn't realize she needed.

Amy returned with their bottle of wine and two glasses. She opened the bottle and poured for them, then left again without a word.

Tina picked up her glass and nodded to Bella to do the same. Bella lifted hers and tried to smile.

"To mothers, and fathers, and knowing you are always loved."

Bella couldn't reply, but she nodded.

Tina said, "Beviamo," and clinked her glass to Bella's, then took a healthy sip. "So good."

Bella followed suit, agreeing wholeheartedly that the wine was delicious.

"Did Albert know about you before you showed up?" Tina asked.

Bella shook her head. "He said he didn't. I believe him."

Tina smiled. "There's no reason for you to doubt your father."

Bella wanted to ask if she meant regarding knowing about her or in general, but she didn't have the guts.

"Has he been good to you since you've arrived?"

Bella nodded. "It's weird at times, but I think it would be under any circumstance. He welcomed me in without a second guess. He's been nothing but kind to me. Except when he found out about Ryan."

"I'm sorry, Bella. All that is stuff you kids shouldn't be worrying about. Obviously, Ryan has filled you in."

Bella nodded. "Albert mentioned it first. I didn't know, Tina. I wasn't here to spy. And I didn't know anything. I swear to you, I didn't."

Tina smiled kindly, but Amy brought their food before

she could reply. Once Amy had plates in front of them and made sure they didn't need anything, she left again.

"I believe you, honey," Tina said when they were alone. "I can see in your eyes that you're upset by all the accusations made against you. It's not fair to you or Ryan that the argument between your fathers is creating a problem for you. That's why I wanted to meet you. The truth is always in a person's eyes. You can hide behind your words and even your actions, but the truth comes out in a person's eyes."

Bella nodded, once again feeling like she wasn't alone. "Thank you."

Tina patted Bella's hand and smiled. "Thank you for being good for my grandson. Ryan is a good man, and he deserves the kind of love his parents shared. My Josephine loved her husband the way I loved my Carmelo. Losing the one you love is the hardest thing a person will ever go through. Ryan was just starting to consider settling down when his father died. He saw the pain in his mother and shut down all thoughts. Not that he'd ever admit it, but it was in his eyes. The way his gaze lingered on his cousins that had found their forever. That look is back since he met you."

Bella couldn't stop her smile. She ducked her head to avoid letting Tina see how happy her words made Bella, but Tina saw anyway.

"I'm happy to see you smiling like that. You care about my grandson."

Bella nodded. "I do."

"Good. Because love truly can conquer all. Even frustrating families. If anyone knows that, it's me."

Bella tilted her head in question.

"My family did not approve of my husband. That's why

we ran away together. I haven't ever told them the entire story, but I think you need to hear it."

Bella nodded and leaned in as Tina started talking about when she met Ryan's grandfather, Carmelo.

~

72 years ago

"I WANT TO MEET YOUR FAMILY," Carmelo said softly.

They were laying together, their bodies still warm from making love for the first time. Tina never knew she could feel the way she felt with Carmelo, but she didn't want to ever let go of it. She wanted to sink into the bliss he brought, but he clearly had different ideas.

"Why?"

"Because that's what a man does when he plans to ask a woman to marry him."

Her eyes filled, and she blinked back the tears. "You were serious about marrying me?"

"Well, if you insist," Carmelo said with a smirk.

Tina slapped him gently. He grabbed her hand and brought it to his lips, kissing each finger them her palm.

"I love you, Tina. I meant it when I said that. And I know I'm not enough for your family, but I want to be. Maybe your father will hire me and let me work for him until he decides I'm worthy of you."

The idea sounded reasonable. Carmelo could work for her father, get to know him, learn his business, then take over when her father was ready to stop working.

Tina had been trying to find a way for them to be together, but she didn't come up with one. Carmelo did, proving once again how perfect he was.

"That's a great idea. My father likes a man who's willing to work. And he's good friends with Mr. Costello. I'm sure they can work something out."

Carmelo nodded and brushed the hair back from her face. "Can I ask you something?"

Tina nodded, smiling up at him. They both worked to get dressed again. It was late, and Tina couldn't get caught out so late, especially with Carmelo.

"Were you supposed to marry Antonio?"

"I already told you no. Why would you ask me that again?"

Carmelo shrugged. There was a reason he asked, and Tina wanted to know what it was.

"What did you hear?"

He sighed and faced her. His pants were low on his hips, unbuttoned, and his chest was still bare, showing off all his muscles. His olive skin glowed in the faint moonlight coming through the windows. She wanted to touch him again. Tina had never felt the way she did with him, but she knew it was so much more than how attractive Carmelo was. He was an amazing man, and he loved her. She never thought she'd be so lucky.

"One of my coworkers said to stay away from you because you were promised to Antonio."

Tina smiled wryly. "And I can see you listened."

A bark of laughter burst from him. His blue eyes sparkled with mischief. He moved closer to her and wrapped his big arms around her waist, pulling her tight to his body once more. "I couldn't resist you. Consequences be damned."

Tina brushed both her hands through his hair and smiled. She'd never been so happy in her life. A future with

Carmelo danced before her. A family. Love. Joy. She could see it all.

"I love you, Carmelo."

He nodded. "I love you, Tina. Now and forever."

"Now and forever."

CARMELO KNEW he was taking a risk sneaking around with Tina, but he couldn't resist her. Meeting her family and asking her father's permission to marry her would legitimize anything they did or had done.

The night came for him to go to her home. He dressed in his nicest clothes even though they were still not enough. Nothing about him was, except, he hoped, his love for Tina.

Carmelo carried a bouquet of flowers for her mother, a smaller bouquet for Tina, and a bottle of wine to contribute to dinner. His stomach was in knots and he thought he might vomit, but he was going to choke it all down and make the best impression he could on Tina's family.

He drew in a breath and knocked on the front door. When no one answered right away, he knocked again. The door flung open, revealing a very unhappy looking man.

"Hello, sir," Carmelo stammered. "I'm...er, I'm Carmelo Richliano. It's nice to meet you."

Tina's father grunted and stepped back. Carmelo nodded at him and walked inside. Once Tina's father closed the door, Carmelo handed over the wine.

"I brought this for you, sir. It's one of the best wines I make."

"You make?" Mr. Vincenzo said, his voice a low growl of disapproval.

"Yes, sir. I work at Costello Vineyard."

"I know where you work, but you're not the vintner. You're not the master behind the wine. You just work in the field."

"I also work in the barrel room, sir," Carmelo said, defending his position. Outside the people he worked with, few people knew the extent of what he did at the vineyard. He loved his job, but he didn't get enough recognition for his work.

Mr. Vincenzo narrowed his eyes at Carmelo. Just when Carmelo was debating running the other direction, a woman joined them.

"You must be Carmelo. Please, ignore my husband and come in. I'm Tina's mother, Maribel."

"Nice to meet you, Mrs. Vincenzo. These are for you," Carmelo said, handing over the flowers.

"Oh, they're beautiful. Peter, why don't you help me put them in water?"

Mr. Vincenzo scowled but followed behind Mrs. Vincenzo. And then there was Tina. In the doorway where Carmelo didn't see her before. She was stunning in a bright blue dress. Her dark hair was pulled back into a long, thick braid that curved over her shoulder. She wore short heels that brought her closer to kissing range.

Carmelo would do anything to be able to pull her close and kiss her until he felt better, but he wouldn't dare disrespect her father in his own home.

"Tina, you look lovely."

The faint blush on her cheeks said his compliment conveyed everything he couldn't say.

"Thank you, Carmelo. You clean up well."

He smiled at her and finally felt better. He could do this. Because it was all for her. Tina was the goal, the dream. She was the reason he existed, and he'd walk through hell for her. Apparently hell was her parents' home.

"Are those for me?" she asked, taking a few steps closer to him.

He nodded and handed them over. "Although they don't do your beauty justice."

Her cheeks pinked again, and Carmelo grinned. *Focus on Tina. It'll all be okay if you focus on Tina.*

"We should probably go in," Tina said quietly. "Otherwise they'll send spies."

Carmelo grinned and gestured for Tina to go ahead of him. She smiled and went the same way her parents did moments before.

The hallway opened into a large kitchen at the back of the house. The kitchen overlooked the large grove of olive trees. Carmelo knew all about her family, but being in their home and seeing the extent of their wealth, by comparison to his lack of wealth, made him feel insignificant and small.

Then he looked at Tina again. Tina. It was all about Tina.

Carmelo drew in a breath and told himself she loved him. She wanted him. She was it for him. Which meant he had to do whatever it took to be worthy of her, not just in her eyes, but in the eyes of her family.

20

Tina was beside herself. She had Carmelo on one side and her mother on the other side of her. Her father sat at the head of the table, like always, and her siblings sat opposite her. It was perfect.

"Tina," her father said, "please say grace."

"Of course," Tina said with a grin. She reached for Carmelo's hand and smiled when he turned his over to press their palms together and threaded his fingers through hers. Then she reached for her mother and smiled at her, too.

Her father cleared his throat and Tina bowed her head.

"Dear God. Thank you for the feast before us and the hands that prepared it. Thank you for the family we are surrounded by and for the gift of Carmelo at our table today. Hopefully it's the first of many meals we have together. And thank you for the gift of your sacrifice and for your unending love."

"Amen," everyone said in unison.

Tina looked at Carmelo when he squeezed her hand. He winked at her, and she smiled back.

Her father cleared his throat again, and Carmelo released Tina's hand. He straightened his tie and picked up his fork.

"So, Carmelo. Tina said she met you in town a few months back," her father said.

Carmelo nodded. "Yes, sir. She was running through town one day, and I happened to be in the fortunate position of being in her way."

"You think it's fortunate to run into a woman in the street?" Peter asked.

Carmelo shook his head. "No, sir. I didn't mean it like that. I just meant I was fortunate to be the one to help her. She was upset, and I was lucky enough to make her smile."

"Upset? What were you upset about?" her mother asked.

Tina drew in a breath. She knew it would come up, but she didn't have a chance to warn Carmelo not to mention that part about when they met. Not that her parents didn't know exactly why she was upset, but she wasn't in the mood to rehash it.

"It was on my birthday," Tina said quietly.

Her mother fell silent, her eyes dipping to the table to avoid glancing at her father. Tina followed suit, finding her plate captivating.

"I didn't realize it was your birthday when we met. You were crying on your birthday? Birthdays are supposed to be good days," Carmelo said.

Tina offered him a smile that she hoped conveyed a shut up look. Carmelo narrowed his eyes like he was trying to figure her out, but her father came to her rescue. Sort of.

"Did Tina tell you she's getting married?" Peter asked.

Carmelo's head swung toward her father and cocked. "Um, yes, we've talked about it."

"And you still feel it's appropriate for you to show up here?"

"Well, I thought we should meet. We've only spoken about it once. I was raised to treat a woman's family with respect, just like the woman herself."

"So since she's only mentioned getting married once, you thought it was okay for you to show up here and touch her and hold her hand and look at her the way you have been," Peter said.

"I, uh, um, uh..." Carmelo stammered.

"He deserves your respect the same as her mother and I do. I for one do not feel it's respectful of you to be here acting as if you're courting my daughter. Especially when she's marrying your boss's son."

Carmelo's head swung to Tina, and she gasped.

"What are you talking about?" Tina asked softly.

"Antonio is going to be your husband. I told you I would be selecting your husband. You didn't choose when you were given the option, so now it's my choice, and I've chosen my friend's son," her father said firmly.

"No, I don't want to marry him. I want to marry Carmelo," Tina declared.

Her father stilled and the entire room followed suit. His head swung from the food on his fork to Tina then over to Carmelo. "Do you dare entertain ideas about my daughter?"

"I, um, we've been getting to know each other," Carmelo said.

"You've been spending time with her behind my back. Behind Antonio's back. You're seducing her when you're not worthy of her."

"Papa! Don't say that. Carmelo is a good man. He works hard. He was hoping you would give him a job here and let him work for you until you decided you were willing to let us get married," Tina pleaded.

"What?" Peter bellowed, pushing to stand. "He comes in here, spending time with my daughter, and then expects me to give him a job and the hand of said daughter. All because he's what? Not good enough as he is?"

"Papa!"

"Go to your room, Tina," Peter declared.

His voice was low and deadly, the voice that told her not to argue or she'd live to regret it. Tina immediately closed her mouth and swung her gaze to her mother for help. As usual, her mother wouldn't meet her eyes, choosing her husband over her daughter.

Tina reached for Carmelo, but her father barked, "Now, Tina," and she knew it would be worse for Carmelo if she touched him.

She held his gaze as long as she dared, memorizing the look of his crystal blue eyes, the way they stared back at her with more love than she felt from every other person in the room. She tried to tell him with her eyes that they would find a way to be together, but she didn't know if he heard her silent vow.

Her father moved, pushing his chair back with a loud screech that had Tina rushing from the room.

Seconds behind her were her siblings, then her mother, which meant Tina had no one who could tell her what was said once she was in her room and completely out of earshot.

CARMELO HELD his ground against Tina's father, but he was terrified. The man clearly ruled his home with an iron fist, one he wasn't afraid to swing. He was fairly certain Mrs. Vincenzo wouldn't stand up to her husband for anything, and Tina shouldn't have to.

Carmelo was raised to respect all people, regardless of who they were. His upbringing had never been tested as much as it was in that room, alone with Mr. Vincenzo, knowing if Carmelo didn't say the right things, there was a good chance Mr. Vincenzo would make Tina pay for their time together.

"My daughter is not yours to touch," Mr. Vincenzo growled.

"Yes, sir," Carmelo said.

"She's marrying Antonio."

"If I may, sir?"

"No, you may not. We do not need to have this conversation, or any. I allowed you to come here tonight because Tina said she was inviting a friend over. She did not let us believe her friend was a man, let alone a man who thought he had a claim to my child. She's my child, and she will marry who I say she will marry. That will never be you."

"Is she no longer given the opportunity to choose?"

Mr. Vincenzo shot Carmelo a murderous look. "No, she is not."

"If we'd met before her birthday, would you have allowed her to pick me?"

Mr. Vincenzo narrowed his eyes. Carmelo made him nervous. He didn't like being challenged or questioned. But that didn't mean he was right.

"My daughter has never made a smart decision in her life. She doesn't know what's best for her. Choosing you at this point is an act of rebellion because she knows a man like you will never be acceptable. She doesn't care about you. She just wants to upset her mother."

"I love your daughter, Mr. Vincenzo."

"How old are you?"

"I'm twenty-two, sir."

"And you think you're in love with a girl who's barely eighteen?"

Carmelo nodded. "I know I am, sir."

Mr. Vincenzo chuckled. "Give it another week. You'll fall in love with another girl."

"No, sir, I won't."

Mr. Vincenzo glared at Carmelo again. "Well, you're going to have to because my daughter is marrying another man. And you'll never see her again."

"Mr. Vincen—"

"It's time for you to leave, Mr. Richliano. Don't make me tell you again."

Carmelo got to his feet and wiped his mouth on his napkin. His manners dictated he follow orders and be respectful, but he wanted nothing more than to tell Mr. Vincenzo where to stick his threats and drag Tina out of that house and run away with her. Somewhere her family and his boss couldn't get to them. "Please thank Mrs. Vincenzo for me, sir. It was nice meeting you all."

Mr. Vincenzo snorted in reply and watched Carmelo until he closed the door between them.

His chest ached at the thought of never seeing Tina again, but he would find a way. He loved her, and even if it wasn't allowed, he would find a way to see her and make sure she knew he loved her and always would.

He just hoped loving her didn't have to mean watching her marry Antonio. He wasn't sure he'd survive that fate.

$\sim$

Present Day

Ryan stumbled into the weekly business meeting feeling like he'd been run over. He worked night shift for the fire department and had been up twenty-four hours straight. They had a busy night, and all he really wanted was a shower and his bed, but he was told he had to be there.

Ryan didn't want coffee since he was going to sleep as soon as he could, but breakfast sounded heavenly. He loaded up a plate and took a seat at a table by himself. The others talked quietly to themselves, and he ignored them all.

Leo walked in a little while after Ryan and sat with him. He didn't say anything, thankfully, but Ryan felt the weight of his looks.

"What?"

"You look like hell."

"Thanks."

"Bad night?"

Ryan shook his head and shoveled another bite of eggs into his mouth. "Busy night, but not bad. Didn't lose anyone."

Leo nodded. He and Ryan had lived together long enough that Leo understood Ryan didn't care how crazy the night was or how quiet, only if everyone was safe.

"How's Bella?"

Ryan glared at his cousin and didn't answer, choosing his breakfast over his cousin.

Thankfully, it wasn't long before Leo sighed and stood to start the meeting. Ryan listened as he finished his food. Everyone gave their updates and shared what was in the works. Kristen had some new connections to partner with for the upcoming summer months. Alyssa was working on updating the website with all the events and new pictures. Andie reported the inn was booked up for most of the spring already. Jake was working on some updates to the bottling building, and Sean was getting started on bottling another run soon.

When everyone shared their updates, Leo surprised Ryan by bringing up Bella.

"By now, we all know Ryan has been seeing Perry's daughter."

"Why the fuck does this affect anyone else?" Ryan growled.

"Because we're all family. Because we're all worried about her," Henry said.

"But," Leo interrupted, "we have been instructed to back off. Ryan, I wanted to address this here and hope you would be willing to talk about it a little."

"Back off? Who instructed you?" Ryan asked, ignoring the other part of Leo's statement.

"I did," Nonna said, making her presence known in the room. "I had lunch with Bella last week. She's a lovely person. I'm so sorry about her mother. She didn't come here to cause problems for us. She's a good woman, and it's unfortunate for her that her father has been less than good to this family, but that's not her fault. I think everyone in this room would agree that we shouldn't judge people based on the choices of their parents."

Ryan was more than a little surprised. He stood and went to Nonna, pulling her into a hug. He whispered, "Thank you," in her ear.

She nodded and said, "I really like your Bella."

"Me, too," Ryan said.

Nonna patted his cheek and slid her hand through his arm. She let him lead her back to his table and took a seat with him, protecting him from his cousins with her presence alone.

"Are we sure we can trust her?" Andie asked.

"No one is going to be completely trustworthy. You included. Did anyone hold it against you when you didn't share that you were pregnant?" Nonna asked.

Andie blushed and shook her head.

"Is she sticking around?" Alyssa asked. "I haven't met her, but I'd like to. If she makes you happy, that's all that really matters."

Ryan nodded at Alyssa and said, "I'll bring her over sometime soon."

"Thank you. I'd like that," Alyssa said.

"I don't like it," Henry said. "You guys can be supportive and forgiving, but I don't like it. The timing is too coincidental."

"You think she's that good of an actress?" Nonna asked.

Henry shrugged. "I think it's possible. We don't know anything about her, and there's no reason to think she's completely innocent."

"Fair enough," Nonna said for Ryan. "But I think you of all people should be willing to forgive and forget. It's not easy, and most of us didn't like you getting involved with Cynthia after the way she hurt you when you were kids. You forgave her quickly and let her back into your world. And now you're denying your brother the same opportunity. To have someone in his life who makes him feel safe and loved."

"He's not alone," Henry argued.

Nonna shook her head. "No, he's not. But your mother and I know that being alone and being lonely are very different things. And we both know that we'd choose the days we had with the men we loved over never loving them.

It doesn't matter how long you love someone, it matters that you love them and they love you. Love isn't perfect, and it never will be, but it's powerful enough to overcome anything and everything. Please don't do to your brother what my family did to me. He will choose Bella over this family if he's pushed. I know he will because it's exactly what I did. Every one of you has made bad choices, has lived with regret, but I promise you all your regrets are nothing compared to the soul-crushing pain that comes from walking away from the person you love because of your family."

Ryan squeezed Nonna's hand. He hated how hurt she sounded. All the stories she'd told about leaving her family in Italy made it sound like she and their grandfather had a whirlwind romance and couldn't choose anything other than leaving, but Ryan never thought about the pain she had to have felt to leave her family behind.

"I'm sorry, Nonna," Ryan said softly. "I'm sorry you went through that."

She smiled at him. "I'm sorry you're going through it now. I hope your cousins give Bella a chance, and I hope the two of you find your happy ending. If you need to talk, I'm always here. Even if you decide here isn't where you need to be."

"Thank you," Ryan said.

Nonna smiled then faced the others. They were staring at Nonna and Ryan with mixtures of shock and guilt. Henry looked angry, but he was the only one.

"I think we're done," Leo said quietly. "Ryan, I'm sorry. I hope Bella can feel comfortable in our house again. Please let her know she's welcome."

Ryan nodded, appreciating the words.

"Tell her I'm sorry," Andie said.

"We're all sorry," Zach said. "Perry is an ass, but Bella isn't him."

Ryan thought about the boxes in Bella's room and Perry moving them. Bella definitely wasn't Perry. She was trying to help him. She wanted to know the truth as much as the rest of them. He wanted to tell his cousins, but he couldn't risk it getting out. For her sake. She was suspicious of her father, and he was acting like a man who had something to hide. Bella was nothing like him.

The others nodded with Zach, all except Henry. He didn't meet Ryan's gaze. He kept his head down, avoiding eye contact with everyone. He wasn't so willing to forgive and forget.

Ryan wanted to be upset, but he felt the same when Cynthia came back. Ryan warned his brother to stay away from the woman who'd already broken his heart once. Henry didn't listen, and Ryan learned to love Cynthia. The roles were reversed, and Ryan couldn't blame his brother for feeling the same way toward Bella.

He just hoped he got the same happy ending Henry and Cynthia got.

21

Bella waited until Albert was asleep to sneak out of the house. She didn't know his regular schedule, but she was fairly sure he wasn't going to get up in the middle of the night.

She let the moonlight guide her through the vineyard to the building that held his office. She expected the doors to be locked, but she figured she'd worry about it when she got there. The knob didn't budge when she turned it, and she swore in the dark.

Bella moved around the building, searching all the doors until she ended back in front of the first one. None of them were unlocked. She circled again, wondering if any of the windows were open. She could just barely reach the bottom of the windowsills, so even if they were, she wasn't sure how she would get herself up and through the window without a ladder.

Halfway around the building, one of the windows moved when she pushed it from the bottom. It didn't go far, but it was the only movement she'd seen.

With a little more excitement than felt natural, Bella

searched for a way to lift herself up high enough to maneuver her way through the window.

No ladders. No steps. Nothing that would make it easy. She drew in a breath, not willing to give up, and jumped. Her fingertips wrapped over the edge, but she didn't have nearly enough strength to pull herself up.

She searched again and saw rocks scattered around the area. She could stack them up high enough that she could stand on them and get herself through the window.

She hoped.

It took far too long, but Bella managed to get a high enough stack of rocks that she could get her forearms on the windowsill. The window lifted easily, and with no screen to impede her progress, she hoisted herself through the window.

She didn't think about her landing on the other side until she was on her belly, halfway through the window, and looking at the concrete floor way too many feet away.

Bella closed her eyes and used every bit of strength she had left to pull her leg through the window opening. She couldn't get her other leg through without falling, but she held on to the window frame and worked her way through as best she could.

When she finally admitted she had to jump, she said a silent prayer that she wouldn't break anything and dropped to the floor.

Her feet stung when she landed, and her knee protested a little, but otherwise, she was okay. She took a deep breath and shook her head, then walked through the quiet building to the office.

Thankfully, that door was unlocked, so Bella was able to walk right in. The boxes were stacked against the wall. Finally, something was easy.

She pulled out her phone and looked at the picture she took last time she went through the boxes. They were all in a different order and some of them were turned around, so the little marks she'd noticed before couldn't be seen. She groaned and decided she needed to go through all of them again.

Bella worked quickly, dismissing the boxes she knew she'd already checked. She only had four boxes left when she found something she needed to get a closer look at.

It was a folder, nearly buried between some other files in the box. It looked out of place given the green color in the middle of all the beige, which was the main reason she found it.

Bella grabbed the folder and pulled it out. There wasn't anything on the front of it, but the first page said *Operating Manual, Amavita Estates.*

Bella gasped and sank onto one of the chairs. She flipped through the book, a book that was marked on each page as *Property of Amavita Estates, not for distribution.* Bella felt like she'd been punched in the stomach. She didn't want to believe it, but Albert lied to her. To all of them. He did take the manual.

Bella finished searching the boxes but didn't find anything else. She closed them all up and stacked them against the wall again. She took the folder with her as she snuck out of the building the way she came in. She closed the window and spread the rocks out again, then headed up to the house as morning cast a sleepy glow over the sky.

The shower was on in Albert's bathroom when Bella got inside. She made a pot of coffee and set the manual on the table in front of her. When Albert came out, he smiled at her.

"You're up early."

Bella nodded once.

"Are you okay?"

Bella shook her head.

"What happened? Did Victor's boy end things with you? I knew he wasn't good enough for you."

Albert chuckled as he poured himself a cup of coffee then walked to the table where Bella sat.

"What's that?" he asked, gesturing to the folder in front of her.

"I think you know what it is," Bella answered.

Albert's brows drew together as his face twisted in confusion. "I don't think I've seen it before. Why would I know what it is?"

"Because I found it in your files."

"What? You went through my files? You know that's illegal, right? To search through the property of someone without their permission. Why would you do that?"

"Because I was looking for this," Bella said.

"What is it? What was so important that you thought searching my things would be a good idea? You could have asked me if you wanted to see something."

"I did ask you!" Bella shouted. She was hurt and tired and angry. She trusted him, and he lied to her face. "I did ask you, Albert. I asked if you stole a manual from Ryan's family's vineyard. I asked you when you told me about it, and you said no. You lied to me."

"I didn't lie to you, Bella. You asked me if I stole a manual. I didn't."

"Then what the hell is this?" Bella asked, tossing the folder toward him.

Albert looked at it, then sighed. He turned the folder toward him and opened the cover. He blanched when he saw the first page.

"Where did you get this?" Albert demanded in a low voice.

"In your files. In your office. I knew when you moved all those boxes out of my room that you were hiding something from me. That you had something to hide."

"I didn't want to worry about Ryan getting into my files. I know how his family feels about me, and I wanted to make sure they didn't do something...something like this."

"No, this is not Ryan's fault. You're the one who stole the manual from his father. You're the one who hid the boxes like a thief. You're the one who did wrong here, Albert. Not Ryan."

Albert shook his head and closed the folder. He pushed it away from himself and looked up at her. His gaze was pained and frustrated, but not guilty. "Bella, you have to believe me. I didn't steal this. I don't know where you found it, but I didn't do this. I moved those boxes because I was worried Ryan might use his access to you to get back at me. Planting something like this in my files makes me look like I stole this. I never did, Bella. Ryan's family has been out to get me since the summer I worked for them. They felt I should have given up my dream of owning a vineyard and just worked for them forever. They've never forgiven me for it. But I didn't steal this from them."

"No," Bella stammered. "You had to have. How else could it have gotten in that box. It was shoved between two files. The box was one of the ones on the bottom."

Albert sighed. "Bella, I never paid attention to where the boxes were. They're all old files that I need to go through sometime. Old tax returns, old personnel records, old data from the previous owners. I kept meaning to go through all of it, but I've never taken the time because it feels like such a monumental task. The box you said was on the bottom could easily have been on the top when they were in your room."

"I didn't do this," Bella said quickly.

Albert shook his head. "I would never think you did. But Ryan was in your room. Is it possible? I hate to even ask that, but I don't know how else that could have gotten in one of my boxes. It had to have been Ryan."

Bella tried to remember the night Ryan showed up. He texted her to ask if he could see her. She was the one who took him to her room. He didn't ask to go in there. And he'd never been in there before. Did she tell him about the boxes? Or did he have the folder under his coat and planned to leave it somewhere in the house. It wouldn't really matter where it was if it was on the property.

Could she have been wrong about him? Was he using her the way his family thought she was using him?

"Bella?" Albert said.

Bella wiped her cheek, surprised to find tears running down.

"Are you okay?"

Bella shook her head. She grabbed the manual and went to her room. She was such a fool.

72 years ago

"Tina," her father called up the stairs, "come down for dinner."

Tina sighed and dropped her pen onto the bed. She folded up the letter she wrote to Carmelo and stuck it between her mattress and the bed. If she ever saw him again, she hoped to be able to give him her letters. To let him know how she felt, and that she was sorry her father was so rude to him.

Tina walked down the stairs and was surprised to hear another voice with her father's. Male. Muffled to where she couldn't make it out clearly, but it was deep. Like Carmelo's.

She rushed the rest of the way down the stairs, hoping her father changed his mind in the last two days, and pulled up short when she burst into the living room and found her father sitting with Antonio Costello. Her supposed future husband.

Antonio stood and grinned widely at her. He was a handsome man with his light brown hair and hazel eyes, but he was a boy she'd played with as a child. She grew up with him the same way she'd grown up with her brother, and thought of Antonio much the same.

"Tina, you look beautiful," Antonio said, reaching for her hand.

Knowing better than to be rude, she let him take it. "Thank you."

"I'm so pleased I could be here tonight to have dinner with your family. My father was thrilled with the invitation, but sadly couldn't join us."

"We understand, son," Peter said. "We know how busy it gets when you're running your own business. It's good for a man, though."

Antonio nodded. "It is. Very good. I look forward to learning more from him and taking over when it's my time. It's good, honest work to be outside and creating something with the fruits God blessed us with."

Peter laughed and nodded. He slapped Antonio on the back then wrapped an arm around his shoulders. "Come on, son, let's see if dinner is ready."

Tina followed behind them, feeling out of place in her

own home. When Carmelo came for dinner, she was the center of his attention. His every move was to make sure she was okay. She was happy and knew he was there for her. Antonio barely spared her a glance as her father led him off to share a glass of something for men only while Tina headed to the kitchen to actually check on dinner.

"I didn't realize Antonio was coming for dinner tonight," Tina said to her mother when she entered the kitchen.

"I was afraid you wouldn't show up if we told you."

Tina rolled her eyes. It was a fair concern, and probably true.

"Take the bread from the oven, Tina. And put water in all the glasses. Your father will open the wine when we get to the table."

Tina nodded and did as she was told. She was trying her hardest to behave, but it wasn't easy for her. Pushing back meant making her father angry, and that meant not getting her way. She couldn't fathom marrying Antonio Costello, but she also hadn't been able to sneak out and see Carmelo since the night he came for dinner. She wanted to meet up with him and tell him she loved him, but her parents figured out that she was sneaking out to see him and had been waiting for her each night.

When dinner was on the table, her mother went to tell her father and Antonio to join them. Tina took her place at the table opposite her siblings and waited for Antonio and her parents to join them.

As they did when Carmelo was there, her father insisted they hold hands for grace and asked Tina to say it.

Tina drew in a breath and felt comforted by the gentle squeeze of Antonio's hand. "Lord, we ask you to bless this family and our friends. We ask you to bless the food we are about to eat and allow it to nourish us. We thank you for the people in our lives, even those we don't see often, and ask you to keep them all safe in your heart until we meet again. Amen."

"Amen," everyone echoed.

Tina said a silent prayer that she might see Carmelo again soon, then passed the plates with the others.

Her father maintained the conversation at the table, asking Antonio question after question about his work and his family. Antonio answered all of them politely. He complimented her mother on the food, and thanked her again for allowing him to join them.

Antonio was a nice man. When he laughed, he tipped his head back and enjoyed himself. He picked on her siblings like they were his own. He spoke to her father with respect and her mother with adoration. And he was kind and considerate of her.

But through all of it, Tina kept thinking he wasn't Carmelo. She missed him. It didn't matter that Antonio would make a fine husband or that he was a good-looking man. He wasn't the one she was in love with.

When dinner was finished, her father asked Antonio to join him on the deck for a cigar. Tina carried plates into the kitchen and helped her mother clean up.

"Antonio is such a nice boy," her mother said softly. "And your father likes him."

"Papa likes that he's from a good family."

"That's important, Tina. I know you don't understand, but being from a good family means you'll be cared for."

"It means I'll have money. It doesn't mean I'll be cared for."

"They're the same thing," her mother argued.

Tina looked at her mother and perhaps saw the woman for the first time ever. Tina blamed her father for forcing her into a marriage she wasn't interested in, but she knew in that moment her mother was just as much to blame.

Her mother wasn't a woman who stood up to her father. She wasn't a woman who had her own voice. She allowed Tina's father to be the one who laid down the law and expected everyone to follow his rules. But her mother had her own set of expectations. Her expectations came in the form of security. She didn't push back because she believed money was the only thing that mattered.

Tina felt an overwhelming sadness for her mother. She'd never known love like Tina shared with Carmelo. She was sure her mother cared about her father, and vice versa, but she didn't believe either of them loved the other. Not in the way she loved Carmelo.

Carmelo was the most important person in her world. She'd do anything to be with him. If her options were a life like her mother lived, or leaving her home, she'd choose to leave if it meant she was with Carmelo.

But she didn't know how she could see him. She didn't know if she could see him.

"You should go speak to Antonio," her mother said. "He's waiting outside for you."

"He's with Papa."

Her mother shook her head. "He's only out there to be polite. You need to go out so the two of you can make plans for your marriage. That's how this works, Tina. Now go. He will be your husband. You need to learn not to keep him waiting."

Tina drew in a breath and did as she was told. Her father left once she was outside, and Tina felt awkward with Antonio.

"Your father would like us to be married soon," Antonio

said, stubbing out his cigar in deference to her. "Within a few weeks. Does that suit you?"

Tina sucked in a sharp breath. "I don't believe I have a choice in the matter."

Antonio nodded. "I understand. Listen, Tina, you're a beautiful woman, and I'll be honored to have you as my wife. I'm not really ready to get married either, but this is our duty at this point."

Tina nodded and forced a smile. "I'm sorry, Antonio. I know I'm not being very kind to you."

Antonio shook his head. "You're not doing anything wrong. We will do as we are told, and hopefully one day we'll know our parents were right."

Tina forced another smile. She knew she would never think her parents were right. They couldn't be right if it meant she couldn't be with Carmelo.

Her heart hurt at the thought of sharing a bed with Antonio. Of never being with Carmelo again.

"How about we get to know each other over the next week. If we decide we don't want to get married, I'll take the blame for it and you can escape this without any harm."

"My father—"

"Will hate me, not you."

"What about your father?"

Antonio shrugged. "My father barely knows I exist most of the time. I can't see this causing him anymore frustration."

"Antonio..."

He shook his head. "It's okay, Tina. You're lucky. You have people who love you and want what's best for you, even if it's in a way you don't appreciate. I haven't had that since my mother died."

"I'm so sorry, Antonio."

He grinned. "Thank you. But it's not what we need to be talking about now. What do you say we meet in town tomorrow. Have lunch, talk, and walk around. Let the town see us, and appease your father. We will get to know each other, and when our wedding day comes, it'll be up to you if you'd like to meet me at the end of the aisle."

"What about what you want?"

He shrugged. "What you want is more important. And I'd never force you into something you weren't sure about."

"Thank you, Antonio. Truly. Thank you."

He smiled and took her hand. He kissed her knuckles the nodded and went back inside. She heard him say goodnight to her parents and leave, and Tina told herself if she did end up marrying him, at least he was a good man.

She just hoped she didn't have to marry him.

22

Present Day

RYAN HAD JUST FINISHED LUNCH WHEN SOMEONE KNOCKED ON his door. He put his plate in the sink and finished his water. Before he made it to the door, whoever it was pounded on the door.

"I'm coming!" he shouted, rushing to the door. "Bella?"

She pushed past him into the house. She walked to the far side of the kitchen then back toward him.

Ryan watched her frantic movements. He closed the door silently behind him and took stock of Bella. Her eyes were red-rimmed, her cheeks splotchy. She wore a black long-sleeved tee under her unbuttoned coat and jeans. Her shoes were definitely shit-kickers, and if the look in her watery eyes was any indication, that's exactly what she'd come to do.

"Are you okay?"

Bella shook her head.

"What's wrong? Are you hurt? Did something happen with your dad?"

She scoffed.

"Bell, talk to me. You're scaring me."

"I found your manual," Bella said, waving around a green folder.

"My what?"

Bella rolled her eyes and shook her head. "Did you really think you would get away with it? That you could hide it in Albert's files and I wouldn't notice it? Well, no, that would have defeated the purpose. I had to notice it, but I was supposed to think he put it there, right?"

Ryan tried to get a look at the folder, but she was waving it around as she spoke and all he could tell was it was green. Other than that, he didn't know what she thought it was.

"Let's sit down and we can talk about this," Ryan said calmly, hoping to get her to relax and explain exactly what was going on.

"No," Bella declared. She finally stopped pacing and sucked in a breath. She looked at him and scowled.

For the first time since they met, Ryan felt like he didn't know her at all. Every time they'd spoken, even the first night, he felt like they had a connection. But looking at her in that moment, with her eyes full of hurt and anger, he had no idea who she was.

"Okay," Ryan said. "We don't have to sit. But can you tell me what's going on?"

"Don't insult me, Ryan. You already used me. Why don't you just admit the truth now and I can get out of your way?"

Ryan nodded. "Okay. The truth is I have no idea what we're talking about."

"Dammit, Ryan! I know you planted this."

She threw the folder onto the table. It slid across the surface and stopped a few feet from him. Ryan looked at Bella then back to the folder.

She lifted an eyebrow expectantly, waiting for him to say something or do something.

Ryan reached for the folder, still wondering what in the hell made her so mad. He lifted it and opened the cover.

Operating Manual
Amavita Estates

Ryan sucked in a breath and risked a glance at Bella. There was no way. He couldn't be looking at what he thought he was looking at. She said it, but he thought she was talking about something else. There was no way.

He flipped to the next page. At the bottom was *Property of Amavita Estates, not for distribution* just like was on all their manuals when they printed them.

Ryan scanned the pages, recognizing notes his father wrote in some of the margins. Those notes were now typed into the version they kept updated on the computer. After the manual disappeared, Victor destroyed all paper copies and put everything into a password protected file that could only be printed by one of them.

Ryan took his time looking through the pages, ignoring Bella as she stood glaring at him. He finally found the proof they needed. Bella found it. She brought it to him. She knew Albert was guilty and she gave him their missing manual.

He closed the folder and ran his hand over the green folder. He'd almost forgotten about it. His dad bought a big box of green folders from the office store when he was a kid. His mom laughed at him and asked what he was going to use them all for. He said he was going to put all of his important information in them and keep them on his desk so he'd have everything right there when he needed it. Jo joked with him that he'd have to go through all of them before he found the right one if they were all the same color. She was right, of course, but Victor never admitted it to her.

"Are you really going to act like you didn't know this was there?" Bella asked after a minute.

"Yes, I knew it was there. Or, I believed it was. God, Bella, how did you find this?"

"It was in one of the boxes, just like you knew it would be."

Ryan nodded. "Wow. I really never thought we'd find it. I honestly had my doubts for a while. I mean, it made sense we would have known something, but even when he was questioned, Perry always said he never stole anything. I think his office was even searched at one point. Did you find this in those boxes that were in your room?"

Ryan looked up at her. He'd forgotten how upset she was when she walked in, but looking at her again, he hated that it caused her so much pain to learn the truth about her father.

"Bella, I'm sorry," Ryan said, leaving the folder on the table and moving around it to go to her. "I wish it didn't have to be this way."

Ryan reached for her, but Bella scooted away from him.

"What's wrong?"

"Why do you think I'm going to forgive you for this? Do you really think I'm that gullible? That stupid? I know I'm not the sharpest crayon in the box, but come on, Ryan. I found it. I found the manual you left. It's time to stop lying."

Ryan took a step back, and all of her words since she walked in finally sank in. She was so frantic and upset when she first arrived that he didn't process all of it. Now, he was. And he finally realized what she was saying. "Lying about what?" he pressed. She had to spell it out for him or he'd never believe what he thought she was trying to say.

She scoffed. "About the manual. I know you stuck it in one of the boxes when you came over that night. I'm guessing you didn't think it would be so easy to slip it into a storage box and you planned to leave it under the couch or something, but I gave you the perfect opportunity to set Albert up."

"Is that what you think?" he asked.

She shrugged. "It doesn't matter what I think. I know it's true. I asked Albert. He said he never stole that. He didn't even know what it was. He said he'd never seen it before. But you knew what it was, didn't you?"

Ryan looked at the woman he thought he loved and nodded. "I did. I've seen this. I won't lie to you about that. My dad used to keep a lot of stuff in these green folders. He loved them. But that doesn't mean I put this in Perry's files."

"Don't lie to me!" she shouted.

Ryan moved toward her again. If he could touch her, hold her, make her see him, she would know he wasn't lying. But when he moved, so did she. She knew it. She knew if she looked in his eyes she would see the truth, so she was staying away from him.

"Wow," Ryan breathed. "I really thought you wanted to find out the truth. I thought you wanted to know what kind of man your father was. I guess you just wanted to fabricate a story to make everyone believe he's a good man." Ryan shook his head. "A good man wouldn't have taken this. I certainly never would have. This is the only one on this property, Bella. Until you showed up, we had none here. My father destroyed all the others years ago, when your father took this. My father didn't want to risk another one of these disappearing. This one was his. It was his personal copy. I know that because it has his handwriting in it. I haven't seen this since I was a kid. And I sure as hell never would have put something that mattered this much to my family in your father's things. I wouldn't take the chance that he would find it and use it."

"So, what was your plan? Tell the cops where it was? Make sure they found it before he did?"

Ryan blew out a breath. "I think it's time for you to go, Bella."

"Really? You're just done. Just like that?"

"You are, so why wouldn't I be?"

"I cared about you. I thought I could love you. Hell, I thought I did love you. But I can't be with a man who would do something like this. This is low, Ryan. You're not who I thought you were."

"Right back at you," Ryan said softly.

Bella shot him a glare then walked past him and straight out his door. She slammed it behind her, and Ryan sank into a chair.

He finally had the proof he needed, but it didn't feel like the victory he'd hoped it would be.

Bella left Ryan's house in tears. She thought he would explain it to her. If nothing else, he could tell her why he did it. She didn't know why she didn't expect him to deny the entire thing.

She could barely breathe by the time she got back to Albert's house. She choked on her tears and rushed past Albert and his worried face.

"Bella?"

"I can't right now. I just can't," was all she said before closing her bedroom door.

She threw herself onto the bed and cried until she fell

asleep. When she woke a few hours later, the sun was sinking quickly. Her stomach rumbled with hunger, but she really didn't want to eat anything.

She got up and used the bathroom. The house was quiet, so she grabbed a granola bar and a bottle of wine and went back to her room.

Bella didn't answer her door when Albert knocked an hour later. She didn't join him for dinner and waited in her room, pretending to be asleep, until he went to bed.

Once the house was quiet again, Bella left her room. She tiptoed to the fridge and grabbed a bottle of water and made herself a sandwich, unable to fight off her hunger any longer. When she finished her sandwich, she snuck out of the house, needing the fresh air and the water.

Bella's heart throbbed in her chest as she worked her way down the driveway and across the street. She stood just on the Amavita Estates side of the road, looking at the water stretched out left to right. She couldn't see anywhere close to the north or south end of the lake, but she could see the other side, the east side. She thought about getting in her car and driving over there, or driving somewhere, but she felt comfortable on the dock.

At least, she did before.

Bella looked around as she walked, hoping she wouldn't run into anyone. The leaves of the trees rustled with the gentle breeze, but otherwise, there wasn't a sound on the property at all.

Bella made it to the bench and lowered herself carefully onto it, bracing herself for the insane cold that instantly seeped through her sweatpants.

She sat on the bench for close to an hour, trying to find some comfort in what happened between her and Ryan. She trusted him, but he betrayed her. And worse, he blamed her father for it. She would have seen it in Albert's eyes if he knew what the folder was. He had no clue until she told him. But Ryan? Ryan admitted he knew what it was.

A whisper of doubt said he didn't recognize it immediately, but she ignored it. She went to Bereton to confront her father. To tell the man who'd abandoned her that she didn't need him, that he was worth as much to her as she'd been to him. She didn't expect to come face-to-face with a man who wanted to know her.

Albert was nothing like what her mother said, but Bella knew time changed people. They knew each other a decade before Albert worked on Amavita Estates. If it was his dream to have his own vineyard, there was no reason he shouldn't have it.

That didn't mean he stole something. Or that he was the man her mom said he was.

Bella finally got too cold to sit outside any longer. She walked back to Albert's, ignoring the disappointment she felt that Ryan didn't show up there. She didn't go there to see him, but a part of her hoped he would try to explain.

Bella slept like shit that night, tossing and turning and barely able to get any sleep before the sun streamed through the curtains she forgot to close the night before.

Bella got up and got dressed. She headed to the kitchen and poured herself a cup of coffee before Albert asked if she was okay.

She shook her head. "No. I don't know what I expected from him, but I didn't think he'd lie to my face."

"I'm sorry, Bella."

She shrugged. "Me, too. I guess I just picked the wrong man to trust. I have a habit of doing that."

Albert looked distinctly uncomfortable with her comment, so she pasted on a smile and changed the subject.

"Is there anything I can help you with today? I need to take my mind off all of this."

Albert nodded. They finished their coffee and went out to the office. "If you're really looking for something to do, how about help me go through all these files finally. I'd hate to leave them here and risk something else happening."

Bella choked back her tears and nodded.

Albert lifted one of the boxes and brought it over to the desk. He carried another over in front of the chair. "Which do you want to start with?"

Bella point to the one on the floor. "I'll do that one."

Albert grinned. "You probably have a better idea of what's in these boxes than I do. I'm sorry I didn't go through them before, but at least now you know who they are."

Bella drew in a shaky breath and nodded. "I definitely do. And I'm done with them. All of them."

Albert nodded once, then they both fell silent and worked. It was exactly the kind of distraction Bella needed to put Ryan out of her mind. With any luck, she'd keep him out for good.

23

———

THE LAST THING RYAN WANTED TO DO WAS TELL HIS BROTHER he was right about Bella. Henry wasn't the type to say I told you so, but Ryan knew he deserved it if Henry threw it out there.

They were supposed to have breakfast with their mom at Henry's house, and Ryan figured that was the best time to tell them about Bella's delivery from the day before. He didn't have the strength to tell them right away, but delaying wasn't going to change it.

After Bella left, Ryan wanted to scream and throw things. He knew Perry lied to her about the manual, but if she wasn't willing to even ask him, just assume he was the monster Perry was, then he was done.

That didn't mean it didn't hurt. He loved her, for fuck's sake, and she thought he was capable of setting her father up. The entire time, he'd been more worried about what would happen to her when they found their proof. He never thought twice about Perry. But Perry was smarter than Ryan ever gave him credit for. He planned the whole thing, probably even stashed the manual in a spot he knew would draw Bella's attention.

Ryan shook his head. It didn't matter what Perry did. They had their manual back, and they were going to make sure it didn't leave their hands again. As long as it was gone, Perry could have made an endless number of copies, but hopefully he wasn't that stupid.

The walk to Henry's was quick, but Ryan took his time, letting the cold clear his mind. He almost went down to the lake the night before, but he couldn't bring himself to go there. So he walked slowly to Henry's hoping it would give him some sense of calm before he walked into his brother's house and told him he was right not to trust Bella.

Ryan knocked on the door then let himself in. Since Henry and Cynthia knew he was coming over, the door was unlocked. Ryan took off his boots and hung up his jacket the same way he'd always done when he walked into the house he grew up in.

Voices told Ryan his mother was already there. They had a rule that their breakfasts were only for the three of them, so even though he heard Cynthia's voice, he knew she wasn't staying.

"Hey, Ryan," Cynthia said, startling him when she walked into the hallway. "How are you?"

Ryan nodded. "Great. You?"

"Good. I'm meeting my mom for breakfast. She and Tim are bringing some honey. I'll save a jar for you, okay?"

Ryan nodded and tried to look happy. In truth, he didn't care. Not because it wasn't good or he didn't appreciate it, but because nothing seemed to matter since Bella walked out of his house.

"Are you sure you're okay?" Cynthia asked again. Her brown eyes narrowed.

Ryan forced his smile to brighten and nodded. "Just didn't sleep well last night. You'd think with my crazy schedule, I'd be used to sleeping anywhere and everywhere, but last night it just wasn't happening for me."

"Sorry to hear that. As long as you're okay, though…"

Ryan nodded. "Absolutely. Enjoy your breakfast."

"Thanks, you too."

Ryan nodded again, feeling like a bobblehead. Cynthia waved and pulled the door closed behind herself. Ryan drew in a breath and admitted he couldn't stall any longer.

He left the manual with his jacket, tucked into his hood, and joined his brother and mom in the kitchen.

"Good morning," Jo said happily. "I was starting to wonder about you."

Ryan smiled. "I'm here. Didn't sleep well last night. Slow to get moving today."

"I'm sorry, honey. Are you okay? Are you coming down with something?" She put her hand on Ryan's forehead.

Ryan shook his head. "No, I'm fine. Just a lot on my mind."

"Like what?" Jo asked.

Ryan shook his head again. "Nothing we need to talk about right now."

Jo shot Henry a look, and Henry shrugged.

Ryan pretended not to notice either and poured himself a glass of water. "Anything I can help with?"

"Yeah, get Mom some more coffee," Henry said.

Ryan nodded and filled his mom's coffee mug up. She enjoyed her coffee. He grabbed the cream from the fridge and the sugar from the container in the pantry, setting both in front of her.

Jo smiled up at him. "Thank you."

Ryan nodded and mentally rolled his eyes at himself.

They were going to know something was wrong in about five seconds if he didn't start acting more like himself.

"So, what's been going on with you boys. How's Cynthia?" Jo asked after she took a sip of her coffee.

"She's good. I think she's still happy here. I'm happy she's here."

"Did you think she wasn't going to be happy here?" Ryan asked.

Henry shrugged. "She always wanted to leave. A part of me worried that old urge would come back one day."

"It's been two years," Jo said.

Henry nodded. "Yeah, and I'm finally less worried. She hasn't even mentioned going out of town for a break. She loves living here, and her mom is happy, which makes a big difference for Cynthia. It's a different situation."

"Which means those same fears don't exist anymore," Jo said with a smile. "You need to worry less. Cynthia loves you. I can see it in her eyes every time you walk in the room."

Henry grinned. "I feel the same. And hopefully one day we'll have some of our old rooms filled up."

"What?" Jo gasped. "You're having kids?"

Henry shook his head. "No, not yet. We've talked about it, but we're not pregnant yet. I'm hoping this year, though."

"Wow," Ryan breathed. "That's awesome. Something big to celebrate. Congrats, man."

Henry nodded. "Hopefully I'll have a reason to accept that congrats."

"You will," Ryan said. "This family needs more babies."

Jo sniffed and both boys turned to look at her.

"Ma?"

She smiled. "I'm happy, but I miss your father on days like this. He would have loved to share this. To see you with kids. And Ryan, to see you so happy with Bella. He was always so proud of you boys."

Ryan's heart ached at the mention of Bella. He knew it was a good opportunity to tell them, but he wanted normal for just a little while longer.

Henry finished cooking breakfast and the three of them moved to the dining room. Ryan took his normal seat to the right of his mom and remembered no matter what, he wasn't alone.

Jo reached for Ryan and Henry, taking both of their hands in hers. Ryan reached across the table to hold Henry's hand, noting yet again that their father missing was a physical ache.

"God, thank you for the gifts you've given our family. The gifts of love, of each other, of family and friends and our health. Thank you for always providing for us, and please say hi to Victor for us. We love you."

"Amen," Ryan and Henry said together.

Ryan took the bowl of eggs and scooped some onto his plate. He added sausage, bacon, potatoes, and two mini waffles. He took a sip of his coffee and realized his mother and brother were staring at him.

"What?"

"Did you forget to eat yesterday?" Jo asked with a smile.

Ryan looked down at his plate and shrugged. He did, but he hadn't planned to admit that. "I'm just hungry. I usually eat by now."

"You never eat by now. What's going on?" Henry asked.

Ryan shook his head. "Just feeling off today."

"Because you didn't sleep?"

Ryan nodded.

"Why didn't you sleep?" Jo asked.

"Can we just eat?" Ryan barked.

Henry's brows went sky high, and Ryan immediately regretted his tone.

"Ma, I'm sorry."

"No," Jo said with a smile that wasn't real. "You're right. I shouldn't be pressing you. You're a grown man, and if something is bothering you, you don't need your mother to bug you about it."

"Ma, it's not that."

"Then what is it?" Henry asked.

Ryan sighed. Guess he wasn't going to eat that breakfast he hoped for.

He pushed away from the table and went to the other room. Henry and his mother called after him, but he ignored their calls and got the manual from his coat.

Henry and Jo were talking quietly when Ryan walked back in.

"I'm sorry," Jo said immediately. "I wasn't trying to push."

"Ma, it's fine. I just wanted to eat before I told you guys about this, but..."

He held up the folder. Jo's eyes widened, and she gasped. Henry looked as confused as Ryan had been.

"What is that?" Henry asked.

"It's what we've been looking for." Ryan handed it over to his brother and nodded at their mother, confirming silently that it was what she thought it was.

Henry opened the cover and drew back when he saw the first page. "Where did you get this?"

Ryan took a breath. "Bella gave it to me. She found it in Perry's files yesterday."

"What?" Henry breathed. "She found this and gave it to you."

Ryan nodded.

"Is it the manual?" Jo asked.

Henry nodded and pushed it in front of her. Breakfast was forgotten as they flipped through the pages Ryan studied the entire day before. Jo ran her fingertip over some of the words Victor had written. Tears filled her eyes, and she wiped them before they fell onto the paper.

"Perry had this. All this time, just like Dad always said," Henry said.

Ryan nodded.

"I can't believe this. He always insisted there was nowhere else it could have been. He felt so guilty thinking it was Albert. Your father wanted to be wrong. So many times over the years I found him tearing apart the house or the office. He would move the furniture, thinking maybe it had fallen behind something."

"That's why he was always rearranging the furniture?" Ryan asked.

Jo nodded. "Yep. He thought as adamant as Albert was that he had to have misplaced it. He wanted to find it and apologize. He really liked Albert the summer he worked here. Said he was a nice guy. That was why it hurt him so badly when this went missing. This was your father's copy."

"His notes are here in the margins," Henry said.

Jo nodded again. "He carried this with him from the day he started here until it vanished. He took it to bed and read it almost every night. He wanted to do your grandfather proud. He knew he had big shoes to fill, and he wasn't sure he could do it, but he was going to try."

"He did it," Henry said, reaching over and squeezing Jo's shoulder.

"I told him that, too. He hoped to pass on all this to you boys. He loved that both of you decided to work in the fields like he did. He felt connected to this place when he was out there. Sometimes I wonder if the stress of walking away was what cause his aneurysm."

"Ma, the doctors said that wasn't it. There was nothing that could have been done, and nothing that caused it. It wasn't you," Henry said.

Jo shrugged. "I know. I just wish he was still here. I wish he could see you boys. It's only been two years, but it feels like a lifetime. Like he's missed so much. Both of you finding love. He always hoped you would settle down one day."

Henry grinned, but Ryan didn't say anything. He couldn't. He was lying to them without really lying. It was tearing him up, and he couldn't handle hearing how happy his father was going to be, especially knowing he wouldn't be after what happened with Bella.

"Please thank Bella for us," Jo said. "It was very kind of her to return this to you so we have it."

Ryan shook his head. "I won't see Bella again."

"What? What do you mean?"

"Perry convinced her I planted this in his stuff. He told her I set it up so she would find it. She didn't even ask me, just came over and threw it in my face and said she knew what I'd done."

"What?" Jo gasped. "No, she didn't."

Ryan nodded. "She did, Ma. She was so angry. I've never seen her look the way she did. It was like looking at Perry. She wasn't interested in hearing what I had to say. Perry convinced her he never stole it, and she trusted him. She said he told her I did it the night I was in her room." Ryan blew out a breath and shook his head. "It's over between us."

"You're better off without her," Henry said firmly.

"Henry!" Jo exclaimed.

"What? If she isn't willing to ask first and accuse later, then she doesn't deserve him. Ryan would never do something like that, and we know it. I wouldn't even think of asking you if you had. I mean, it would be a great idea, but the only way for something like that to matter would be if you got the cops there. You knew Bella was looking at those boxes. Why would you hide it there?"

"I didn't!"

Henry nodded. "I know. I'm just saying it doesn't make any sense. If we wanted Perry caught, you'd put it somewhere it could be seen."

"I don't think that's the point," Jo said softly.

"What do you mean?" Henry asked.

"It matters that she didn't believe him. Not that if he did it he would have done it differently. It's that she believed her father over Ryan without giving him a chance to defend himself."

Henry looked at Ryan. Ryan nodded. "Ma's right. If Bella had come over and asked, I would have told her I wouldn't do that, but she just said she knew I did it."

"Then you don't need her in your life. I know that hurts, but you told me the same thing about Cynthia. You said if she couldn't see who I was and didn't want me, then it wasn't worth being with her. You were right," Henry said.

"But you and Cynthia are together," Ryan argued.

"Yeah, because she wanted me. Bella doesn't want you," Henry said matter-of-factly.

Ryan winced. Just hearing the words hurt. He knew Henry was right, but he didn't want to think about it. Bella said she thought she was in love with him, that she thought she could have loved him. If she ever actually did love him, she never would have accused him of planting the manual.

"Henry," Jo said gently. "Give me a minute with your brother."

Henry looked between them and nodded. He left the room without arguing, and Ryan met his mother's gaze.

"I'm sorry about Bella," Jo said.

Ryan nodded.

"She's why you didn't sleep?"

Ryan nodded again.

"You love her, don't you."

Ryan nodded once more.

"People can struggle to pick sides when there's no way for both to win. It's not an easy position for her to be in. She found something that proves her father isn't the man she hoped he was. Accepting that is much harder than accepting that you were using her."

"I wasn't!"

Jo nodded. "I know, honey. And in time, I think she'll realize that, too. For right now, Bella's still hurting. It hasn't been that long since she lost her mother, and if she doesn't believe Albert's lies, then she loses her father, too. Your parents are supposed to be the people who love you unconditionally. The people who are always there for you. If she doesn't have either of them, what does she have?"

"She would have me," Ryan said.

Jo shrugged. "Maybe, but do you know that for sure? Love fades. People drift apart. I wish love was the answer to every problem in the world, but we both know it isn't. If it was, I would have loved your father back to life. I would have died for him if I could have. Unfortunately, love wasn't enough that day. And if Bella doesn't know you love her, it's definitely not enough for her."

"Are you saying I should tell her I love her?" Ryan asked, incredulous.

Jo shook her head. "No, because you have to decide when the right time is for something like that. What I'm saying is I understand why she chose her father. I think you need to give her some time. Don't count her out just yet."

"She didn't trust me, Ma."

"I know, honey. And that's not easy to accept, but I think maybe she'll come around. Just think about giving her another chance when she does."

Ryan nodded but wasn't sure he would be able to put aside the hurt. He was stubborn, and he didn't do second chances very well. And he definitely didn't do second chances with women who didn't give him a first chance.

24

---

72 years ago

CARMELO SPENT EVERY NIGHT LOOKING FOR TINA. HE WASN'T
ready to give up on her, but he didn't know what to do. He'd
gone to her house, but her mother refused to let him see
her. He was getting desperate.

He was also working. He wasn't good enough for her as
far as her family was concerned, but he wasn't going to stop
working and live on the streets. He had to keep working,
keep earning, keep trying.

He and Joey took the truck into town for supplies. Joey
was bugging him for the last week about his attitude, but
Carmelo refused to tell him what was going on. Joey
guessed it was about a woman, but Carmelo wouldn't say
anything. Just in case, he wasn't willing to rock the boat.

Carmelo and Joey split up once they were in town. Joey
did the grocery run, and Carmelo went looking for tools.
They had some new equipment coming in and they needed
to replace some of the older tools they used on a regular
basis.

He wandered the aisles of the local hardware store and searched for everything he was going to need. It wouldn't be long before the weather turned and they were in the fields every day. When that happened, the weekly field trips would cease and Carmelo would barely make it to his bed at night. He feared if he didn't see Tina before then, he'd miss his chance with her.

Carmelo thanked the clerk and grabbed the bag. He walked out of the store just in time to run into Regina.

"I don't even warrant a hello anymore?" Regina said with a scowl. "You choose someone else and I'm invisible."

"Hello, Regina," Carmelo said with a smile. "How are you today?"

Regina grinned like she had a secret. "I'm doing great right now."

Carmelo didn't want to waste any more time with her than he was forced to, so he nodded and went to leave.

"Although I'm not nearly as good as she is," Regina added with a nod behind Carmelo.

He turned and saw Tina tip her head back in a laugh. The long column of her neck made him want to rush over and nuzzle against it. He drank her in, his eyes flowing over her breasts to her waist, down her legs then up again to where her gaze lingered on the man next to her.

Carmelo finally realized Tina wasn't alone. In slow motion, he looked at the man who possessed Tina's hand. Her elegant fingers, fingers that had caressed his chest and held him as he slid into her body, wrapped around Antonio's forearm.

They looked at each other like no one else was in town. They were talking, and clearly the conversation was one that made them both happy because they were laughing together. A private, secretive conversation meant for their ears only.

"Wasn't that the girl you ran out of my shop to chase? The chubby one?" Regina tsked. "I guess she had her eye on a bigger prize. You know what they say, though. Start at the bottom and work your way up. She definitely worked up."

Carmelo would have slapped her if she was a man. He wanted to tear his gaze away from Tina and Antonio, but he couldn't. They kept walking, oblivious to his presence on the opposite side of the street. He turned as they passed him and continued to watch them.

The view from behind was just as painful. Tina's round bottom shifted side to side as she walked, stretching the material of her skirt. He ached to touch her, to hold her in his arms. To kiss her and love her and make her forget the asshole he worked for.

"She really didn't give you much of a thought, did she? Maybe you should have told her you defended her to me. Then she would have at least glanced your way. Or maybe not. I don't know how women like her operate. Me? I'm more of a quality woman than anything else. I know a man who'll make me feel alive, and I don't care how much money he has."

Regina slid her hands up Carmelo's back. He shivered at her touch, hating that he ever found it appealing. He turned his head and looked at her, thinking about it. Sleeping with her would be sex only. He didn't care about her. He didn't want her.

But he couldn't even think about sex with her. Not as long as Tina was out there could Carmelo consider being with another woman.

He plucked Regina's hand from his shoulder and dropped it. "I don't think so."

Regina scowled at him. "You'll come crawling back when they get married. It's soon. Just a few days. Then you'll know she's too good for you and finally accept that you belong with someone like me."

"I don't belong with you, Regina. Not now. Not ever."

Carmelo stalked away, letting Regina fume behind him. The woman refused to understand he wasn't interested in her anymore. He hadn't been able to think about another woman since he met Tina.

But she was marrying Antonio, his subconscious whispered.

Carmelo shook his head. He had to find a way to talk to her. Regina could have been lying. It wouldn't have been the first time.

Carmelo was sitting in the truck when Joey returned. He had the engine running and the windows rolled down, and he was looking at the town. Tina and Antonio didn't make another appearance, but even if they had, Carmelo knew he couldn't approach her when she was with his boss's son.

"You good?" Joey asked.

Carmelo nodded. Joey knew things. He would know if Regina was lying.

"Is Antonio engaged?"

Joey snorted. "You live under a rock. How do you not know about this?"

Carmelo shrugged but didn't say anything.

"Remember that woman I told you to stay away from? Tina Vincenzo?"

Carmelo nodded absently, pretending he didn't remember her well and didn't really care.

"I told you he was going to marry her."

"Yeah, but is it official? I mean, last time I spoke to him

he was bragging about all the women trying to get him to marry them. Is she just another one in line?"

Joey shook his head. He grabbed a pastry out of the bag on his lap and shoved it into his mouth. He offered one to Carmelo, but Carmelo shook his head.

"She's not?" Carmelo prodded.

Joey shook his head. "Nope. They declared last week. The wedding is this weekend."

Carmelo absorbed the words of his friend and thought he was going to be sick. No, it wasn't a thought. He really was.

He pulled the truck over and threw it into park. He jumped out and ran to the edge of the road and emptied his stomach into the ditch next to the road.

"What the hell?" Joey barked. "Are you sick? I can't get sick."

Carmelo wiped his mouth with the back of his hand. He was definitely sick, but it wasn't something anyone would catch. It was heartbreak, plain and simple. And he was going to have to learn to live with it because it wouldn't be long before the woman he loved was going to be his boss's daughter-in-law. And one day his boss.

Present Day

RYAN TOLD Henry he could tell everyone about the manual and Bella's accusations at the next family meeting. Ryan wasn't sure he could get the words out, and he knew Henry would have no problem at all.

Ryan sat in the back of the room with a cup of coffee and a roiling stomach. Leo tried to sit with him, but when it was clear he wasn't going to say anything about what Henry was going to tell everyone, Leo moved to sit with Zach.

When Leo started the meeting a few minutes later, Ryan seriously considered walking out. He wasn't sure he could sit there and listen to Henry tell them all that he was right and Bella was just as much a threat to them as Perry.

They would all be there for Ryan. They'd stand up for him and defend him. They'd surround him and protect him. They'd do whatever he needed. He just fucking hated that he needed it.

"Henry has something he wanted to share with everyone. Dillon is calling in to hear it, too," Leo said. He turned on the laptop he brought to the meeting and nodded at Henry when Dillon showed up on the screen.

"Hey, everyone. Hi, Dillon. I'm not going to beat around the bush here. We have good news. We finally have the manual that was stolen from us back in our possession," Henry said. He pulled the folder out with a flourish, holding it high for everyone to see.

As expected, there were gasps and questions and a whole lot of confusion. Everyone wanted to know how Henry got it back, where it was, how he found out about it, and what was going to happen.

Ryan told Henry he didn't want to talk. He didn't want to address the family. He knew they'd ask him questions, but he wasn't willing to explain everything.

Henry looked at him, and Ryan shook his head. He knew his brother wanted him to say something. He thought Ryan should be the one to tell the family what happened, but he couldn't. He just couldn't.

"All right," Henry said loudly, holding up his hand. "One thing at a time. First, how it happened. The room Bella was staying in with Perry was stuffed with boxes when she got there."

"Ryan's Bella?" Sean asked.

Henry nodded. "Once Perry found out Ryan had been in the room, he moved the boxes. Bella searched them and ended up finding the manual in one of the boxes."

"Wow. That's amazing. She was willing to help us? Betraying your father has to be tough," Alyssa said. Alyssa was the only one of the cousins who didn't grow up with her father in her life. Her mother had a summer fling with one of the guests shortly after her father died, and Alyssa was a product of the fling. She always knew her father, but he lived in New York City and didn't visit often.

Ryan never thought before how Alyssa could relate to Bella. Two girls raised by single mothers without a father in the picture on a regular basis. If he still cared about Bella, he might ask Alyssa to talk to her.

But he couldn't care about her. Not after the things she said.

"That's not exactly how it happened," Henry stated. "Bella did go looking because she was suspicious. She thought it was odd that Perry moved the boxes out of her room after he found out Ryan had been there. Unfortunately, when she found the manual, she showed it to Perry and he convinced her he'd never seen it and that Ryan planted it in his files."

"What?" the room gasped.

Ryan didn't want to look at their faces. He had no interest in seeing the pitying looks or the eye rolls from those who wanted to say I told you so. Ryan just wanted to ignore all of it. If he was lucky, there would be a fire somewhere and he would have to go. Immediately.

He sat in the silent room and felt guilty for yet again

wishing someone started a fire just to get him out of a shitty situation. He really needed to work on that.

He finally closed his eyes and lifted his head. When he opened them, his cousins were all watching him. There was a hint of pity in their gazes, but more than anything there was understanding and compassion. They'd all been through their fair share of crap. Relationships gone wrong, misplaced trust, betrayal. They got it.

He hated that any of them had ever felt the way he did in that moment, but yet again, it reminded him he wasn't alone. He had an entire family of people who were there for him. Who wanted the best for him. Who would drink a beer with him and help him put his heart back together.

"Bella brought the manual to Ryan," Henry continued, drawing the attention back to himself instead of Ryan. "She told him what Perry said, but we all know it's another of his lies. Ryan never had an opportunity to plant the manual, and even if he did, that's not who he is. We wanted to find proof that Dad was right, and Bella delivered it to us. We all know he destroyed these, but this one has his handwriting. It's the one he looked for, the one he knew Perry took."

The room erupted again. Everyone started asking more questions, wanting to know what they were going to do with the manual. Some were out for blood, others wanted to forgive and forget.

Ryan just wanted the whole thing to be over. For the first time in his life, he seriously considered leaving Amavita and Bereton. Every day he saw Bella. She was in his bed, in his home, on his vineyard. She was everywhere. He had no idea if she planned to stay in Bereton or not, but he didn't want to run into her regularly for the rest of his life. Not with the way he felt.

Ryan looked at his cousins and hated that he had any

part in upsetting them. If he'd never gotten involved with Bella, they never would have found the manual, but she also never would have betrayed them.

"Everybody, shut up," Dillon said loudly from the laptop at the front of the room. Dillon always could command a room with a word and his presence. Even without being there, he was in charge. "First of all, Ryan, are you okay?"

All the heads in the room swung to Ryan. He nodded once, but it was obviously no one believed him.

"Ry, listen, it's okay to be pissed off right now, but I want you to remember that she's caught in the middle of this just like we all are. This was between Uncle Victor and Perry. Obviously, we all took Uncle Victor's side, and rightly so, but it was never our fight. It's not Bella's either, but she put herself in the middle. And if she was looking for something, I have a feeling she had a reason to believe she would find something."

The others nodded in agreement.

"I know I don't know her, but from what I've been told, she really seemed to care about you. I think she will eventually realize she made a mistake by accusing you of this, but it'll be your choice if you can forgive her."

Ryan nodded once.

"If you do, please know you have my support. Love doesn't have to make sense, and it sure as hell isn't ever perfect, but love makes life worth living. So, if you decide Bella is the one for you, and you want her in your life, I'll be there welcoming her into the family."

"Thank you," Ryan said softly. Of all the things he expected from his cousins, he didn't think he'd hear forgiveness and acceptance. Anger, yes. Vindication, yes. Even understanding, yes. But Dillon's words, and the nodding heads of agreement from his cousins...his throat swelled with emotion.

"Now, second, Henry, does anyone outside the family know about this?"

Henry glanced at Ryan. Ryan shook his head.

"Just Bella," Henry said, "and Perry, of course."

"What are our options? If we're going to turn him in, we will need Bella to report where she found the manual. Do you think she'll do that?" Dillon asked.

Again, all eyes swung to Ryan.

He cleared his throat and said, "I honestly don't know. I doubt it. If she thinks I'm the one who put it there, she isn't likely to help us prove it was her father."

"Is there a way to prove it wasn't you?" Andie asked. "Can't they take fingerprints or something?"

Leo nodded. "They can, but a box in an office that's God knows how old isn't going to be that reliable. There's no telling how many people have touched it. And if it's been moved a few times since Ryan allegedly stuck the manual in there, it would be inconclusive at best for his prints."

"How do you know all that?" Sean asked his brother.

Leo shrugged. "I like to watch cop shows."

"He's right, though," Dillon agreed. "It's unlikely we'd have any proof that Ryan didn't touch the box. What I'm worried about is that we'll never be able to prove he did this."

The murmured agreement around the room made Ryan's chest ache. He gave up Bella for this. He let her walk away without fighting for her. He watched her leave his home and his life. And now they can't even hold her father accountable for what he did. She's forever going to think he told her the truth. She'll always believe Perry. Without proof, she'll never consider that Ryan was telling the truth.

"There has to be a way," Ryan said. "He can't get away with this. He's ruined too many things, too many lives, with his lies and deception. He destroyed Dad, and now he's stolen Bella from me. He can't just get away with it."

The room was silent after Ryan's outburst. He breathed heavily and looked around the room at his cousins. They all looked just as determined as he was, but none of them had any answers.

"He won't get away with it," Nonna said from behind Ryan. "But we're not going to send him to prison either."

Ryan turned and saw all the aunts and uncles with Nonna. And in the middle of them was the man they were all discussing, standing there like he belonged.

"What the hell do you think you're doing on my property?" Ryan growled at him.

"He has something to tell us, son," Jo said. "And we're all going to listen."

25

"Ma?" Henry said from the front of the room.

Jo stood tall, defending Perry. "We need to listen to him. Please. For your father."

Of all the things she could have said, asking them to listen for Victor was the last thing Ryan wanted to do. The man made his father insane. He was considered by many people in town to be a liar. They all believed Perry was innocent, but he wasn't. And of all things, his mom said they needed to listen for his father.

"I know you're mad," Jo said. "You have every right to be. But we should listen. We should all listen."

Ryan didn't like it. He sat back in his seat, arms crossed, and glared at the man who'd not only hurt his father but had taken Bella from him, too.

Perry walked farther into the room. He looked older in just a few weeks, like the stress of lying was finally getting to him. His gray hair was thinning and his face wasn't as happy as it once was when he was on their property. Gone was the cocky asshole who thought he could do anything.

"Please, Albert, tell the kids what you told me," Nonna said.

Perry looked at her, and she nodded. Ryan scoffed, but he didn't say anything.

"The summer I worked here was the first time I felt like I knew who I was. I'd always wanted to own a vineyard, but I didn't know nearly enough about it. I didn't want to be a money guy and just hire people to do it, so I needed to learn."

"So you took advantage of our father," Henry said.

"Henry," Jo scolded.

"It's okay," Perry said. "I did. It wasn't entirely my intention, but that's how it ended up. When he hired me, I knew I was looking for a vineyard, but I didn't tell him. I didn't want him to know because I thought if he knew, he wouldn't teach me everything. I've only ever known people to play a zero-sum game. But Victor was never like that."

Jo smiled and looked at Henry and Ryan. Ryan didn't like hearing Perry speak about his father like he actually knew him. Perry didn't know his father. If he did, he never would have treated him the way he did.

"Victor gave me the manual that Bella gave you. He gave it to me that summer. I didn't realize how valuable it was at first. I took it home to read through it, and in all honesty, I forgot about it."

Ryan snorted and rolled his eyes.

"I know you don't believe me—"

"Why would we?" Sean asked.

"Sean!" Aunt Pauline said.

Perry took a breath and shook his head. "You have no reason to. I know I've never given any of you a reason to trust me. But Bella did. Bella fell in love with this family the same way I did.

She knew there was something special. But I was angry. I was jealous. I didn't want her to choose you over me like so many people did. It's not an excuse, but it's the truth. I've been bitter because I thought buying a dying vineyard and turning it into something would win me points in Bereton, but people still look at Amavita Estates as the top vineyard in the area. And they should. But again, it's my zero-sum mindset. If you're the best, then I'm the worst. There is no middle ground. We can't both be great. One of us wins, which means the other loses."

"That's not how everything has to be," Dillon said from the screen.

Perry nodded. "You're right. And it's only been since Bella came into my life that I've accepted that. She saw something special here. She fell in love. And I ruined that for her. I ruined it because I took something on accident and never owned up to my mistake. I feared being ostracized by the town, so I hid the truth. I thought eventually it would all blow over, but it never did. I antagonized all of you because it was the only connection I had left. I brought all this on myself. All I can say at this point is I'm sorry."

Ryan shook his head, not believing much of anything Perry said. Yeah, he admitted he was wrong, but he blamed Victor as much as he blamed himself. He convinced himself Victor was the bad guy and would turn the town against him. It was all in his head, but it was a self-fulfilling prophecy.

"Why should we just say no big deal and let it go?" Leo asked. "Why shouldn't we turn you in right now?"

Perry had the nerve to look at Ryan. Ryan glared at the other man, not giving him an inch. If he wanted an ally, he wasn't about to find it in the person who'd lost the most because of Perry.

"You don't have to. I'm going to tell the police what I did.

I had planned to go there and confess, but I wanted your family to hear the truth from me first. I wanted all of you to know Victor was right. It doesn't matter that I didn't take it on purpose. I took it, and I hid it. And when it was discovered, I lied again. I turned Bella against Ryan and all of you so easily I barely felt guilty."

Perry took a step toward Ryan, and Ryan leaned back in his seat.

"She's devastated without you. She came here to find me, but she fell for you. You are the reason she thought about staying. I was angry that she chose you over me. That she went searching for evidence against me because it was what you wanted."

Ryan opened his mouth to say he never asked her to do it, but Perry held up his hand.

"I know you didn't ask her to. You never would. You're as honorable as your father. You're a good man, and Bella was lucky to have found you."

"Bella tossed me away. She doesn't want to see me anymore."

"Bella knows the truth now," Perry said sadly. "Luckily for me, she didn't tell me she hated me and storm out, but I'm pretty sure she considered it."

"You would have deserved it," Ryan muttered.

"Ryan!" Jo exclaimed.

"He's right. It's exactly what I deserve. I never should have lied to any of you. I never should have told Bella Ryan hid it in there. I should have been honest from the beginning, and none of this would have happened. All I can say at this point is I'm sorry. I've already changed my will and power of attorney. Bella is in charge of everything now, but there is one stipulation that if she marries Ryan, this entire family becomes part owners of Perry Mount Vineyards."

"Why would you do that?" Dillon asked.

"Because if I go to jail, I want to make sure my vineyard is in good hands. I should have handled everything since I came here differently, and I'll always regret it, but I'm getting older. I know one day I won't be able to run Perry Mount. When that happens, I want people who love making wine to continue making wine. And I hope that means changing our relationship," Perry said.

Shocked didn't even begin to describe how Ryan felt. He was blown away. Short of Bella walking in the door and saying she loved him, nothing could have surprised him more than Perry wanting him and Bella together.

"All right, kids," Nonna said, stepping forward. "I think we have an opportunity here. We can hang him out to dry and let him turn himself in, or we can accept that it started as a mistake and ended as poor judgement and let it go. What do you all want to do?"

72 years ago

TINA SMILED her way through the rehearsal dinner and kissed Antonio on the cheek when she had to. Her stomach was upset the entire night, so she didn't eat much.

Her mother was beside herself with excitement. Tina couldn't remember ever seeing her so happy. It made her feel a little guilty, but not guilty enough to change her plans.

Her father was welcoming and friendly, acting as though it was his party instead of one for Tina and Antonio. His father hung back and let the party happen.

The doors were flung open on the back of the house, letting guests go from outside to inside with ease. The scent of the newly blossoming olive trees filled every inch, making Tina sad.

The entire night was an exercise in balance. Enjoying the time she had with her family in the home she spent her whole life in and looking forward to her future as a married woman.

Guests stayed until well past dark. Tina was tired, but her mother wouldn't let her go to bed until the last guest walked out the door. Antonio was under the same orders, and he stuck to her side the entire night.

"Are you doing okay?" Antonio asked after her hundredth yawn.

Tina nodded. "Tired. It's been a long day."

"Tomorrow is going to be another long day," Antonio said with a smile.

Tina met his gaze and nodded. "It is."

"But tomorrow will be your wedding day," Maribel said. She put her hands on both their cheeks and grinned.

Tina smiled, choking back her tears. Not too much longer and she'd be able to go up to her room for the last time. She was already packed to move in with Antonio after their wedding. Her mother made sure Tina had everything a woman could possibly need, which was frightening, but Tina let her mother have the moment.

As the clock struck midnight, the last of the guests finally headed for the door. Tina and Antonio followed her parents to the door and thanked them for coming. Tina took a deep breath and closed her eyes. It was all becoming real. She was going to be married soon. And she was leaving the only home she'd ever known.

"Antonio, you should head home," her father said to him. "Tina, say goodnight."

Tina smiled at him and said, "Good night."

"Good night, Tina," Antonio said with a kiss on her knuckles. "I will see you very soon."

"Aw, they're so cute," her mother gushed. "You two are going to be so happy."

Tina's stomach tipped over again. She smiled at her mother and let her father guide Antonio out of the house.

"Are you feeling okay?" her mother asked when the men were out of earshot.

Tina nodded. "Just nervous, I think."

Maribel grinned. "Tomorrow is a big day. You're going to look so beautiful in the dress. And Antonio is a good man. He'll take good care of you."

Tina nodded, agreeing with her mother completely. "He is a good man. I was lucky you and Papa chose him."

Maribel clapped her hands together and drew up her shoulders. "You two will make beautiful babies. Soon, too. This should be a good time for you to get pregnant."

"Mama, I'm not even married yet."

"No, but you will be tomorrow. Now, you should head up to bed so you have enough sleep for tomorrow. We wouldn't want you looking tired on your wedding day."

Tina nodded and turned to go. She stopped on the bottom stair and turned back to her mother. She rushed over and hugged her. "I love you, Mama."

Her mother hugged her back for a second, then pushed her off. "Go to sleep, Tina. You have a big day ahead of you. The biggest of your life."

Tina nodded and released her mother. She drew in a breath, memorizing the scent of olives drifting through the house, and went upstairs.

Tina washed her face and brushed her teeth. She braided her hair and changed her clothes. She double checked that she had everything she was going to need in her bags. Then she sat on her bed to wait.

Her siblings had gone to bed earlier, but her parents were still awake. Her mother hired people to clean up from the party, and Tina was sure that's why her parents were still up.

She chewed on her nails and fidgeted with the bedspread. She looked around her room and debated taking something else, something that would remind her of home, but there was nothing she wanted.

Her parents finally went to their room, and Tina held her breath, waiting for the sounds of them getting ready for bed to silence.

She was tired. Exhausted. She wanted to lie down in her bed. But she couldn't.

When she finally thought she'd waited long enough for her parents to be asleep, Tina eased her door open. The door swung silently on well-greased hinges. No one was in the hallway. The bedroom doors were all closed.

Tina grabbed the one bag she planned to take with her and closed her bedroom door behind her. The note she left on her bed wouldn't make things better, but at least her family would know she was safe. She didn't want anyone to blame Antonio.

Tina tiptoed down the stairs and through the house to the back patio. She slid the door open, then closed it behind her. Tears filled her eyes at the realization that she'd never again set foot inside the house.

She didn't have time for tears, or second guesses, or regrets. She had to hurry.

Tina took off across the grove, running as fast as she could with a bag bouncing on her back. She held her most prized possessions to her chest in a purse her mother gave her when she turned sixteen.

At the end of the grove, Tina turned toward town and rushed toward the building Antonio told her to meet him in.

"Tina, thank God. I was starting to worry about you," Antonio said in a rush of breath. He pulled her into his embrace and kissed the side of her head. "Are you okay?"

Tina nodded, letting the tears she'd been keeping at bay flow. "I thought it would be easier to leave."

Antonio smiled gently. "Leaving is never going to be easy, but if this is what you want, then you have to."

Tina wiped at her tears and nodded. "It is. I know it is."

"Okay, then we need to go."

Antonio grabbed Tina's bag and her hand. He checked the street before they ran to his truck. Tina laid on the seat to make sure no one saw her, but no one was out in the middle of the night.

The drive was only a few minutes, but with Tina's heart throbbing in her chest, it felt like it took forever. "We're here," Antonio said quietly, and Tina's heart thumped even harder.

Antonio parked his truck and told Tina to stay put. She promised she would and put all her faith in Antonio.

It wasn't long before they were back. Tina stayed hidden under the blanket, like she promised, but it killed her to do it.

The truck started again and a hand fell on the back of her head, patting her reassuringly. She breathed a little easier, but fear filled her as they drove.

Twenty minutes later, Antonio pulled the truck to a stop. He opened the door, and immediately, Carmelo was asking him why he was doing this.

"I worked hard for you. I've always done what's been

asked of me. Why are you firing me? In the middle of the night when I have nowhere to go?" Carmelo asked. "And tonight, of all nights."

He sounded like a man who'd lost almost all his hope. Tina ached to just flip the blanket off, but she had to know the truth.

"Do you love Tina Vincenzo, the woman who's supposed to become my wife tomorrow?" Antonio asked harshly.

Carmelo didn't answer, and Tina's heart throbbed painfully.

"Do you?" Antonio asked again. "Because I've seen the way you look at her when you think I'm not looking. I've heard rumors that the two of you spent time together. That she invited you over to dinner with her family. That her parents weren't willing to let her be with you."

"That's true," Carmelo said. "I wasn't good enough."

"Does that mean you no longer love her?"

Carmelo exhaled loudly enough for Tina to hear. Her whole life depended on what that one sound meant.

"No, it doesn't."

"So, you love her."

"Yes, I do."

"And if she wasn't married to me, you would do everything you could to keep her safe and make her happy? You would love her until you died? You would make her your first and only priority?"

"Yes, sir," Carmelo said, sounding pained.

"You would even leave this place if it was what she wanted?"

Carmelo sucked in a sharp breath. "Is that what this is? She wants me gone? She doesn't want to see me again?"

"Answer the question," Antonio said. "Would you leave here, go to another country, if that was what Tina wanted?"

"Yes," Carmelo said softly. "I would do anything for her, even leave the country."

Tina's breath locked in her throat. Tears streamed down her cheeks. Every cell of her body ached to touch him again. To be his again.

"Good," Antonio said. "Because that's exactly what she wants. But there is one condition."

"Anything," Carmelo said quickly.

Antonio yanked the blanket off her and grinned at her. "You have to take Tina with you."

"What?" Carmelo gasped.

Tina crawled onto the seat and slid across to where she could get out of the truck. She flung herself at Carmelo. He caught her without hesitation and buried his face in her neck, drawing a long breath.

"Is this real?" he asked.

Tina nodded against him. "It is. Antonio found out about us. He wanted me to be happy, for us to be happy, but we both knew our parents wouldn't back down. He's arranged for us to leave the country together. Tonight. If you're willing."

Carmelo looked from Tina to Antonio. "You're not firing me?"

Antonio shrugged. "That depends. If you don't go with her, I might fire you just for being stupid."

Carmelo breathed a laugh.

"This is your choice, Carmelo," Tina said carefully. "If you don't want to go, it's okay."

"Do you really think I don't want to spend the rest of my life with you? I was trying to figure out how I could steal you away from my boss without someone coming after me."

Antonio chuckled, but Carmelo kept his gaze focused on Tina. She smiled. "You were?"

He nodded. "I love you, Tina. I wasn't ready to give you up."

"Good. Then you're coming with me?"

He nodded. "I'll follow you anywhere you want to go."

Tina grinned. "I like the sound of that."

Carmelo leaned in, but just before he kissed her, Antonio cleared his throat.

"Sorry to break this up, but you two need to get going. Someone is going to realize Tina is gone soon, and the farther away you are, the better," Antonio said.

Tina nodded. "You're right. Thank you, Antonio. We couldn't have even considered this without you. Are you sure you'll be fine?"

Antonio nodded. "I'll be good. I'll milk the whole left at the altar angle to get extra sympathy from all the single women in town."

Tina rolled her eyes. "I'm happy we're both going to get what we want. You get to stay single, and I…"

"Get the man you love. Have a good life, Tina," Antonio said. He pulled Tina close in a hug, one that always felt like she was hugging her brother. Antonio let go of her and kissed her cheek, then shook hands with Carmelo. "I'm sorry to see you go, but love seems to be worth giving up one of the best employees we've ever had."

Carmelo nodded. "Thank you, Antonio. Thank you."

"Take care of each other," Antonio said.

Tina and Carmelo thanked him again then headed for the bus he drove them to. They waved once they were onboard, then started the rest of their lives together.

26

Present Day

BELLA WALKED OUT OF HER ROOM DRAGGING HER SUITCASE behind her. She wanted to get out of town. She was ready to leave. She promised Albert she would keep in touch and think about coming back to visit, but she wasn't sure she'd ever set foot in Bereton again.

She was happy Albert told her the truth. She was willing to forgive him, but it hurt. If he hadn't told her Ryan planted the manual, they might still be together. But Bella didn't deserve another chance with Ryan. She should have given him a chance to explain, but she bought Albert's lies. She was so desperate for a family that she didn't stop to think about what he was telling her. She just believed him, and she couldn't see a way to believe both Ryan and Albert. She chose wrong, and she would spend the rest of her life regretting it.

"Are you ready to go?" Albert asked her when she left her suitcase by the door.

Bella looked down at it and nodded. "Yeah."

"Are you heading straight back to Binghamton?"

Bella nodded. "I told Julia I'd come back for a few months. We both know I can't stay there long term, but Julia needs some help training new people and I need somewhere to start."

"I really wish you'd consider staying here," Albert said softly.

Bella wanted to consider it, but she had to learn to stand on her own two feet. She spent too long letting her mother support her, and she wasn't going to lean on Albert the same way. She smiled at him and said, "Thanks, but I just can't."

Albert nodded. He understood. "Think I can talk you into going somewhere before you head out?"

Bella checked the time on her phone. If she left immediately, she'd get back to Binghamton before dinner. If she stuck around much longer, it would be dark before she made it.

"How long?"

Albert shrugged. "As long as you want. I just want to show you something."

Bella took a breath and nodded. "Okay."

Albert grabbed her suitcase and put it in her trunk for her. When he led her to his truck, she resisted the urge to run back to her car and just leave. She didn't want to risk seeing Ryan or his family.

"Um, where are we going?" Bella asked as Albert eased down his driveway.

"I want to show you something. It won't take long," Albert said.

Bella nodded. She looked out the window at the lake beyond Amavita Estates. It was a beautiful place. She could have lived there her entire life and been happy. But it wasn't meant to be.

Bella didn't realize until Albert stopped the truck that he'd driven across the street and onto Amavita property.

"What are we doing here?" Bella demanded, her voice shaky and her heart lodged in her throat.

"Let's go inside, Bella," Albert said.

Bella shook her head. "No. I...I can't. I don't want to. This...No."

"I really think you should."

Bella shook her head again. "Albert, please. I can't see them. I know I should apologize, but I don't think I can see Ryan and not beg him to give me another chance. I don't deserve another chance. He hates me, and he has every right to. I'm not going to make him feel like any of this is his fault."

"I told all of them everything," Albert said.

Bella looked at him, more than a little surprised. "When?"

"A few days ago. I went to Tina and told her the truth. I told all of them. The family...they decided not to press charges against me. They should have. I wouldn't have blamed them a bit. But they're amazing people, Ryan included. They invited us here today. It's Tina's ninetieth birthday party. She wanted us here."

Tears ran down Bella's cheeks. She thought she ran out, but more kept coming every time she thought about Ryan's family. Tina welcomed her in. His cousins were mad she lied, but they accepted her. And Ryan...

"I don't know if I can do it," Bella whispered. "If he sees me...I don't think I can survive being in the same room as him and not having him smile at me or kiss me or—"

She broke off at a knock on the window. Bella looked up into the eyes of the man she missed more than she'd miss her next breath.

Ryan crooked his finger, telling her to get out.

Bella shook her head.

Ryan cocked an eyebrow and nodded.

Bella shook her head again.

Ryan reached for the handle and opened the door before Bella could lock it and keep him out.

The rush of cold air wasn't the only thing stealing the breath from her lungs.

"Get out of the truck, Bella."

Bella squeezed her eyes shut. "I'm sorry. I should have trusted you. I should have given you a chance. I had no reason to doubt you, and I'm sorry. Now, I need to go."

"You're not going anywhere," Ryan said. "I'm not letting the woman I love walk out of my life."

"What?" Bella gasped.

"I'll give you two a minute," Albert said. He got out of the truck, the door closing behind Bella the only way she knew he was gone. She could only stare up at Ryan.

RYAN HAD a whole speech planned out. How he was going to tell her he loved her and wanted her in his life. How he forgave her for not trusting him and wanted her forgiveness for not fighting harder to get her to listen to him. It all went out the window the second he saw her.

Ryan drank her in like a man drowning. She was gorgeous, even through the sadness that clung to her. Ryan ached to wash it away and see her eyes light up again. To see her smile. To feel her lips and body against his.

First, he needed to convince her to get out of the truck.

"Nonna would like you to come inside."

Bella shook her head.

"No? You're saying no to Nonna?"

She shook her head again and opened her mouth. "You don't love me. You can't."

Ryan chuckled. "Why not?"

"Because I was horrible to you. I said awful things. You should hate me, not love me."

Ryan shrugged. "I don't."

"Why?"

"Because you make me laugh. Because you make me feel like I can breathe. Because I don't have to hold back with you. Because you're amazing and smart and beautiful. Because you're everything to me. I've always wondered if I'd find the kind of love my parents had. The kind of love that makes you feel like nothing else in the world matters. My grandparents had it, my parents had it, my cousins and brother all have it. I thought maybe I was broken because I'd never felt even a little of that. Until I met you."

"Ryan," she breathed.

"If you're not there, that's okay. If you know you'll never get there, I'll let you leave. But if there's a chance you might one day get there, I want you to come inside and celebrate my grandmother's birthday with us."

Bella took a breath and a single tear slid down her cheek. Ryan waited, not very patiently, for her to say something.

Bella finally turned and looked up at him. The pained look in her eyes made his heart sink. She was rejecting him, but she was doing it face-to-face, so he'd accept her words and wish her well and wonder for the rest of his life if he'd missed out on the best thing that ever happened to him.

"I never believed in love. I never saw it. My mom talked about my dad like he was a horrible person. I don't know if it was pain that he didn't choose her or if she really thought so poorly of him, but it didn't matter. She thought she was in love constantly, but she never was. It never lasted. Love had no place in my life outside family. Meeting you was different. Meeting you felt like meeting myself. You felt a part of me from the first night. I know I'll spend my life apologizing to you, but I'd rather spend my life doing that than anything that doesn't have you in it."

Ryan's breath caught in his throat as her words sank in. "Are you saying you'll stay?"

Bella nodded and the first ghost of a smile appeared. "I'm staying. But that's not all."

Ryan was half a second from reaching for her, but he balled his hands into fists and let her finish.

"I love you, Ryan."

"You do?"

She breathed a laugh and nodded. "I do. I have for a while, but I didn't trust it. I won't doubt us again."

Ryan grinned. "Can I kiss you now?"

"Yes, please."

Ryan scooped Bella up and lifted her to him. He didn't waste any time sealing his lips over hers. He licked his way into her mouth as his family broke into cheers from the porch.

Bella pulled back with a laugh and looked over her shoulder at the crazy group of people cheering.

"They're just as happy as I am," Ryan said.

Bella nodded. "Me, too."

"Good. Now let's go inside and party. And tonight?"

"Yeah?"

"You're coming home with me, Bella."

"I'm already packed." She froze and shook her head. "I didn't mean it like that. I mean..."

"It's okay, Bell. I know what you meant. And I know you have to go back to help Julia for a while."

Bella nodded.

"I was thinking maybe I could come with you. We could come back here on the weekends sometimes, but I don't want to let you go, even if it's just for a few months."

"Don't you have to work?" Bella asked.

Ryan grinned. "Of course, but I can be away for a couple of months. Especially if it means I get to be with you."

Bella nodded. "I like the sound of that."

Ryan pulled her in for another kiss, one that wasn't interrupted by his family. He tilted his head and kissed her deeper. He stirred in his jeans, missing her with every inch of his body.

When he finally pulled back, they were both breathing heavily.

"Maybe we should skip the party and go straight to bed," Ryan suggested with a smirk.

Bella shook her head. "Your grandmother only turns ninety once. We have the rest of our lives to spend in bed."

"I'm going to hold you to that," Ryan teased.

Bella laughed. "Come on. Let's go see everyone."

Ryan smiled and took her hand. They walked into the inn together, and he knew he'd finally found the love he hoped for. With the last woman he'd ever expected.

TINA LOOKED around at all the people there to celebrate her birthday and smiled. She'd lived a good life. She'd made a good life. With Carmelo and their family.

She couldn't help but think about him on every birthday, but her ninetieth was even more of a reminder. When they were on their trip to the United States, he talked about when they were both ninety. He said they'd have a home filled with children and grandchildren and great-grandchildren. He couldn't wait to see all of them.

Tina never once doubted their decision to leave. The life they built together, the love they shared, it made so many things possible.

"You doing okay, Ma?" Jo asked, coming to stand by her.

Tina nodded. "Just thinking about your father."

Jo smiled. "He would have loved this."

"He was a sucker for a big party," Tina said. "I think he always felt like he had to distract me from what we left behind, and if we were surrounded by people, I wouldn't think about the people who were missing."

"I'm sorry, Ma," Jo said. "I'm sorry your parents didn't let you love him."

Tina turned to her and smiled. "I'm not. Nothing can stop love. I was scared when I ran away with your father, but I knew he'd always protect me and love me. My parents did their best, but they didn't understand love. I felt sorry for them when I left because they'd never known what I felt."

"I can't imagine marrying someone I didn't love."

Tina nodded. "That's what we wanted all of you to know. That love matters. Money and status and so many other things that people value don't matter. Love matters."

Jo smiled. "I think they all figured it out, too."

Tina grinned as she looked at her family. Four daughters, nine grandchildren, and just the beginning of great-grandchildren...more coming all the time. Love filled the walls of their home and overflowed into the vineyard.

"Are we over here celebrating?" Marie asked, bringing Tina a glass of wine.

Tina took it happily and sipped it. "We're always celebrating. We have a lot to be thankful for."

"We were talking about Dad and love," Jo added.

"Love," Marie said. "I love this place."

"Not that kind of love," Jo said drily.

Marie shrugged. "Maybe true, but I didn't have a great love in my life. I never found the man who made me think I'd rather be with him than here. I love this place. I feel Daddy here every day. And Victor. I'd insist on being buried here if it was legal."

Jo and Tina laughed.

"What's so funny?" Christina asked.

"Marie wants to be buried here," Jo said.

Christina blanched. "Um, I definitely missed something."

Tina hugged her daughter. She spent all her time with Marie and Jo, which she loved, but she missed her two middle daughters.

"Are you having fun, Ma?" Christina asked.

Tina nodded. "I am. I wish your father could see this."

"He would have loved it," Pauline agreed, joining them.

"He would have," Tina said. "He would have loved all of this."

"He started it. The two of you. If you hadn't come here, none of this would have happened," Jo said.

"It was meant to be," Christina said.

The others nodded in agreement.

"I love you, girls," Tina said suddenly. "I don't think I tell you often enough, but I love you all. And your father did, too. He was so proud of all of you."

"Ma, why are you telling us this?" Marie asked.

Tina smiled. "Because we never know how much time we have. I've been blessed with a lot, but we all know my time will end one day. It could be soon, it could be another decade or longer. But I want to make sure you all know how much you are loved."

"Are you feeling okay?" Christina asked.

Tina nodded. "Healthy as a horse."

Jo put her hand on Tina's arm and said, "I know what Ma's trying to say. When Victor died, it made me realize how fragile I was. I never thought I'd see a day without him. But without him, I have to be both mother and father for my boys. It doesn't matter that they're grown, they'll always need their parents. Just like we do."

Tina nodded. "You guys should listen to your little sister more. She knows what she's talking about."

The older three rolled their eyes and groaned. They all laughed.

"It's good to have Albert back," Jo said suddenly. "Victor would have loved seeing him here."

"He knows," Tina told her. "He helped make it happen."

Jo nodded. "I'm sure he did. If anyone could make that happen, it was definitely Victor."

The five of them were silent for a long moment. Tina smiled as Andie nuzzled her daughter's neck and handed her off to Cody. Alyssa looked tired as she chased her son around. She also looked like she might be pregnant again, especially if the hand Jake slid over her belly meant what Tina thought. Sean and Erin kissed and shared a private word. Leo and Sara laughed with Kristen and Zane. Gianna and Zach were talking to Summer and Emily, who were waving their hands around describing something. Henry and Cynthia held hands as they walked across the room toward Ryan and Bella. Tina held her breath until the four of them embraced. A tear slid down Bella's cheek, and Tina knew she was right about her.

The only ones missing were Dillon and Katherine. Tina wished they could have made it, but Katherine's tour schedule was tough. She understood. They'd be back in another few weeks and the whole family would be together again.

Michael and David walked over, kissing their wives and squeezing the hands of the others.

"You should say something, Ma," Michael said. "Everyone is here for you."

Tina nodded. "I probably should. At least a thank you."

Jo picked up her glass and tapped the side with a fork. The others followed suit until the room fell silent, all of them staring at Tina.

She grinned. "Seventy-two years ago, I met the only man I've ever loved. My parents told me I needed to get married and they were going to pick my husband. I was upset and ran off, and ran straight into Carmelo. He picked me up and made me laugh, and a part of me fell in love with him instantly."

Tina looked at the four beautiful women behind her. "It wasn't an easy road to get to where we are today, but Carmelo and I knew as long as we had each other, we could get through anything. I've watched this family grow. From one daughter to four. From one grandchild to eighteen."

Everyone laughed.

"And now great-grandchildren. It's what Carmelo and I always dreamed of. I'm sad that he isn't here to see it, and I wish Dillon and Katherine were here—"

"Did you really think we'd miss this?" Dillon asked from behind her.

Tina turned and tears flooded her eyes. Her family was complete.

Dillon hugged her, and Katherine was right behind him. Her belly was round, and she was beautiful, as always.

"How did you get here?"

Dillon laughed. "I'm married to one of the biggest stars in country music. All she has to say is jump and people ask how high."

Tina turned to Katherine. "Thank you."

Katherine nodded. "We couldn't miss this."

Tina hugged them and turned back to everyone else. "It doesn't get any better than this. Love each other. Share that love with the world. And don't let anyone tell you not to believe in love because love built this vineyard. And love will always run it."

Tina raised her glass and said, "Beviamo!"

THANK **you** so much for reading Love Is Thicker Than Water, and the rest of the Raise A Glass series. I always wanted to find a way to bring Perry into the family again, and I knew the only way to do it was to bring Bella and Ryan together. I also had a fabulous time telling Tina and Carmelo's story!

Ready for something new? Mandy is a curvy girl who doesn't need, or want, a man in her life. Xander is sexy and determined to get to know Mandy, no matter how many times she runs away from him. Read Chubby & Charming for free now!

WANT something that keeps you up at night? Lily's best friend goes missing, and the only person she knows that can help is his brother, who also happens to be a former SEAL.

The last thing Archer wants is to go back home, but he owes his brother. His brother's curvy, sexy best friend is just a bonus, one Archer can't resist. Pick up Freedom today.

AMBER MADE one big mistake in her life and blames the officer who arrested her for changing the course of her future. Caleb has been merely existing since he lost his best friend, but meeting Amber feels like she's someone who's meant to be in his life. When their shared past comes to the present, they both have to decide if they can salvage what they started. Read Playing By The Rules now.

ABOUT THE AUTHOR

USA TODAY Bestselling Author Mary E Thompson spent most of her childhood wishing she had a few less curves. She hid in the pages of books because her favorite characters never cared what size her clothes were. Now, neither does Mary, and she writes stories that celebrate women like her. Real women who have curves, chase dreams, and find love, because we should all be happy, no matter our dress size.

Mary spends her non-writing time with her husband and two kids, watching too much TV, cheering for her hometown football team (Go Bills!), and hiding chocolate from her family.

Visit https://MaryEThompson.com/ to sign up for Mary's newsletter, **Romancing the Curves**. Subscribers get free ebooks and other fun stuff, like exclusive, members only content and giveaways, plus are the first to know about new releases and sales!